"I've been evening

"I have no objecti

"Good," Troy murmured, and bent his head.

This was a full-out, hungry demand. Apparently he wasn't a tentative kind of guy.

He was the one to stiffen and lift his head. Only belatedly did Madison realize she'd heard the scrape of furniture on the floor behind them. Oh, heavens—she sneaked a peek to see that a waiter was upending chairs and putting them on tables. He very tactfully had his back to them as he worked, but he must have seen them kissing.

"It's probably just as well we were interrupted." Madison wasn't sure she meant it. "I'm usually, um, a little more cautious than that."

Wow. Getting swept away like this might make her giddy, but it was more than a little scary, too.

So what? she thought with an unaccustomed feeling of boldness. In her opinion, she was past due to take some risks—at least with this man.

Dear Reader,

The idea for these two linked stories came to me, I think, because I loved my college years. I had excellent reason to feel entirely at home at Wakefield College and in the small town of Frenchman Lake. I was born in a college town much like this, because my father taught at Whitman College in Eastern Washington. I later went "home" to Whitman, where I earned my degree in history.

Of course, I also grew up listening to talk of tenure, department politics, grades, problem students and the annoyance of having an eight-o'clock class scheduled for you. After graduation, I worked briefly in Admissions at Whitman College and then Registration at a community college, gaining a glimpse into the world of college administration. Quite different from the student's viewpoint, I assure you!

As a student I don't recall ever worrying about my personal safety. I'd walk across campus at night without a second thought, swim laps late at night at the athletic center. And who didn't pull all-nighters during finals week? Having now put two daughters through college, I'm well aware that college campuses aren't as safe as they were when I attended—or perhaps I should say, as safe as we imagined they were.

Wakefield College has been haunted for thirty-five years by the memory of a student struck down at a time and place where he never would have imagined he wouldn't be safe. What a way to make everyone feel vulnerable!

Sometimes as a writer it's fun to research a background or profession completely new to me. But going home to the familiar and giving it a small (oh, well, maybe big, or even brutal) twist, that's fun, too.

Welcome to Wakefield College, where a voice from the dead resurrects a very old crime. And look for my next book set at Wakefield College, coming in August 2013 from Harlequin Superromance.

Happy reading,

Janice Kay Johnson

PS—I enjoy hearing from readers! Please contact me through my publisher at Harlequin Books, 225 Duncan Mill Road, Don Mills, ON M3B 3K9 Canada

Where It May Lead

JANICE KAY JOHNSON

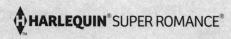

Recycling programs
for this product may
not exist in your area.

ISBN-13: 978-0-373-71848-1

WHERE IT MAY LEAD

Printed in U.S.A.

HARLEQUIN®
www.Harlequin.com

ABOUT THE AUTHOR

The author of more than seventy books for children and adults, Janice Kay Johnson is especially well known for her Harlequin Superromance novels about love and family—about the way generations connect and the power our earliest experiences have on us throughout life. Her 2007 novel, *Snowbound,* won a RITA® Award from Romance Writers of America for Best Contemporary Series Romance. A former librarian, Janice raised two daughters in a small rural town north of Seattle, Washington. She loves to read and is an active volunteer and board member for Purrfect Pals, a no-kill cat shelter.

Books by Janice Kay Johnson

HARLEQUIN SUPERROMANCE

SIGNATURE SELECT SAGA

*The Russell Twins
**A Brother's Word

Other titles by this author available in ebook format.

CHAPTER ONE

MADISON LACLAIRE HAD hoped no one would mention the murder. It was the one pitfall in what she believed was otherwise a great idea.

"Wasn't that the same year as the murder?" Linda Walston, current dean of students, asked promptly after Madison's presentation.

Didn't it figure.

Heads turned toward her around the long table in the conference room. Several mouths were agape. The dean— a small, intense woman who was well-loved as a professor in the philosophy department—was possibly the only member of the Wakefield College administration who had been here thirty-five years ago, when a student was murdered on campus.

The murder itself wasn't the stumbling block, Madison reflected; the real problem was that no arrest had ever been made.

No expensive, private liberal arts college wanted parents of current or prospective students thinking their precious offspring wouldn't be safe on campus. Madison's impression was that, after the police had thrown up their hands and designated the case inactive, the crime hadn't exactly been hushed up, but close enough.

Her father certainly hadn't liked to talk about it, and he had been a student at the time, not an administrator. She supposed that was because he knew the victim.

"I don't think we need to be too concerned about it," Madison said smoothly. As director of alumni relations, she would be masterminding the special alumni weekend she was proposing, which would include a full slate of activities like a wine tasting, dinner at the president's house and more. She glanced around. "For those of you who weren't aware anything like that ever happened here at Wakefield, it was an awful crime. A senior named Mitchell King was bludgeoned to death in the McKenna Sports Center sauna during first semester finals week."

There were some sharp intakes of breath.

"Just as it is now," she continued, "the center was open all night for students who needed a break from studying. At that hour, it was deserted enough that no one saw or heard anything. The police investigation got nowhere."

"If he was a senior," Babs Carmichael, director of admissions, pointed out, "every single alumnus coming back for the opening of the time capsule would have known this Mitchell King. Wasn't the student body even smaller then?"

"Yes." Everyone here knew that Madison's father had also been a student at Wakefield at the time. "But the victim wasn't an English major. He wouldn't have contributed to the time capsule even if he'd lived."

She saw a subtle relaxation in the half-dozen people involved in the discussion. This whole thing would definitely have been trickier if Mitchell King had put an item in the time capsule tucked into the foundation of the then brand-new Cheadle Hall, which housed the English department.

Only a couple of weeks before, Cheadle had suffered irreparable damage in an earthquake that startled local residents awake but otherwise barely shattered a dish. Consultants determined that the building, built in the early

1980s, had been erected on a flawed foundation that had required only a mere nudge to make it shift and crack.

The news that it would have to be demolished and rebuilt from the ground up was pretty much a disaster. College administrators had hoped to build a new Student Union building next. The existing cramped and dated one was commonly left off the tour given to prospective students and their parents. Tour guides would wave vaguely in its vicinity and say, "Our SUB is over there," while hustling their charges along to the music building, which was impressive with its stained glass and soaring ceiling.

Back when students in the English department had been invited to put items in the capsule, the plan was to open it fifty years later. Fifty was a nice, round number, and the then-students would only be in their late sixties and early seventies when it came time to open it. But only thirty-four and a half years had passed. The original assumption was that the capsule would be removed and carefully put back in the foundation of the new building to be erected this coming year. It was Madison who saw the premature opening as a splendid excuse to bring a host of well-to-do alumni back to the Wakefield campus, where they would be wined, dined, entertained and given opportunity to reminisce fondly about their college days.

They would also be given plenty of opportunities to write checks to help replace Cheadle Hall so that the current and upcoming classes of English majors would benefit from the same experiences they had had at Wakefield.

"Remember," Madison continued, "that the students all came back to Wakefield for spring semester despite the murder. And that the majority of the students who did put something in the time capsule had at least another year left here, some more than that. They won't have forgotten the murder, but it won't be the first thing they remember about Wakefield, either. As you know, some of our more prominent alumni from that era often express public gratitude to the college for providing them with the springboard to their current success. Clearly, the murder didn't taint *their* memories." She paused. "Sooner or later, the time capsule will be opened. If we don't do it now, we're only postponing the issue for another fifteen years."

"That's true." The president of the college, sitting at the head of the table, nodded thoughtfully. "Tell us more about what you have in mind for the weekend."

She did. By the end of the discussion, everyone in the room looked energized. They were all excited about the prospect of bringing in a significant amount of money to replace Cheadle Hall.

The president looked around. "Anyone opposed?"

No one stirred.

"Then it's a go if you think you can pull it off this fast," he said with a nod. He smiled warmly at Madison. "I like your creative thinking."

"Thank you," she said with composure, although privately she was rejoicing.

"Okay, any issues with residence hall advisors?" he asked, and talk flowed into the current preoccupation of most administrators: the first day of fall semester, one month away.

Fast indeed, Madison thought with trepidation. Cheadle Hall was scheduled to be demolished in late September, as soon as it was emptied of its contents and stripped of some salvageable material, including wood paneling and copper roofing. She had slightly less than two months to pull her event together.

It was all she could do not to leap up and dash out to get started. Instead, she tried to maintain a patient, interested expression while her mind whirred.

IGNORING CLUMPS OF students parting to pass around her, Madison stood on the sidewalk that wended its way through the campus of Wakefield College and contemplated the handsome brick building currently wrapped in yellow tape that proclaimed, "Keep Out." She held a clipboard ready to jot down any last-minute to-do items.

Seven weeks had passed since her proposal was approved. The big event was happening this coming weekend.

The tape had to go before alumni started arriving on campus, Madison decided. It was unsightly, even tacky. She made a note to speak to someone on the maintenance crew. She saw no reason a dignified sign on the door wouldn't be adequate.

Leaving the sidewalk, she stepped closer to the cracked foundation. She knew exactly which block hid the time capsule that was the raison d'etre for this weekend's event. Madison had come to envision the time capsule as a lemon that, when properly squeezed, would make some excellent lemonade for the college.

She felt really good about how everything was coming together. There were only a few final details needing her attention.

Smiling with satisfaction, she turned away and started toward the building that housed administrative offices. One of her student assistants had called five minutes ago to tell her that the box of programs for attendees had arrived from the printer. And this afternoon she had a meeting with the city police department liaison to discuss any security issues that might arise. She couldn't imagine there would be any—this *was* Frenchman Lake, after all, a small Eastern Washington town with tree-lined streets and graceful older homes. It was true that downtown Frenchman Lake wasn't the same place it had been ten years ago when Madison was a student here, thanks to the conversion of wheat fields surrounding the town to vineyards. At last count, there were thirty-eight wineries in and around Frenchman Lake. Tasting rooms, bed-and-breakfasts and high-end restaurants had mushroomed in a town that had never been on the tourist path before. In fact, Madison was taking advantage of that new fame by including a wine tasting tour on the itinerary for visiting alumni.

Fortunately, crime had not increased, despite the many outsiders who flooded the small town seasonally. Making sure the police department was prepared to back up the college's small security force in the event of a problem was only a precaution—but she believed in being cautious. She hoped the officer assigned to work with her had a good attitude.

After a glance at her watch, she walked more briskly.

PRIVATE LIBERAL ARTS colleges claimed to offer the finest in undergraduate education. They prided themselves on cutting edge labs, sophisticated online databases, professors who had searched for medicinal plants in the Amazon basin, served as Under-Secretary of State or come up with a revolutionary algorithm. Much was invariably made of the fact that this was where tomorrow's leaders would be trained.

So why, Detective John Troyer pondered, did those same colleges always appear as if they hadn't altered so much as a brick or trimmed the ivy since 1890? Seemed to him there was an implication of tradition and even stodginess in the look. But what did he know?

Troy nodded at a group of passing coeds who were noticeably staring at him. He contemplated the three-story, granite block edifice—complete with bell tower—that housed the administrative offices of Wakefield College.

The sound of that bell ringing the hours was part of his childhood. His family home where his mother still lived was only ten blocks away from the campus. Although his father was a Wakefield grad, Troy had rebelled and attended the University of Washington in Seattle—on the other side of the mountains. He'd been desperate to escape the small town where he'd grown up for the imagined delights of urban living. He knew how disappointed his father had been that his son chose not to follow in his footsteps.

On a beautiful day like this when the campus looked its best, Troy had his own regrets. He'd enjoyed his years at UW, but his experience didn't have much in common with what students found at Wakefield. With enrollment of only 1,400, the students all got to know each other and the professors knew them individually almost from the moment they arrived.

The UW also had plenty of brick buildings festooned with ivy, but the dorms at Wakefield were a lot nicer-looking, he reflected, admiring Harris Hall with its long gambrel roof and arched, small-paned windows.

And then there was the fact that he didn't like thinking he'd disappointed his dad.

Shaking off the grief that thoughts of his father brought, Troy let his gaze rest briefly on a few girls wearing skimpy shorts while sprawled in the shade of an old leafy tree studying. *Nice legs,* he thought, but without much interest. At thirty-two, he'd discovered recently that college students looked like kids to him.

He scanned the two dorms and the half-dozen classroom buildings that ringed Allquist Field until his gaze landed on the building that was the cause of his visit to the campus. Cheadle Hall was scheduled for demolition at the end of the month. He understood the English department was being forced to hold classes in miscellaneous rooms elsewhere on campus, including some that had formerly been used for storage. A new building would go up on the same site—the college hoped to complete it by next fall.

To his cop's eye, the yellow tape suggested a crime scene. He grinned at the thought. College administrators must find the sight exceptionally jarring.

He was on his way to meet one of those administrators, the director of alumni relations who had come up with the scheme that involved Troy. Troy's captain had made clear that this assignment was not optional.

"You're the logical choice," he had informed Troy. "If you have anything urgent on your caseload, hand it off."

Fortunately, Troy hadn't been immersed in the aftermath of a recent murder, kidnapping or rape. The idea of a few days spent hanging around the college hadn't been unwelcome, especially since he'd be here for part of the festivities anyway in his father's stead.

Aware of speculative stares—guns weren't a common sight on this campus—he cut across the plush green lawn and climbed the broad granite stairs to enter Memorial Building, which was fondly known at Wakefield and in town as "Mem."

A receptionist behind an antique oak counter directed him to a staircase that led to the third floor. Admissions, Financial Aid and the president's office took up much of the ground floor. Made sense, he supposed, as more prospective students and their parents visited campus than alumni, who tended to show up only for their reunions. He was amused to see that Career Planning and Resources had been relegated to the basement. Students were unlikely to have their parents with them when they plunged into the bowels of Mem.

Of course, he reflected, the basement was probably

the coolest level of the building on a day like this. In the
third week of September in Eastern Washington, tempera-
tures were still climbing into the nineties. The lower floors
had felt as if they might be air-conditioned, but when he
emerged from the stairwell, he found the third floor to be
hot and stuffy.

Alumni Relations was stenciled in gold on the glass
inset of the second door. It stood open, and he saw that
the tall casement window was open, too, in an apparently
futile effort to create a cross-draft. The outer office contained rows of tall oak filing cabinets, bookcases and an
old desk with a very modern computer on it.

"Hello?"

"Hi, come on in," a woman called through another door,
from an internal office.

Troy circled the large desk and entered this second office. His first impression was of elegance—warm woods
that might have been cherry or mahogany, a desk with
Queen Anne style legs and a Persian rug that looked like
the real, gently-aged thing and not a recent knock-off.
Then he focused on the woman and, stunned, lost interest in their surroundings.

A brunette with warm brown eyes, she stood maybe
five foot five and was curvaceous enough to be considered
a little plump by today's standards. That body, poured into
a red suit, was perfect by his. Her hair was cut bluntly at
her shoulders, thick and glossy, currently tucked behind
her ears. As she looked back at him, he caught a glimpse
of surprise and maybe a touch of nerves on her face before she offered a bright, professional smile.

Not altogether professional, he decided, or if it was, it
was damn good. Her entire expression was now welcom-
ing. He felt like the lucky guy basking in the only available beam of sunlight.

He gave his head a brief shake to clear it. "Ah…I'm looking for Ms. Laclaire. I've been assigned as liaison from the Frenchman Lake P.D."

"Oh, good." Sounding delighted, she held out a hand. "I'm Madison Laclaire. And you are?"

"John Troyer. Troy, to anyone who knows me." He gently squeezed her hand—delicate but strong—then reluctantly released it.

"Please, call me Madison. You're not in uniform," she observed, gesturing him toward a seating area furnished with a sofa, a low table and a couple of comfortable looking chairs.

"Plainclothes." He lowered himself into one of the chairs and watched as she settled at one end of the sofa. "I'm a detective in Major Crimes."

"Dare I ask how you got assigned to this gig?" Madison asked.

Her snug skirt meant she had to sit primly, knees together, but the hem rode up her thighs anyway. She wriggled, as if to persuade it to cooperate, but instead managed to bare another inch of her legs. He found them a hell of a lot more intriguing than the legs of the eighteen- or twenty-year-old coeds he'd spotted out on the lawn.

Tearing his gaze from her knees and the shadow above them, he reminded himself that she'd asked him a question.

"My father is a Wakefield grad." He smiled. "In fact, Dad was an English major who contributed to the time capsule. I would have been at the opening in any case."

"Troyer." Tiny lines in her smooth, curving forehead cleared. "Oh! I should have recognized your name right away. Joseph Troyer. You'll be attending in his place, I gather."

That was a nice way, he thought, of saying she knew his father was dead.

"That's right," he agreed. "Dad's been gone less than a year, and Mom…still isn't getting out much."

"I'm sorry," Madison said softly. "He wasn't very old."

"No. Sudden heart attack." Troy grimaced. "Lifelong smoker, which might have had something to do with it."

"You must miss him."

"I do." In the past couple of years since Troy had returned to his hometown, he'd come to think of his dad as his best friend. Saying he missed the man was hopelessly inadequate to describe his sense of loss. He hid his shock and grief better than Mom did, but Troy knew he hadn't even begun to adjust.

Apparently sensitive enough to guess he'd just as soon not chat any more about his father, Madison nodded. "As it happens, you and I have something in common. My father was also an English major here at Wakefield, and put something in the time capsule. He's in Tokyo on business and was happy to have me take his place." She smiled. "He claims not to remember what his contribution was."

"Dad never said either."

"Maybe we'll both get some fantastic insight into our parents' characters."

"We can hope." Damn, she had a pretty smile. Merry and open, making a man want to agree to anything she asked. Troy bet she was really good at extracting big bucks from wealthy alumni.

"I'm grateful the P.D. offered you to help with any security issues," she said more briskly, getting down to business. "It's unlikely there will be any problems, of course, but I want to be particularly careful given that two of the returning alums are well-known enough in their respective fields to be minor celebrities."

"So I understand. Why don't you give me the specifics?"

She handed him the schedule that would be given to each attending alumnus. She had to excuse herself to grab a pair of black-framed reading glasses from her desk. Seeing his expression, she made a face.

"You're supposed to be at least forty before you need these, aren't you? There's no justice."

Personally, he liked the way the frames set off her brown eyes. He hid a smile at her disgruntled expression. He would have replied, but she had already returned to business.

Responses to the invitation and news that the capsule was to be opened fifteen years earlier than planned had been greater than anticipated, she told him with satisfaction. Out of the 118 students who had put an item into the capsule, 83 had so far expressed the intention to be here or send a representative.

"Some of those are sons or daughters of the students, as in our cases. But most are alumni. Naturally they're bringing wives, husbands, partners, other family. The wonderful thing is that the lectures Gordon Haywood and Ellen Kenney have agreed to give are drawing a number of additional visitors to the campus, as well. And the current students are excited, too, naturally."

Haywood, Troy knew, was a third-term senator from the state of Utah. There was talk of a run for the White House in his future. Given the guy's politics, Troy wouldn't vote for him, but he was often described as charismatic. Meeting him and hearing him speak would be interesting. Ellen Kenney had sold her first novel before she turned twenty-five and had earned accolades and what had to be pretty impressive royalties ever since. She walked that tricky line between admired literary fiction and books regular people actually want to read. Troy had read her most recent, which on its surface was a murder mystery involving a windsurfer on the Columbia River. The characters had real depth, the background was well researched and he'd found even the police work believable. He hadn't loved it so much he'd delved into her backlist, but he'd been impressed. He wasn't surprised that alumni were popping out of the woodwork for a chance to hear both Kenney and Haywood talk.

The two were shimmering stars in Wakefield College's firmament. It was pure luck that both had been English majors, students on campus here when Cheadle Hall was being built and the time capsule inserted behind a block in the foundation.

Besides the lectures, as he scanned the program, he saw the weekend included a reception at the president's house, a tasting tour at half a dozen local wineries, a golf tournament, a casual lunch with grilled burgers and hot dogs to be held on Allquist Field and finally a formal dinner Saturday night.

Madison told him that security concerns on campus had grown in recent years, but not to the extent they had on urban campuses. Female students, she explained, were encouraged not to walk across campus in the dark; if a girl was alone and needed an escort, say to return to her dorm late at night, she could call a number and one of the male volunteers on shift would turn up to walk with her. She'd rarely have to wait more than five minutes before her escort arrived. So far theft, vandalism and the like hadn't been huge problems.

Madison gave him the name and phone number of the head of the small campus security department. She admitted that so far more attention had been paid to parking issues than anything else. The security plan, such as it was, consisted of having one or two members of the force mingling with the crowd at each event.

Troy couldn't argue too much. Police snipers on rooftops and cavalcades of escort vehicles seemed over the top.

Stretching his legs out, he had a thought. "Do you suppose the senator travels with any bodyguards? He's a lot more likely to be a target of a threat than Ms. Kenney."

"She wrote a book a couple of years ago that was rather controversial, though. It was her one foray into true crime. I never read the book, but I know it generated a lot of anger. I think there were some ugly incidents at book signings. Someone threw a bucket of cow blood on her at one."

He frowned. "Yeah, I'd forgotten that. I didn't read the book, either."

"You don't read true crime?"

"I get my fair share of the real thing. I like fictional crime better. It's more fun."

She laughed, a low sound that—damn it!—turned him on. He shifted to hide his response.

"Do we have enough major crimes in Frenchman Lake to keep you busy?" she asked.

"Sure," he said, interested to see how surprised she looked at his answer. "Me and three other detectives. Homicide still isn't common—we only had three last year, but we're up to four already so far this year. Mostly we deal with crimes like assault, sexual abuse and breaking and entering. The vineyards have brought a good-sized population of migrant workers to Frenchman Lake, which has increased crime overall, but people who live in gracious old houses right around the campus sexually abuse their daughters, beat their wives and get robbed, too." He shrugged. "Then there are the tourists."

"I had no idea." She sounded shocked. "I was just thinking smugly how lucky we are that crime isn't a significant problem here. I suppose I pictured police officers mostly giving speeding tickets or scaring the daylights out of teenage shoplifters."

"Hate to disillusion you," he said, "but people here are pretty much like people anywhere. You know there was an ugly murder right here on the Wakefield campus back when our fathers were students. Same year Cheadle Hall was built and the time capsule was filled, as a matter of fact."

She frowned, and he guessed she would rather not think about her beloved college connected to a brutal killing.

"Yes, we had some discussion when we scheduled this event. I hope you don't intend to bring up the subject over the weekend."

"Me?" His gaze never left her face. "Why would I? But I think it's safe to say there'll be talk about it, anyway. They're all going to be thinking about it, you know. Murder isn't the kind of thing anyone forgets."

CHAPTER TWO

"No," MADISON ADMITTED. "People like to talk about murder. I'm just trying not to think about it. You won't be surprised to know the college discourages reminders, especially since no arrest was ever made. I gather the assumption was that a transient committed the crime. Anyone could have wandered in."

"Sure, but why would they? To take a sauna?" Troy shook his head. "I skimmed the original reports when I first came on the job here. There wasn't any obvious thread to pull, so I didn't suggest reopening the case. But my impression was that the original investigators thought the victim was killed by another student."

"But…that's…"

When she didn't finish, he did it for her. "Impossible? Because Wakefield students are the cream of the crop?"

She must have heard the irony in his voice because she flushed. "I suppose that is what I was thinking. And yes, I know that rich people sexually abuse their daughters and beat their wives, too. You don't have to tell me again. Still…"

"What could possibly have triggered an assault that brutal? No idea. Nobody so much as came up with a theory back then." He frowned. "Dad said he knew the victim, Mitchell King, but not well. I seem to remember he was some kind of science major. Bio or chem, maybe?"

Madison nodded. "My father said he hadn't had much to do with Mitchell, even though they were both seniors."

"My father's classmate."

"Yes."

"Funny that we're both here, involved in this thing."

"Yes. Well, I dreamed up this *thing,* as you put it." She smiled at him. "In fact, it makes sense that I'm here. Quite a few employees of the college are alumni."

Smiling at her was no problem. He was pleased that she was apparently as curious about him as he was about her. "You asking what my excuse is for ending up back in Frenchman Lake?"

"I would have put it more tactfully."

"I worked for Seattle P.D. Got frustrated with some of the policies in the department, the attitudes that were too prevalent. I almost quit without job hunting first, but had an attack of common sense. When I started looking around, I guess the small-town boy in me emerged. I wanted a town where I could get to know people." He shrugged. "I grew up here, you know."

"I saw that this was your father's last address."

"Turned out that having connections in Frenchman Lake didn't hurt when it came to getting a job. As far as I was concerned, it was time to come home. I was glad to have a chance to be closer to my parents." He grimaced. "Lucky, as it turned out."

"For your mother," Madison said gently.

"Yeah." Rather than let himself descend into bleak thoughts of how little good he'd actually done his mother, he decided it was time to get back to business. "Have we come to any conclusions here?"

She studied him carefully and with a perceptiveness that was a little unnerving, but she clearly chose to go along with his effort to close the subject. "You haven't said whether you think our preparations have been adequate."

"How long have you held this job?" he asked.

"Um." Her pursed lips suggested she was momentarily disconcerted. "This is the beginning of my second academic year."

Troy nodded. "I imagine you've handled a dozen events involving alumni, then."

"Oh, more than that if you include our 'On the Road' events. We hold a dozen or more every year across the country to keep our graduates involved. Here on campus, the biggest was the summer alumni college and, of course, the spring reunions."

"I don't suppose you had any security problems at either of those, did you?"

She smiled. "No."

"I doubt we will this weekend, either. I think my role is going to be an exciting one. I'll hang around. Maybe even play golf."

Her laugh this time was as contagious and unintentionally erotic as the first. "Do you play golf?"

"Poorly," he admitted. "I've got a hell of a slice. On the other hand, from a security standpoint, having me lurking off in the rough probably isn't a bad plan."

She giggled. "I'll look for you there."

"You'll be playing, too?"

"No. Actually, I'll be frantically finishing arrangements for the luncheon and dinner while you're sweating on the golf course."

Troy grunted with amusement. "Smart. I hear it's going to be sizzling by Saturday."

"So they say. Fortunately, the formal dinner is the only dress-up occasion."

"You mean, I can wear shorts and a muscle shirt the rest of the weekend?"

Her nose crinkled. "*You* can wear anything you want."

"No such luck for you." He grinned at her. "What's that saying about how ladies don't sweat? That they can only glow?"

"I suspect I'll be sweating like a pig Saturday." She frowned. "Do pigs sweat?"

"I have no idea. Never considered farming a career option."

"Me neither." She rose gracefully to her feet. "Thank you for coming, Detective Troyer."

"Troy." He stood, too.

A smart man would probably bide his time, not make any move until after the alumni weekend. He didn't want her to be uncomfortable with him when they had to work together. Troy had always thought of himself as a pretty smart guy. He'd had the grades and SAT scores to get into Wakefield. Turned out he wasn't as smart as he'd thought he was, he discovered. Either that, or his store of patience was severely lacking.

Seeing that she had started to turn away, probably with the intention of politely escorting him out of her office, he cleared his throat. Madison paused, lifting her eyebrows in inquiry.

"So. I was wondering." Slick. Really slick. *Get on with it,* he ordered himself. "Any chance I could talk you into having dinner with me?"

Madison blinked. "Do you mean…tonight?"

Tonight, tomorrow night, every night. Startled by the instant thought, he cleared his throat again. "Tonight would be good. Or tomorrow night." He hesitated. "Unless you're too busy getting ready for this weekend."

She scrutinized him for a slightly unnerving moment.

Then her expression melted into another sunbeam of a smile. "I would love to have dinner with you tonight, Troy. As long as we make it casual. I can hardly wait to change out of this suit."

"Yeah, I can see why."

He had noticed that she was glowing. In fact, tendrils of her dark hair looked damp enough around her face to be sticking to her skin.

He smiled. "You could have said something. I wouldn't have minded if you'd ditched the jacket."

"I'm more anxious to rip off the stockings." She rolled her eyes. "I had meetings this morning. Otherwise I wouldn't have bothered."

Troy definitely liked the idea of her ripping off the stockings. Better yet, he'd be glad to do it for her.

Down, boy.

"Casual works for me."

She suggested they meet at the restaurant; he threw out the idea of Bannister's, housed in an old brick building downtown and known for everything from pizza and burgers to quiche and the best damn fettuccini Alfredo he'd ever had. Madison agreed, and he left before he did something stupid. Like kiss her.

He was grinning as he took the stairs two at a time, as if he was twenty years old again. She'd said yes. He *felt* young. Half-aroused, too, a common state for twenty-year-old guys.

He would definitely be kissing her tonight.

MADISON STOOD JUST inside the outer office and listened to the thud of Detective Troyer's feet as he took the stairs with the same enthusiasm most of the students did. She made a face. He might be in a hurry because it was so blasted hot up here.

She glanced at her watch and squeaked. She'd spent a lot longer talking to Troy than she'd expected to devote to the police department liaison, and the president of the college expected her in his office five minutes from now.

She grabbed her handbag and hurried to the ladies' restroom on her floor. There she carefully splashed her face with cold water, then patted it dry with a paper towel. Whatever makeup she'd started the day wearing was history, but she didn't want to be beet-red when she sat down with her boss. In the depths of her purse she found an elastic band and, after brushing her hair, devised a simple knot on the back of her head that got the hair off her neck while looking reasonably classy.

Despite the need to hurry, she paused and looked at herself in the mirror. Her eyes, she couldn't help noticing, sparkled with excitement. Truthfully, she was almost vibrating with it. She didn't think she'd ever reacted to a man quite the way she had to John Troyer.

She would have been crushed if he'd nodded politely and left without expressing any personal interest in her.

She permitted herself one small squeal and a bounce before resuming her dignity. She returned to her office to stow her bag then started down the stairs to the first floor. It wasn't the meeting she was thinking about on her way. It was Troy.

He was so much more physical than any man she'd been involved with. Not that he was huge and beefy; he wasn't, though he was a good deal taller than her. Maybe six feet, she guessed. Broad-shouldered, with muscles she couldn't help but notice. A man's muscles. Troy wasn't as lean as a runner. He was more solid than that. She suspected he could still move plenty fast, and would have no trouble restraining most suspects once he caught them.

His hair was a medium shade of brown that the summer

sun had lightened and streaked. By midwinter, it would probably darken. His hint of stubble had definitely been darker. His eyes, a charcoal-gray, had captivated her from the moment they met hers. Gray eyes should be clear, like blue ones, right? His didn't have any hint of other colors that would make them hazel, but they were somehow smoky, as if they hid secrets.

She shivered a little, possibly because the temperature had plummeted as she descended two floors in Mem, but more likely it was another symptom of her excitement. Only a few more hours and she'd see him again. Find out if they had anything at all in common beyond the fact that both their fathers had been English majors at Wakefield College. Madison frowned, trying to remember what his father's profession had been. Hers was a very successful businessman with an MBA from Harvard. He was snob enough she had no doubt he'd look at John Troyer with disdain. Dad wouldn't be able to imagine why she might want to date a cop. Her father admired success, defined by wealth or acclaim. She had never been able to envision him as an English major, of all things. She didn't even think he read novels anymore.

To heck with whether Dad would approve, she thought in a moment of defiance. She was sometimes uncomfortably aware of how much her father's approval meant to her. She would be very glad to quit caring. She never earned his unqualified approval anyway. Madison often asked herself why she bothered trying.

With some exhilaration, she discovered that she didn't give a flying you-know-what whether Dad would like Troy or not. *She* liked him, and that was what mattered.

More than liked him.

Delight rose inside her in a tide that made her want to skip. Only long practice and the fact that one of the assistant directors of Financial Aid was coming down the hall toward her kept her steps sedate. She smiled at Kyle Matthews and opened the door to the president's outer office.

MADISON CROSSED HER arms on the tabletop. She and Troy had been seated upstairs in the loft at Bannister's, which was busy tonight. A group of students sat nearby, but half the tables were taken by townies. She hardly noticed—all she saw was Troy, lounging comfortably across the table from her. His gaze hadn't left her since they sat down.

"You didn't go to Wakefield," she said.

Troy's smile held satisfaction. "You tried to look me up."

She hoped the warmth she felt in her cheeks didn't show. "I hope *you* didn't look me up."

"In law enforcement databases?" He grinned and relaxed back in his chair, his big hand wrapped around a glass of beer. "Checking out women that way is discouraged." He paused. "Would I have found you?"

She made a face. "I'm afraid so. I've been known to drive a little too fast."

"Ah." There was amusement rather than disapproval in his eyes. "Not good for your insurance rates."

"No." She sighed. "My premium shot way up after the second ticket."

"How many tickets have you had?"

"Only two—well, two recent ones, but both were in the past year." Her face was heating. "You know how empty the highway is past the Tri-Cities."

His mouth twitched. "Not empty enough, apparently."

Remembered annoyance made her frown. "The state patrol officers are really good at hiding."

"Yeah, that's one of the things taught in police academies."

"Seriously?"

He laughed. "No. You learn your first year when you're partnered with an experienced officer who passes on the collective wisdom of whatever police force you've joined."

"Well, it's ridiculous," Madison said indignantly. "I don't speed when it's not safe. I never do in town, for example. But, honestly, when the highway is straight for miles on miles and there's hardly any traffic, seventy or, well, seventy-five is perfectly safe." *Or maybe eighty.*

Although there was still a trace of humor in his eyes, he'd quit smiling. "See, anyone in law enforcement has worked traffic accidents. They're really ugly. Once you've scraped a kid off the pavement or used the Jaws of Life to pry a body out of a flattened car, your idea of 'safe' driving changes. Seventy-five miles an hour on a two-lane highway that is pretty damn narrow *isn't* safe."

The pictures he'd drawn were all too vivid. She winced. "You've made your point."

"Good."

"Back to you," she said hastily. "Didn't your dad try to talk you into going to Wakefield?"

"Sure he did." He contemplated his beer, the set of his mouth wry. "I told him I'd rather go to a community college in North Dakota. Why would I want to stay in the most boring town in America? I wanted excitement. I wanted to *live* a little."

Madison chuckled. "Did he understand?"

"Yeah, I think he actually did, which didn't mean he wasn't disappointed." His face had relaxed. "You get the family pressure, too?"

"My father simply *assumed* I'd be going to Wakefield. There was never even any discussion. It never occurred to me to dig in my heels." She rarely admitted as much to anyone. She was embarrassed to have been so docile and ashamed when she wondered whether she would still be.

"A good girl who drives too fast," Troy mused. He took a swallow of his beer, his eyes never leaving hers.

"That was a long time ago. I was seventeen when I sent my application to Wakefield." *Excuses, excuses.*

"Would you tell Daddy, 'Hell no,' now?"

"The trouble is, I had a fabulous time during my four years here. Look at me." She spread out her arms. She'd worn a snug-fitting, jewel-necked Wakefield College T tonight. "I loved it so much, I came racing back as soon as there was a suitable job opening."

"Yeah, I guess that was an unfair question." He smiled, his eyes lingering on the words *Wakefield College*—or perhaps on her breasts, outlined by the forest-green cotton knit. He looked up, the smile having become crooked. "Truth is, I was thinking just today that I'm a little sorry I didn't stay here for my four years. I had an okay education, but it might not have been the equal of what I'd have gotten here. I went to UW," he told her, "and for an undergrad it's a completely different experience than a student gets at a small school." He grinned. "Dad might have been smarter to sneer at the idea of me applying to Wakefield. Tell me I couldn't get in. Or that I belonged at a state school."

"A little reverse psychology."

He laughed. "Teenagers are dumb enough for it to work."

"True enough." She couldn't remember smiling so much, or feeling such a fizz that never subsided. "You notice I don't work in Admissions. I work with adults."

"I noticed today how young the students look. Maybe we see ourselves as eternally young, but I couldn't help realizing I'm not as young as I used to be."

He looked so disconcerted, she couldn't help laughing at him. "Kind of like finding your first gray hair?"

"Something like that."

His lips were clean-cut, not too full or too thin. They were more expressive than his eyes. It was hard not to look at his mouth and imagine how it would feel covering hers.

Hoping he hadn't noticed she was staring, she took a hasty sip. "How old are you?"

"Thirty-two. You?"

"Thirty-one."

Their meals came, a curry chicken crepe for her, a burger with bleu cheese for him. Conversation never lagged as they ate. She told him about grad school at Duke, about her first jobs in college administration.

"I had a student job in Admissions here at Wakefield," she said, remembering. "I loved every minute of it. I didn't realize I'd already decided what I wanted to do with my life by the time I graduated, but I had. I started out at Carleton College in Minnesota in Financial Aid. I was so cold all winter, I started job hunting by spring. After that I worked in Admissions at a small college in Northern California then moved into Development. Begging for donations wasn't quite my thing either, but I was getting warmer."

His lips quirked. "In more ways than one."

"No kidding. When I saw the opening here, I knew it was perfect." She leaned forward. "I love the idea of helping alumni feel connected—of giving them opportunities, either here or close to home, to immerse themselves in the kind of intense educational experience they knew at Wakefield. And, yes, to help the college by ensuring those same alumni maintain a financial commitment."

He nodded as if unsurprised, at which she was able to

relax a little, relieved he hadn't made a joke out of her passion. She hadn't intended to speak so strongly.

Madison made an attempt to prod him into talking about why he'd gone into law enforcement. "Is it a family thing?"

"As in, my dad, a cop?" He laughed. "Not a chance. He was a banker. He actually grew up on a wheat farm outside town. His father was disappointed he didn't want to take over the farm. Like with a lot of the other wheat farms around here, times got tougher and eventually the land was sold."

"Is it growing grapes now?"

"Yep. It's part of the Frenchman Lake Vineyard & Winery. It feels strange to drive by. I'll think 'Grandma and Grandad's place is right around this bend,' only it's not. Yeah, the house is still there, but nothing looks the same." He shrugged. "Even Grandad eventually admitted that Dad was smart to find another way to make a living."

"Did Dad ever decide *you* were smart to do something else?"

His lashes veiled his eyes. "He never put it quite that way, but he claimed to be proud of me. He and Mom were a lot happier when I left the Seattle P.D. for Frenchman Lake, though. Not only because I'd be close to them."

"Because they thought you'd be safer," she said gently.

"Parents."

"If you had kids, would you want them to follow in your footsteps?"

He frowned, and she saw that he was taking her question seriously. "I don't know," he said finally. "I tend to feel pretty protective of anyone I care about. That might be a struggle for me."

She almost hesitated to ask again. Maybe he didn't want to tell her why he'd become a cop. Or maybe she wouldn't like his answer. He could like the power trip, having the right to swagger around carrying a gun. Or what if he was an adrenaline junkie?

Well, it couldn't be that, or he wouldn't have quit his big-city job to come home to small-town policing, would he?

He was definitely hesitating about telling her, though. He set down his burger at last and leaned back in his chair. "It was something that happened when I was at the UW. I saw a homeless guy get beaten to death."

She made an involuntary sound.

"I was walking home from a party late one night. I'd had a couple of beers, but I didn't have more than a buzz. I'm not much of a drinker," he said matter-of-factly.

Madison nodded. She'd noticed how he was nursing the one beer along.

"I saw this flurry of motion up ahead, maybe a block and a half away. At first I was only curious. I was within a block when I got a bad feeling. I started walking faster. I saw a couple of guys kicking something in the doorway of a closed business down the street. Next thing I knew I was running." Tension imbued his voice. "They saw me coming and took off. I might have caught them if I'd kept after them, but I stopped to see what that was in the recessed doorway."

"And he was already dead."

"Yeah. Jesus. It was sickening. I was naive as hell, but even I knew it was too late to try to resuscitate him. I called 911 and waited for the cops."

"Did they ever make an arrest?"

His mouth twisted. "No. That upset me." Clearly an understatement. "It sort of ate at me. Eventually I decided *I* could have caught the sons of bitches. I went straight to the police academy after graduation."

"What did you major in?" Madison asked, her curiosity irresistible.

The question seemed to erase his dark mood. He reached for his burger again. "Guess."

"Hmm." She mulled over the possibilities, studying him. "Psychology."

"Not even close."

Her eyes widened. "English?"

That earned her a bark of laughter. "Not a chance."

"Biology." Head shake. "German." A laugh. "Oh, for Pete's sake. Computer Science. Horticulture. Political Science." More head shakes and a whole lot of amusement. She threw up her hands. "I give up."

"Art."

She was the one to laugh this time. "Were you serious? Or was it part of your rebellious phase?"

"Oh, probably a little of one, a little of the other. Dad couldn't say much, though. After all, he was an English major. What's more useless than that?"

"Not much, if you look at it in practical terms."

His gaze sharpened. "Don't tell me you were an English major."

"No, Psych. I envisioned myself doing counseling, except I never seriously pursued that route." She frowned. "Wait. You're not off the hook. Tell me about you as an artist."

He grimaced. "There's not much to tell. I wasn't going to take the art world by storm. I do still work with clay, mostly as a hobby. I have a wheel and kiln in my garage. It's how I relax."

"That's fascinating. What do you do with your pieces?"

He shrugged, looking uncomfortable. "Mostly, give 'em away. These days, I'm selling some. I'm not doing anything artsy. I do vases and bowls, plates." He shifted under her stare. "Lately I've been experimenting with teapots."

"Teapots."

"I don't like the way you say that."

Madison laughed. "I was expressing astonishment. It's the dichotomy. Tough cop who goes home and glazes a teapot."

He scowled. "This is why I don't tell people."

"I think it's wonderful," she said honestly. "It makes me like you even better than I already did."

After a minute, one corner of his mouth lifted. "Then I'm good with having told you."

"Did I mention that I don't have a single artistic bone in my body?"

His chuckle was a bass rumble. "No, you didn't. What do you do for fun? Or to reduce stress?"

"A lot of days I swim half a mile before I go home. I listen to music—I love jazz. I can't carry a tune, though." She loved his smile. "I cook, although only when I'm in the mood."

"I hope you get in the mood one of these nights soon."

"Once this weekend is over," she promised. "I should warn you I don't eat much meat."

Troy glanced at his plate. The burger was gone, but he was still working on the fries. "I'm not exclusively a meat and potatoes guy. It just sounded good tonight."

"I wasn't trying to make you feel guilty."

"Wouldn't have worked if you were. But I'm happy with a vegetarian meal, too."

"Good," she said, pleased.

Eventually the waiter took away their plates. Troy ordered blueberry cobbler à la mode and asked for a second fork. They split it and kept talking. It seemed as if there was never a lull in conversation. Madison found she wanted to know everything about him, and the feeling seemed to be mutual. She was getting way more tingles than were justified, given that he hadn't touched her since laying a hand on her back to steer her to the table. It had to be anticipation. Every so often she lost track of what he was saying because she was watching his mouth instead. Or his hands. He had great hands—big, strong, with long, blunt-tipped fingers. They weren't hairy like some men's. She tried to imagine them shaping clay into a delicate piece like the spout of a teapot, and then envisioned one wrapping the butt of his gun.

Or touching her. She kept imagining that, too.

Every so often his eyes would narrow or she'd see a flicker of heat in them. Either he could tell what she was thinking, or he was doing some imagining of his own. She had the giddy thought that the night felt like magic.

She couldn't possibly fall in love this fast, but it felt an awful lot like a beginning. Or at least it didn't feel like anything that had ever happened to her before.

She flushed with the realization that she had no idea what they'd been talking about and that Troy was watching her with amusement and something more electric.

"Where'd you just go?" he asked.

"Oh, I…" She could say her mind had wandered and leave it at that. But she felt unaccustomedly reckless. "I was thinking about you," she heard herself say. "How glad I am you were assigned to work with me. We might never have met otherwise."

"Unless I pulled you over for speeding." His voice was a little gritty. He reached across the table and took her hand. "I'm glad, too." He looked around. "I think they'd be glad if we left."

Madison was shocked to see that the tables around them were empty. She hadn't even noticed other people leaving.

At the moment, they were completely alone, although she could still hear voices downstairs. "Oh, no! We're lucky they didn't whisk the tablecloth off while we were still sitting here."

Troy laughed, stood up and tugged her to her feet. He kept pulling until she bumped into him. "I've been wanting to kiss you all evening, Madison Laclaire."

"I have no objection," she managed to say.

"Good," he murmured, and bent his head.

She rose on tiptoe to meet him, gripping his shoulders for balance. Their mouths connected, and it wasn't the tentative brush of lips she'd expected. The kind that asked, *do you like this?* and that she'd answer with a nibble that said, *oh, yes.* This was a full-out, hungry demand. Apparently John Troyer wasn't a tentative kind of guy.

Washed away by sensation, Madison discovered she felt demanding, too. Her fingers dug into the sleek muscles in his shoulders and she parted her lips to accept the thrust of his tongue. Her knees wanted to buckle. She leaned against his solid frame and tasted beer, salt and something distinctly him. His thighs were so strong, his hands powerful but still careful as he positioned her to suit him. She was melting, too aroused to remember where they were.

He was the one to stiffen and lift his head. Only belatedly did Madison realize she'd heard the scrape of furniture on the floor behind them. Oh, heavens—she sneaked a peek to see that a waiter was upending chairs and putting them on tables. He very tactfully had his back to them as he worked, but he must have seen them kissing.

Troy gently kissed her again then eased her away. He was smiling, but the heated glow in his eyes told her he hadn't liked having to let her go any better than she did. "Didn't mean to get so carried away," he said.

"It's probably just as well we were interrupted." Madison wasn't sure she meant it. "I'm usually, um, a little more cautious than that."

His hands momentarily tightened on her arms. The next moment he loosened them very deliberately. With a nudge he started her between tables toward the top of the staircase. "I don't suppose you have a lot of spare time the next few days."

"You think?"

"I'm meeting with your head of security tomorrow. Can we have coffee if I stop by your office afterward?"

Madison discovered she hated the idea of not seeing him at all tomorrow. "Yes. If we can make it iced coffee. It's supposed to top a hundred tomorrow."

His hand moved in a gentle circle on her back. "Far as I'm concerned, we can go sit in the shade and do nothing but hold hands."

This feeling, as if champagne bubbles were popping in her bloodstream, was an entirely new sensation for her. "That works, too," she admitted and made sure she had her hand on the railing as she began to descend the stairs. Her legs still weren't quite steady.

By the way he hovered, Madison felt fairly certain Troy wouldn't let her fall. Modern woman that she was, she ought to be disgusted to discover she felt reassured and even…cherished.

Knowing he couldn't see her face, she frowned. Wow. Getting swept away like this might make her giddy, but it was more than a little scary, too.

So what? she thought with an unaccustomed feeling of boldness, already looking forward to tomorrow. In her opinion, she was past due to take some risks.

CHAPTER THREE

"I SAW A PICTURE of your dad," Madison said.

Troy made a lazy sound in his throat that she took as an inquiry.

He lounged next to her on a stone bench in the shade beside the duck pond, his long legs stretched out and crossed at the ankles. The shade wasn't doing an awful lot of good. Leaves hung limply. Even the usually aggressive ducks hadn't stirred themselves to beg for handouts. Conversation had been desultory at best. Each of them had been sipping at the iced coffees he'd brought, as promised.

"I studied some of the reunion photos," she explained. "Putting faces to names. Think how impressed they'll be if I recognize some of them as they arrive."

Troy turned his head and smiled at her. "I'd be impressed."

She sighed. "Of course, the last reunion of our fathers' class was five years ago. Everyone has probably gained weight or lost hair or something. I probably won't recognize a one of them."

"Dad was definitely losing his hair."

She'd noticed. This morning, Madison had squinted for some time at her computer monitor. Eventually she'd zoomed in on the faces that interested her, including Joseph Troyer's. His hairline had undeniably receded. What hair he had left was graying, but she thought he'd been blond. At the time the picture was snapped, he was still a solid, well-built man.

"He looked like you."

"More accurate to say I look like him."

"Well, I guess that's true." She hesitated. "Your mother was in the picture, too."

He grunted, looking uninterested. "What about your dad? Was he there?"

"No. He's never bothered with a reunion." He'd come to her graduation from Wakefield, but she had a feeling that might have been the only time he'd returned to French-man Lake since his own graduation day. She hadn't visited the campus prior to applying to Wakefield College. Moving-in day still stuck in her mind. Most of the incoming freshmen had arrived with parents who helped settle them into their dorm rooms. Her father hadn't seen any reason she needed him. He had seemed surprised when she timidly asked whether he intended to bring her. She had a car, after all, and would surely want it, he'd pointed out.

Troy was watching her now. "You close to him?" he asked.

"Yes and no." She shrugged as if the subject wasn't a sensitive one. "I mostly lived with him after my parents divorced. But he's not what you'd call warm and fuzzy."

Troy's arm had been lying along the back of the bench behind her. Now his big hand gently squeezed her shoulder. "Your choice to live with him?"

"Yes." She gazed ahead, where a mallard duck dived midpond. "Mom remarried right away and started another family. I felt like the square peg. It was probably my fault more than hers." She'd said that so many times, she almost believed it.

"You see much of her?"

"Very occasionally. I hardly know my half sister and brother."

"Hmm."

She chuckled to relieve some of her tension. "You sound like a therapist."

"I'm lacking the goatee to stroke."

"So you are." She liked the way his hand kept kneading her shoulder. She wasn't nestled close to him, both because this was, after all, her workplace, but mostly because sweat would probably have glued them together if they dared get too close. She'd have been tempted to plunge into the pond with the lone mallard had the water not been so murky. "All roads seem to lead back to our parents," she commented.

The skin beside his eyes crinkled. "Then let's talk about something else."

"Did I mention the golf course manager informs me I don't have the tee times I thought I did? We may edge the lunch back so the golfers have a chance to finish their rounds."

"Glad to hear that. I'll be starved by the time I beat my way out of the rough."

Madison laughed. "The caterer for the reception failed to locate the quality of asparagus she wanted and for some reason that made her rethink several of the hors d'oeuvres, even ones that have nothing to do with asparagus. I've gotten calls from half a dozen alumni who are miffed because they didn't make reservations soon enough and now they're going to have to stay at a hotel not up to their standards. Oh, and the president's wife is coming down with a cold."

"Is it possible to get a cold when it's this hot?" Troy peeled his polo shirt away from his body. "I'll bet she could bake the virus crispy dead if she played eighteen holes midday."

Madison muffled a laugh. "I'll be sure to suggest that." She took the last slurp of her drink and sighed. "I ought to get back to work."

His fingers circled the ball of her shoulder one more time. "Sounds like you have everything in hand."

"Knock on wood." She glanced at the iron bench. "Oops."

He rose to his feet and looked down at her. "Tomorrow's the big day."

"Yes. You'll be at the reception at the president's house?" She knew he was skipping the wine-tasting tour, as was she.

"Wouldn't miss it." He smiled at her. "I'm looking forward to seeing you in action."

"Hiding panic at every glitch, you mean."

"I seriously doubt that. You're too well organized to permit glitches."

Pleased by his faith and by the fact that he seemed to be more than okay with the idea of her being really good at her job, she said goodbye and parted from him. She couldn't resist the temptation to turn and watch him stride away. Although he clearly wasn't in any hurry, he moved purposefully and his head turned to take in his surroundings. It wouldn't be easy to take him by surprise. Probably that was characteristic of cops.

Walking back to Mem, Madison speculated on what it would be like to be involved with someone in law enforcement. Did he talk about his job? He hadn't so far, but then she hadn't asked. Would he be moody when he came home after seeing awful things? Had he ever shot anyone? She'd read that cops had a high divorce rate and a high rate of alcoholism, too. Troy had made a point out of mentioning that he wasn't a drinker. The subject of previous marriages hadn't yet arisen. At his age, it was entirely possible he had a divorce behind him, she thought, not liking the idea.

Reality check. They'd had one date. One coffee break. She was getting way ahead of herself.

Still, as the afternoon went on she found herself thinking about both Troy and, perhaps inevitably, their respective fathers. How well had the two known each other? They had surely been in a number of classes together. She realized that it bothered her more than ever how little she knew about her father's years here. Why it mattered she couldn't have said, but it felt weird that he would have known all the alumni arriving tomorrow. Chances were that there were former friends of his among them, even girlfriends. Madison's last name was uncommon, so someone might make the connection. She hated to have to say, "Gee, no, Dad never mentioned you."

She gave serious thought that evening to calling him, but he was in Tokyo and she had no idea what the time difference was. He was undoubtedly asleep in his hotel room during her waking hours. He'd be irritated if she happened to get him awake but when he was doing business, which included all meals. And…what would he say, anyway?

She could hear him irritably admitting he knew Joseph Troyer. *What did he end up as?* He would grunt when she told him. *A small-town banker sounds about right. No ambition.* Her father did condescension very well.

Why, she asked herself, *do I even* want *to call my father?*

As always, she was embarrassed by the answer.

Because he's all I have.

TROY HAD BEGUN to think he wouldn't like either of Madison's parents. He doubted she had any idea how much

she'd given away when she was talking about her mother.
It had been enough to make him hurt for the little girl
she'd been. Or had she been older? A teenager, maybe?
He would have to ask.

He'd reserve judgment where the dad was concerned.
Somebody had to have done something right, or Madison
wouldn't be the woman she was. Did an unhappy child
ever learn to smile with unalloyed delight the way she did?

Troy put in a few hours at his desk at the station, finishing up reports and making phone calls, but she stayed on
his mind. She'd been there since he first set eyes on her,
and he wished like hell they were having dinner again tonight. He didn't like knowing they wouldn't be able to do
more than exchange a few words at the crowded reception
tomorrow night, either.

Patience, he told himself. Madison wouldn't always
be as busy as she was this weekend. He should be glad
to have the chance to watch her at work. He'd learn more
about her that way than he would on a dozen dinner dates.

Not a day passed that he didn't wish his father was
still alive. The need to talk to Dad was even fiercer than
usual right now. Driving home, Troy thought about everything he wished he could ask. He was curious what his
father thought about these classmates, starting with Guy
Laclaire. He'd have liked Dad to meet Madison. And he
was bugged that he hadn't pushed harder when Dad said
so little about the long-ago murder.

Damn it, had he really not known Mitchell King very
well? For some reason Troy kept thinking back to their
conversation. He hadn't felt dissatisfaction then, but he
suspected now that Dad had been holding back. It would
be like him to be reticent if, say, he hadn't liked King.
Troy's easygoing father never wanted to admit he didn't
like someone.

Troy grabbed fast-food meals more often than he should, but tonight he made the decision to stop at the grocery store—air-conditioned, thank God—and then grill a steak and make a salad once he got home. He cleaned the kitchen then called his mother, as he did a lot of nights when he wasn't stopping by the house to make sure she was all right.

But he dreaded these phone calls.

This conversation was typical.

He asked how she was.

"Fine." She sounded vaguely surprised he'd asked. "Just fine."

Of course she was fine. She'd never admit to anything else even when he heard tears in her voice.

Had she gone anywhere today? Why no, but she'd had to water all the plants on the patio, you know, and that took forever.

Oh, the time capsule was being opened this weekend? Goodness, she'd forgotten all about it.

She didn't want to talk about it any more than she had the last time he mentioned the weekend activities.

Troy could never pin her down. There was a lot she didn't want to talk about, including how she felt or the fact that she scarcely left the house. The weight she'd lost since Dad died wasn't open to discussion. Sometimes he wasn't sure she'd notice if he quit calling altogether. For a while there, he'd been doing her grocery shopping, but once she discovered one of the stores delivered, she'd opted into the service. Mainly, Troy suspected, so he couldn't critique what—or how little—she ate.

And, hell, maybe he wasn't handling her grief well. Probably because he was male, he'd always been closer to Dad than he was to her. Whether Mom might have found it more acceptable to lean on a daughter than a son, he didn't know. What he did know was that he was all she had, whether she liked it or not.

There were days he wanted to give up, but he knew he'd never let himself. He understood his mother's devastation. She and Dad hadn't spent a night apart from their wedding day on. They'd had the kind of marriage he wanted. The love between his parents had been so palpable, he'd sometimes been embarrassed by it when he was a kid. Nobody else's parents looked at each other the way his mom and dad did. He'd never been able to imagine one of them without the other. None of them had expected something so sudden and shocking. There wasn't even time to say goodbye.

And yeah, there was a secret part of him that resented her determination to make the grief exclusive to her. She didn't want to hear that he hurt, too.

Troy had no trouble imagining her stare of complete incomprehension if he tried to say, "I feel like I've lost my mother, too."

He gave brief thought to saying, *I met a woman who is special,* but if that didn't get a rise he didn't want to feel the disappointment. It was too soon anyway, he told himself. He hardly knew Madison Laclaire.

Although, damn, he did like what he knew.

A STEADY STREAM of alumni arrived from early Friday morning on to pick up the schedule of events that included a map of the wineries on this afternoon's tour and directions to the golf course that hadn't existed when they were students here. Madison had had tables set up beneath the trees outside Mem, one for check-in and the other holding a coffee urn and pitchers of lemonade. The day's heat was already making itself felt, but the huge old trees and the velvet green lawn, still slightly damp from last night's sprinklers, at least gave an illusion of cool.

Senator Haywood was an early arrival. Rather than tasting wine, he would be speaking to an upper level political science class that afternoon, in addition to giving a second, open lecture this evening after the reception. Madison had no trouble recognizing him since she'd looked up current images online.

Silver at the temples and an overall dusting of silver set off his styled dark hair. He had a charming smile she couldn't help returning.

He shook her hand, his eyes keen on her face. "You wouldn't be Guy Laclaire's daughter?"

"I am indeed," she confessed. "Unfortunately, Dad couldn't be here this weekend. He's in Tokyo on business."

"He's done well for himself." He shook his head admiringly. "I saw mention of him in the *Wall Street Journal* the other day. I'll make a point of giving him a call."

He was clearly making a mental note. She didn't tell him Dad was stingy with donations, but in this case he might surprise her. His politics were more conservative than hers.

Haywood introduced his wife, a stylish, attractive woman whose smile was as bright and probably as insincere as her husband's. Madison chided herself for being a cynic. She wouldn't have thought any such thing if she hadn't known he was a politician.

She talked briefly with the senator about his two speaking engagements and told him how much the students were looking forward to hearing him. She already knew he and his wife were staying at the home of one of the college trustees, who owned a good deal of downtown Frenchman Lake, rather than in a hotel.

The college president deftly took the senator off her

hands and she turned to greet the next arrivals. The woman's face looked familiar.

"Let me think. Marcia Skiles?"

The woman chuckled. "Very good! Marcia Skiles Armstrong now. I've remarried since that last reunion." She introduced her husband, after which they told Madison how excited they were about visiting some of the wineries.

"We've become connoisseurs," she said, "in our small way."

Some of the alumni expressed an intention to play in the informal golf tournament on Saturday morning, but the greatest enthusiasm was expressed for the wine tasting tour. Frenchman Lake wines weren't yet as acclaimed as Walla Walla Valley wines, but some were beginning to receive high ratings from *Wine Spectator* and other sources.

Madison murmured agreement when people waxed rhapsodic over the wine, although she never had picked up on hints of licorice or tannin or wild huckleberry. As far as she was concerned, expensive wines usually tasted better than cheap ones. Full stop. It was safe to say no one would call *her* a connoisseur.

She had the comforting thought that Troy probably wasn't one either. He hadn't seemed at all interested in the wine tasting portion of the weekend.

Of course, that might have been because he was focused on security, impossible to provide when the alumni were driving themselves to the many wineries throughout the valley.

"Any relation to Guy Laclaire?" the latest alumnus in front of her table asked.

Her gaze dropped surreptitiously to the name tag he'd affixed to the front of his striped polo shirt. It was embarrassing to have forgotten his name quite so quickly.

Del Trzcinski.

That was even *more* embarrassing, as she had also just had him pronounce his name for her.

She smiled at him. "His daughter." This was the fifth time someone had asked and she'd had to explain that no, Dad wouldn't be here this weekend. The day had barely begun. Thank God no one had yet assumed she'd know way more about her father's acquaintances than she did.

One man mentioned that he and Guy had been doubles partners on the college tennis team for two years. She knew her father had played varsity all four years at Wakefield. He'd been on the debate team, too, which had reached finals in the national competition his senior year.

So, okay, she did know *something* about his years here. More than something—out of pure nosiness she'd looked up his academic record, and learned that Guy Laclaire had graduated with a 3.85 GPA. Not perfect. There were several Bs sprinkled throughout his freshman and sophomore years. All were outside his major, in classes he'd been required to take to demonstrate breadth.

Still…not perfect. She'd been stunned. As long as she could remember, he'd been driven, impatient with anyone else's frailties and demanding of perfection. She wondered if he'd hated graduating without a perfect 4.0, or whether he'd actually allowed himself to have fun during his four years at Wakefield.

Her mind boggled at the idea of her father having "fun."

She smiled at the woman who stepped up to the table. "And you are?"

OSTENSIBLY THE EVENING reception at the college president's house was casual, but Troy had known better than to show up in chinos and polo shirt. A few men did, but their polo shirts had discreet and pricey little logos on the breast. A fair number of the women wore linen, cool and probably also expensive but wrinkled anyway. He wasn't a clothes-horse; in fact, most of the time he didn't give a damn what he was wearing. Even so, he couldn't quite figure out why anyone wanted to wear something that looked like it had been wadded up under the mattress all night long.

His heart skipped a beat when he caught a glimpse of Madison across the room. Her gauzy little dress with spaghetti straps was the color of a peach picked ripe from the tree. The fabric was airy instead of crisp or wrinkled. With strappy, high-heeled sandals, her legs were nicely displayed. When the crowd shifted and he could no longer see her, he shifted, too, using his shoulders to wedge his way past clusters of attendees sipping cocktails and chattering. He noticed a few faces that had gotten more sun today than they should have. One woman was *really* red and he winced sympathetically.

Ah. There was Madison, laughing at something being said by the suave-looking guy leaning into her. The next second, Troy recognized the senator. He was pretty damn sure Haywood's gaze was locked on Madison's cleavage and not her face.

Just like a politician.

Troy moved to her side and planted his left hand on the small of her back, even though one date, one kiss, didn't give him any right to be proprietary. At the moment, he didn't give a damn. "Hey," he murmured. "Sorry I'm late."

Her face brightened with relief or pleasure or both, causing some more strange bumping sensations under his breastbone. "Troy!" She didn't move away from him. "Oh, good. I was afraid something had come up. Troy, have you met Senator Gordon Haywood yet? Senator, this is Detective John Troyer. You may have known his father, Joseph."

The two men shook hands.

"Sure, sure. I was real sorry to hear that he'd passed

away." Haywood grimaced. "I've been paying a little more attention to my cholesterol since then."

"Dad ate well and was fit, but he was a smoker," Troy explained. "Never could quit."

"What a shame." The senator shook his head sorrowfully. "A real shame. He was a good man."

Since to the best of Troy's knowledge, Senator Haywood hadn't had any contact with Dad in thirty-five years, it was a little hard to figure how he knew Joseph Troyer was a good man. But hey, a guy had to say something.

The senator excused himself a moment later to clap a hand on a man's back and exclaim, "Fred! Great to see you."

"Creep," Troy muttered.

Madison only laughed at him. "Now, how do you know that?"

"Isn't the guy married? He won't make the White House if he's stupid enough to ogle women like that very often."

"I don't know." She sounded thoughtful. "Politicians seem to get away with things like that for years before they get caught. Although I was starting to get offended. And, as it happens, he's not only married, his wife is here." She tipped her head toward the group the senator had joined.

Troy saw that the guy now rested his hand on the wrinkled-linen-clad back of a woman thin to the point of looking breakable.

"In fairness," Troy conceded, "you have a very fine cleavage."

Her eyes widened and she clapped a hand to her chest. "Oh, no. Is this dress too…too…"

When she failed to come up with a word, he supplied one. "Sexy? No, your dress is pretty and perfect for a hot evening." He bent his head closer to her ear. "It's *you* that's sexy."

She blinked at him, tiny creases appearing between her eyebrows. "Thank you. I think."

Troy smiled. "You look beautiful tonight. Don't worry. He's a dirty old man."

Madison spared a glance the senator's way. "He's only fifty-seven. Or maybe fifty-eight."

"And married."

"Well, yes. He is married. You're right." She nodded. "He's a creep."

"Ellen Kenney here?"

"Yes, holding court by the bay window."

Mostly, Troy could see a whole lot of backs. Heads were nodding. The author was presumably doing the talking. Hard to resist, when so many people were hanging on your every word.

"She actually seems to be really nice," Madison said. "She and the senator both spoke to students today. I stuck my head into the classrooms. She had the kids enthralled. He had a little more trouble, because the students here tend to be liberal and they were throwing some tough questions at him. He seemed to take it in stride, though."

Troy accepted a glass of champagne from a passing waiter. "I'd intended to go hear him tonight."

Their eyes met and they both laughed.

"From a security standpoint, I probably should go," he said reluctantly.

"Absolutely." She grinned at him. "You can tell me all about it."

They were both laughing again when a particularly penetrating man's voice cut through the babel.

"Hard to believe they never arrested anyone for killing Mitch."

Madison turned and Troy saw her alarmed gaze meet

the college president's. "Into the fray," she said softly to Troy, and started briskly toward the speaker.

Troy followed but hung back, curious how she'd handle this.

The answer was: very smoothly.

She joined the group, commented on how shocking it must have been back then to have a fellow student killed right here on campus, then within moments had them rhapsodizing about wine and kidding each other about who was going to play under par in the morning.

Troy reflected that Madison's professional instincts and his were exactly opposite. She wanted to stifle all speculation, pretend the whole ugly thing had never happened. When it came to murder, he was all cop. He'd always been especially intrigued by cold cases. There was nothing he'd have liked better than to encourage talk.

Half the people in this room had known Mitchell King and maybe some of his secrets, assuming he had any. Those same people might conceivably have known the killer, too, assuming you didn't buy the stranger-who-happened-to-be-passing-through-town theory—which Troy didn't. It was even possible, he reflected, that the killer was one of these people, although on second thought he decided that was unlikely. If some twenty or twenty-two-year-old kid had been in a rage great enough to drive him to bludgeon Mitchell King to death, you wouldn't expect that same student to become the kind of alumnus so fond of his college experience he enjoyed regular visits to the campus, now would you? Since he presumably wasn't a psychopath who enjoyed killing—or at least he was hiding it real well if he was—the guy would be more likely to have clutched his diploma in sweaty hands and sworn never to set foot on this campus again. He probably did his damnedest not even to *think* about Wakefield College and what he'd discovered about himself while he was here.

Yeah, that made sense. Troy had been scanning the room as he pondered, his gaze going from face to face. Now his mouth tipped up in a faint smile. Madison wouldn't be thrilled if she knew what he'd been thinking. Or maybe she'd be okay with it as long as he kept his mouth shut, which he fully intended to do.

It was damn tempting, though, to reopen that cold case when there were actually some potential witnesses gathered right here rather than spread across the country. Even better, though, when there was a full reunion of King's classmates.

Of course, college/town relations were always a little delicate, and that might sour them here in Frenchman Lake for the next quarter century or so. No, Troy wouldn't get anywhere suggesting any such thing unless he found an interesting end of a string to pull.

Forget it, he told himself.

He automatically sought Madison. She stood with her back to him, but he found plenty to admire, anyway. With her hair piled on top of her head, he had a fine view of her slim neck and the delicate string of vertebrae that disappeared beneath the plunging back of the dress. Her shoulder blades were beautifully constructed, too, he decided. And, while the dress didn't cling quite as well as the red suit she'd worn that first day, it still suggested an ass as lush as the breasts Senator Haywood had leered at.

She was a lot more interesting than a murder that had happened thirty-five years ago.

She glanced over her shoulder right then, those warm brown eyes rolling with just a hint of desperation, and he obeyed the summons. He was getting to spend more time with her this evening than he'd expected.

It had been a while since he'd been able to think smugly, *life is good.*

CHAPTER FOUR

THE CROWD WATCHED, breathless, as two workmen used crowbars to pry out the foundation stone that hid the time capsule.

Troy bent his head to place his mouth close to Madison's ear. "You know, this could be a big oops. What if somebody stole the capsule twenty-five years ago?"

She allowed herself a small grin. "You think I'm that dumb?"

Amusement glinted in his eyes. "You checked."

"You bet."

She hadn't been about to set all this up only to find, at the penultimate moment, that the capsule had disappeared at *any* time in the past thirty-five years.

With a grinding sound, the block of granite was inched backward until it hung out of the foundation so far that Madison held her breath. Finally the two workmen leaped backward and the stone fell, landing with a perceptible thud. Even she jumped a little.

Troy's chuckle made her want to stick out her tongue at him. Of course, *his* poise never wavered. The two of them had positioned themselves near the front, but to one side in the shade cast by a huge, ancient maple tree. Madison felt a little like the wizard of Oz right now, pulling strings from behind the curtain. The designated front man was the president of the college, well accustomed to being on stage.

Lars Berglund *looked* like a college president should,

with his snowy hair cut stylishly, his blue eyes percep-
tive, his tall body trim from daily workouts. He had the
gift of seemingly focusing all his attention on the one person who was speaking. What could be more flattering?
He exuded charm, charisma and brains. It went without
saying that he had the requisite background: while a professor of political science and international relations at a
couple of different, prestigious private colleges, he had
published well-reviewed articles and books, including one
that was a standby college text in the area of comparative
African politics. He still wrote and published. His personality made him a natural for administration, however.
Wakefield felt lucky to have lured him from a larger Mid-
western university.

Now he stooped to peer into the dark opening. He murmured to one of the workmen, who handed him a glove.
After donning it, Berglund groped within. He allowed a
dramatically elongated moment before triumphantly drag-
ging out the rather odd capsule. Made of shiny metal, at
first sight it had looked to Madison as if it ought to hold
nuclear material or something else space-age and possibly dangerous.

A few cries of delight, some catcalls and piercing whis-
tles preceded a round of applause as the president set the
capsule carefully on the table placed for that purpose.
Pleased at the response, Madison turned her head to look
around.

The size of the crowd was augmented by the many
family members as well as curious students, administrators and professors. Most had been able to find a place
in the shade. Chairs had been set out but were only half-
occupied. Most people chose to stand or, in some cases,
sit on the grass. She recognized the majority of the alumni
in attendance by now. She ought to—she'd tried to talk

to all of them. If she hadn't found them at the reception, she'd sought them out today during the lunch served not far away on Allquist Field.

Ellen Kenney seemed to have acquired a permanent entourage made up of classmates and students. Senator Haywood and his wife had found a prominent position at the front. Others clustered in relaxed groups, obviously enjoying the production. A few seemed to make a point of standing alone or with only one companion.

President Berglund put on his dark-framed reading glasses so that he could see the slip of paper Madison had earlier given him. The capsule had not only been mortared into the foundation of Cheadle Hall. It was also closed with a combination lock.

The president, while joking with the crowd, now dialed the combination. In her determination to dodge any possible embarrassment, Madison had secretly done this in advance, too, although she hadn't let herself study the contents.

As near as she was to the front, she heard the click as the lock surrendered. President Berglund rotated the lid to one side and the crowd roared with delight.

"As you know," he said, "the plan is for me to remove items one by one. I'll call out the name, and the individual in question—or his or her representative—will then come up and accept whatever item was deposited in this capsule on that long-ago day." His hand delved into the long metal container. Eagerness silenced the buzz.

"Rob Dayton."

A tall, lanky man, almost entirely bald, stepped forward and accepted the 8 ½ by 10 inch envelope. It had appeared to Madison, when she peeked, that most inclusions had been sealed into similar envelopes.

To the sound of good-natured jibes, Dayton retreated to his wife's side.

No one was there to claim the next couple items, which Berglund set aside. Several more alums came forward and accepted theirs.

Madison noted that one of the envelopes was rather lumpy and obviously held something more than the writing samples most of these English majors had probably chosen to save for posterity. This one was accepted by an attractive woman around her own age. Madison had barely had a chance to chat with Amy Nilsson, who had explained that her mother was in Australia for two years.

"I thought it would be fun to pick up whatever she put in the capsule," Amy had said that morning. Now, carrying that fat manila envelope, she retreated back to the side of the man who had accompanied her. Madison would have presumed he was her husband, except that Amy hadn't introduced him as such and they didn't seem to touch casually the way people comfortable with each other physically did. Friends, maybe.

"Jeanne Wellborn."

"Mary Jo Warren."

"Ellen Kenney."

Curious stares followed the noted author as she accepted a rather thick envelope.

"An entire book manuscript?" Troy said softly. "Do you suppose it's a masterpiece that the world would have been deprived of for another fifteen years if you hadn't decided to do this early?"

Madison laughed. "More likely, the painful drivel of a too-earnest adolescent."

"Tut, tut. Doesn't Wakefield promise to ignite genius?"

"Nobody said ignited genius doesn't also require a maturing process."

"Aging, you mean? In oak casks?" he asked politely.

She laughed. "That sounds easy and more peaceful than what we all go through, doesn't it?"

He gave her a sharp look, as if she'd betrayed something she hadn't meant to. Madison didn't even know why the comment brought a pang of sadness along with it.

"Guy Laclaire."

Troy nudged her. "That's you."

Startled, she stepped forward. She'd almost forgotten she was to collect something of her father's.

President Berglund grinned at her. "Hope he didn't leave something that will shock you."

She smiled at him. "I almost hope he did."

A couple of nearby people overheard and laughed. She went back to Troy's side.

Berglund next drew out something that *wasn't* contained in an envelope. "Well, well," he said. "Now tell me, who plans to claim these?" He held up a handful of packets that Madison realized, after a puzzled moment, held condoms. The president grinned contagiously. "If you do claim them, I recommend caution. I suspect they're past their use-by date."

Ribald comments and slightly crude accusations flung among the gathering and laughter loosened the atmosphere. It was almost a surprise to hear the next name.

"Joseph Troyer."

With their upper arms brushing, Madison felt Troy's new tension. His expression, she saw, had closed down entirely. The occasion and the simple act of accepting something his father had most likely written and perhaps never intended any other eyes to see was far more complicated for Troy than it had been for her. He must feel his father's absence with painful clarity as, after only the briefest hesitation, he walked forward.

His envelope looked like all the others, but was one of the thinnest, as if it held only a few pages. Maybe Joseph Troyer had written poetry, Madison speculated. She'd have to ask Troy later.

The calling of names continued. The pile of unclaimed envelopes grew. Some people had opened their contributions and were sharing what appeared mostly to be writings with their companions. There was a lot of laughter. Madison told herself she was saving her dad's for later because she was in charge of the event and couldn't afford to get distracted. Troy, she couldn't help noticing, made no move to slide his finger under the flap of the envelope he held either. In fact, although he'd returned to her side he now stood a couple of feet away. His posture was nowhere near as relaxed. His face remained impassive. No more humorous murmurs in her ear.

Madison became edgy when she realized that expressionless gaze was repeatedly sweeping the crowd. Had he seen something to awaken the cop in him? she wondered in alarm.

"What's wrong?" she asked in an urgent undertone.

Dark gray eyes met hers. "Wrong?"

"You look…" She hesitated.

"No," he said flatly. "Nothing's wrong."

"Gordon Haywood," President Berglund said, and the senator wasted no time in claiming his contribution.

The list of names went on. At last Berglund upended the capsule and smiled when one small object fell onto the table. "A petrified Tootsie Roll," he informed the crowd, who laughed.

"If you'd like to linger, visit with old friends, maybe hold public readings—" more chuckles "—catering staff have brought out beverages and cookies to hold you until dinner." One last brilliant smile. "I look forward to see-ing you all this evening."

"Well," Madison said, feeling awkward with Troy for the first time. "I'm afraid I have to stay."

Troy nodded. "I'd better, too, although it looks like most people aren't going to hang around."

Senator Haywood and his wife were already making tracks, Madison couldn't help but notice. His wife was all but scuttling to keep up with him and seemed to be pro-testing, although they kept their voices low. He was among the relatively few who *hadn't* opened his envelope. Madi-son had a sudden, intriguing thought: What if the young Gordon Haywood had written something that would now be scandalous, or at least embarrassing? He wouldn't have dared not come to claim it, in case somebody peeked. Maybe, she thought in amusement, he'd brought a por-table shredder in his suitcase.

And maybe I just don't like him.

Almost everyone else visited the refreshment table, by common consensus bypassing the coffee urn for the gen-erous cups of lemonade that staff served from big punch bowls. It was so blasted hot out, though, that people were departing immediately thereafter with lemonade and cook-ies in hand. She didn't blame them. Her small house with its trusty window air conditioner sounded really good. And a cool shower, she thought longingly. But no—she was obliged to stay until the bitter end.

She consoled herself with the thought that she'd have a chance to shower when she went home to change for the formal dinner.

"I'm going to go lock this in the trunk of my car," Troy said, not really looking at her. "I'll be right back."

She watched as he walked toward Mem with no apparent haste but a ground-eating stride that took him past departing alumni. He spoke to no one.

He hadn't actually done much mixing this weekend, she realized. She had introduced him to a few people at the reception and the luncheon, he'd gone to hear Ellen Kenney speak, and at his request he'd been assigned to a foursome for the golf tournament, but he seemed mostly to maintain that watchful, aloof stance.

Because he's working, Madison reminded herself. Her job was to be friendly, his to be observant. She had moments of forgetting that he wasn't here as her date. She thought he would have lingered at some of the events because he liked her—he'd certainly kissed her last night after walking her to her car as if he liked her a whole lot— but she doubted he would be returning now if he wasn't working. From the moment his hand closed on that envelope, he had retreated into himself.

While he was at the car, would he read what his father had written?

No, Madison decided. He'd be wary of any emotional punch.

Apparently we have something in common, she thought wryly. She'd already decided not to look at her father's contribution until tonight, after the formal dinner. It wasn't as if she expected any big revelations—her father had sounded too indifferent about the whole thing to give her any reason to believe otherwise. Even so, she had complicated enough feelings about him—she didn't want to be left confused or troubled or even just distracted when she still had to be "on" until the end of the evening.

Then she had another thought. Maybe Troy had no intention of opening the envelope at all. He might consider that right to be his mother's, not his. Madison hadn't been able to tell how he felt about her refusal to be here today, but very likely they'd open the envelope together and shed more tears about their mutual loss.

The idea of Troy holding his mother, gently drying her tears, gave Madison a peculiar pang of… No, not envy, of course not.

Loneliness.

And she didn't even know why.

TROY SAT DOWN in his recliner at home with the damn skinny envelope in his hand. *Joseph Troyer* was scrawled on the front. Dad's handwriting had changed, but Troy still recognized it.

He'd been asking himself the same question since this afternoon: give this to Mom unopened, or rip it open now and find out what words his father had thought most significant thirty-five years ago?

Troy wouldn't have even asked himself if his mother had seemed the slightest bit interested. But he had no doubt if he stopped by in the morning with the envelope in hand she'd gaze at it in vague puzzlement and then say, "Oh, you mentioned something about a time capsule, didn't you?"

To hell with it, he thought. He must have made the decision earlier, because he had brought a letter opener with him when he settled into the recliner. A beer, too. He paused and took a long swallow then lifted the bottle in a salute. "To you, Dad."

He slit the top of the envelope, set down the opener and reached inside. Something in him tightened when he realized there was only one page there, typed single-spaced with narrow margins. Perturbed, he peered in. Nope, that was it.

What the hell…?

No *To Whom It May Concern* or *Dear Older Self.* Dad had jumped right into it.

I've kept a secret that I probably shouldn't have. By writing this down, I think I'm trying to absolve myself of responsibility. After all, if I put this in the time capsule, then it will all be exposed someday, won't it? I keep thinking I should go to the police now—it's only been a few months, which isn't too late, and they often keep witnesses' names confidential, don't they? But I suppose having my name come out isn't really what's bothering me. I don't want to make trouble for a friend. And I keep telling myself what I'm thinking is all in my head. Guy of all people wouldn't do something like this—

Stunned, Troy reread that first paragraph. His father, the most upright man on earth, had withheld information from the police? About what?

But Troy knew. He knew.

Here's what happened. It was first semester finals week. Guy Laclaire is one of my best friends. I live in a senior apartment, Guy in a house off campus. The two of us arranged to meet at two a.m. for a game of racquetball. Not like either of us would be sleeping, given that we both had two big exams on Thursday and Friday. I was coming from the library where I'd been studying when I saw somebody rush out of McKenna and tear by me. Guy. I caught one good glimpse of his face. He had something in his hand like…I don't know. Not a book or a towel or a gym bag like I had. Something solid. It didn't *fit* and I kind of thought *what's that?* I called out his name, but he didn't hear me. So I figured he'd forgotten something and would be back. I sat down on the rim of the fountain and waited for at least fifteen minutes. He never came back. I froze my ass off and was pissed and went back to my apartment and to bed.

By morning, the campus was buzzing. Mitch King had been found dead, bludgeoned to death, in the sauna in McKenna Center. The police think the crime happened between 1:30 and 2:15 a.m., when Steve Kaplan found him. A few other students had shot baskets in the gym or used the pool during that time, but Steve was the first to go into the sauna. Nobody admitted seeing an outsider or a fellow student who seemed agitated or was covered with blood or anything. It sounds like there was a lot of blood. Police were asking for help.

And I'm thinking, oh man, I did see someone who was agitated. Someone running away from the gym, carrying a length of wood or a bat or—I don't know, but something that could have been used to beat a person's skull in. And I know that someone really (underlined twice) didn't like Mitch King.

But I don't want to get Guy in deep shit he doesn't deserve either. I don't think he had blood on him, although I didn't get that good a look at him either. Mostly his face under the light. So I ran him down and complained because he didn't show last night. He said he was sorry, he guessed he'd fallen asleep. He hoped I hadn't waited long for him.

He lied.

But Guy wouldn't do something like that. I really believe that. So I'm keeping my mouth shut, but part of me is howling "No-o, that's wrong!"

I figure this is something, right?

Okay, it's going into the envelope.

But I'm thinking, now that I read it all here in black-and-white, that I will talk to whoever is investigating.

Troy read the page several times. The close-packed words kept blurring. He wished his father had double-spaced. He wished Dad had been more matter-of-fact, hadn't put so much of his personality and panic into this.

He wished his father hadn't kept a secret of this magnitude.

"Goddamn it," he said aloud, to his silent house.

Most of all, he wished the fellow student Dad had fingered wasn't Madison Laclaire's father.

Eventually he slipped the shocking revelation back in its envelope and put it in the small locked safe where he kept his service weapon. He went to bed and really tried to sleep, even though he knew before his head touched the pillow that it would be a no-go.

WELL.

Madison slipped the pages of the short story back in the envelope. She'd mail it to her father. He might find it amusing. More likely, he'd barely glance at it then toss it in the recycling bin.

It wasn't a *bad* story. In fact, Dad had written exceptionally well. No surprise there. All the same…when Guy Laclaire decided to go for his MBA instead of trying for the Great American Novel, the literary world had not lost a great talent. Presumably this was the writing he considered his best at the time. He'd been striving for dark, moody and world-weary, and ended up sounding pretentious and derivative.

His professors must have known that, but he'd never received anything lower than an A in a class within his major. Most, of course, required analysis of great literature, not original creative writing.

Smiling, Madison wondered if Dad had ever had visions of himself as the next Norman Mailer: eccentric, brilliant and admired. Probably not, or if he had he'd given up those aspirations before he placed this story in the capsule. After all, by then he'd have already applied to Harvard and maybe even have been accepted into the MBA program.

No deep revelations about her father here, she thought, setting the envelope aside and reveling in the cool flow from the air conditioner on her body. Although she did sort of like knowing Dad *wasn't* brilliant at everything he tried. After reading his smugly self-satisfied writing, she could laugh knowing how full of himself he'd been at that age.

Go figure. It turned out Guy Laclaire had been normal after all. Madison found she rather liked that idea. The father she knew was arrogant, all right, but with reason. *She'd* never caught him in a mistake, never seen him fail. He was morally unbending, impatient of other people's follies, indecision and screwups. He was still a handsome man with a full head of hair barely touched with gray. A daily run or game of racquetball or tennis kept him in excellent physical condition. He never seemed to need more than about six hours of sleep a night, and had no understanding for why other people—including his daughter—did.

Madison had the funny thought that maybe Dad never failed because he wasn't willing to try anything he *might* fail at. She'd never seen him in the water, for example. Was that because he didn't swim very well? He certainly didn't sing, not even to join in "Happy Birthday" or "Auld Lang Syne." He'd perfected the art of appearing faintly contemptuous while other people indulged in anything he deemed a waste of time. Maybe, she thought, bemused,

Dad couldn't carry a tune. She'd presumably inherited her own tin ear from one of her parents, after all.

The knowledge flooded her. Dad wouldn't like knowing she'd read his short story, because if *he* troubled to read it he'd see that it wasn't very good. Most of the alumni on the field this afternoon had been having a really good time laughing at their youthful selves.

Dad wouldn't have been able to do that. So of course he hadn't attended.

She felt…odd. And, strangely, a little bit mad. The weight of her father's disapproval was with her even when he wasn't. Because she had always worried about whether she should stick to doing the things she wasn't great at. She'd felt the pressure when she was a kid and wanted to play soccer, for example, or join the swim team or stick with band even though, okay, the sounds that came out of her trombone were more like the cry of a wounded walrus than music. But mostly, once it became apparent she would never excel at whatever it was, she would quietly give it up and concentrate on her schoolwork, where she did excel.

"Why waste your time?" was one of Dad's favorite lines, always accompanied by a supercilious flick of one eyebrow.

But I wanted *to swim on the high school team,* she thought now, still defiant. *So what if I wasn't the best?*

"So what if I wasn't?" she said aloud, slowly.

What was wrong with doing something just because it was fun?

Dumb question—it wasn't the Laclaire way.

Of course, the Laclaire way meant she was a perfectionist. It made her good at her job. This weekend's event had gone without a hitch because she'd worked so damn hard to foresee every possible pitfall. And no, that wasn't a bad thing.

Suddenly, though, Madison wanted to sing. Sing so loudly her neighbors couldn't miss hearing her and flinching at every discordant note.

Damn it, I like to sing.

Well, all right, she'd sing in the shower, she decided. Maybe someday she'd sing in the shower even if she was sharing it with someone else.

Carrying her strappy evening shoes in one hand, she padded into the bedroom, where she shimmied out of her snug black dress. The *someone* she envisioned in the shower with her was John Troyer. She had a feeling he wouldn't mind at all that she couldn't carry a tune as long as she was happy singing.

But then, singing probably wasn't what she'd be doing if Troy joined her in the shower, Madison thought with a private smile.

As she reached in to turn on the water, she wondered again whether he'd read whatever his father had left in the time capsule. And if so…was he feeling sad?

She wished he'd called her. She was a little startled to realize how much she would like to be the person he did call when he felt distress or triumph or anything at all he needed to share.

CHAPTER FIVE

TROY CONTEMPLATED HIS face in the mirror. After a sleepless night, what he saw wasn't pretty. He'd expected shaving would help, but if anything he looked worse now. The stubble had drawn the eye from the deepened lines and creases that were now so apparent. The fact that he'd nicked himself meant his jaw was decorated with a couple of tiny wads of toilet paper. And yeah, the bags and shadows beneath his eyes were almost as bad as the time a punk who didn't want to be arrested had planted a fist in Troy's nose.

Making a sound in his throat, he scrubbed a hand over his face and turned away.

Goddamn it. He didn't see that he had any choice but to take what he now knew to the department, however much he hated to expose his father's lousy judgment. No, worse than that. His father's stunning, damn near criminal, ethical failing. It stung, remembering how proud Dad had been when Troy made the decision to become a cop. He'd been there to see the badge pinned on. He'd rejoiced to see his son come home to Frenchman Lake to enforce the law.

And all that time, he'd been hiding the knowledge that he had shielded a murderer because they were *friends*.

Troy's mind still boggled at what he'd read last night. He would have sworn he knew his father inside and out. He'd looked up to him, measured his own decisions and accomplishments and rectitude by his father's. *What would Dad do?* he would ask himself. *What would Dad say?*

Goddamn it, he thought again, as he took his first swallow of coffee, desperately needing the caffeine hit. *Dad, how could you?*

So, okay, a lot of twenty-one-year-olds weren't very mature. Dad believed in loyalty. It was apparent in what he'd written that he had desperately wanted to believe in Guy Laclaire's innocence. He'd tried hard to dismiss his suspicions.

It was also apparent he hadn't succeeded. If he had, what he saw that night wouldn't have weighed so heavily on his mind months later, when he typed that single, stark page and chose to insert it in the time capsule.

But I'm thinking, now that I read it all here in black-and-white, that I will talk to whoever is investigating.

So why hadn't he?

Hell, maybe writing the confession and knowing it would be read someday had given him some sense of absolution.

Everything in Troy rebelled at the idea that his father had sighed in relief and gone on with a clean conscience.

He found himself wondering what had happened between Guy and Joe Troyer the last semester of their senior year, after Guy had lied about being at McKenna Sports Center the night of the murder. Had they stayed buddies, same as always, Dad pretending to Guy—and maybe even to himself—that he'd never seen a thing? Had they ever had it out? Or maybe they just drifted apart? And if so, had Guy ever wondered why Joe had changed toward him?

All questions, Troy realized, that only Guy Laclaire could answer.

What Troy did know was that the two men hadn't stayed friends after graduation. Troy had never heard Guy's name until Madison mentioned it. After his mother's complete collapse, Troy had been the one to take responsibility for calling, emailing or writing everyone in Dad's address book. Some friends from college who Dad hadn't seen in years were in there. Guy wasn't.

"Shit," Troy said, thinking about his mother. She wouldn't like the idea of any wrong Dad had committed being exposed to the eyes of the world.

Or was he misjudging her? Troy frowned. As he was growing up, Mom had been as firm as Dad was about what was right and what was wrong. What if he talked to her about this?

His every instinct said, *No.* There might have been a time when Mom was capable of placing an abstract concept of justice and ethics ahead of her love for her husband, but that time wasn't now. It was almost a year since Dad died, and as far as Troy could tell, all she did was cling more tenaciously to his memory. God forbid Troy criticize Dad. He was beginning to think she regretted not climbing into the coffin with him and holding tight to his lifeless body as the soil thudded down and buried them together. She sure as hell had no interest in life.

This decision is mine, he realized, and knew it wasn't a decision at all. He was an officer of the law. He'd loved his father, but there was only one choice he could make.

There was no urgency, though, and he had to talk to Madison first.

His belly felt hollow, and it wasn't all because of his conflict about his father, his disappointment in the man he'd admired above all others. No, what scared the shit out of him was the fear that this would kill any chance he had with Madison, who, while obviously having some ambivalent feelings about her own father, also clearly loved him.

Yeah, arresting her dad for murder probably wasn't the way to get the girl.

He groaned and reached for the phone.

WE HAVE TO TALK, Troy had said.

Talk about what? As she waited for him to arrive, Madison restlessly paced her living room and fretted. He'd sounded strange, and when she wanted to know what was wrong, he only asked if he could come over.

What could he have to say that would impact her? The visiting alumni had all departed this morning to drive home or catch flights. And wouldn't he have said something at the formal dinner last night if he'd learned anything worrisome?

Did he think she'd been too manipulative in bringing everyone back to the campus, with a goal of extracting money from them?

Damn it, I was doing my job. No more and no less.

Everyone had fun. She knew many *had* written checks, but she had yet to hear the total.

No, that was silly anyway—she'd been up front from the beginning about her goals and Troy had seemed okay with them. He knew how important fund-raising was for a private college.

So what did he want to talk about?

She growled in frustration, then stiffened at the sound of a vehicle pulling up outside. Whirling, she raced for the bathroom. Her ponytail was still smooth. Take it down or leave it up...? The doorbell rang, and she jumped.

Losing interest in her hairstyle, she hurried to open the front door. On the other side of it, Troy was imposing, as always, his tall, solid body dwarfing hers. But her heart bumped in alarm at her first sight of his face, haggard and grim.

"Something *is* wrong."

"Yeah, I guess it is." He raised his eyebrows. "Can I come in?"

"Oh. Sure." She backed up. "I'm sorry."

"No, I'm sorry to be mysterious with you." Having followed her in, he glanced around her living room.

She felt a little self-conscious, since the home she'd created for herself was bound to give away facets of her personality she hadn't yet shared. He could probably tell right off that, while she wouldn't describe herself as a slob, she had rebelled in her modest way after moving out on her own by refusing to be fixated on perfect order either. A couple of magazines lay on a sofa cushion; books and the Sunday newspaper littered the coffee table. Books were jammed into the pair of bookcases flanking the fireplace, too, not arranged with restraint or even—her father would shudder—alphabetically. But the house was basically clean, and she liked the paintings she'd hung, the combination of bright colors that, to her eyes, worked. She'd done classic decor in her office at the college. Here at home, she'd suited herself.

Funny—more than once she'd had the thought that Dad wouldn't like it. But then, he never visited her here. She always went to Seattle to see him.

"Please, have a seat," she said, scooping the magazines off the sofa and adding them to the heap on the table. "Would you like a cup of coffee?"

"Maybe in a little bit." His grimness hadn't abated. "I have something I need to tell you."

She sank onto one end of the sofa, a leg curled under her, and he chose a chair facing her. For the first time, she saw that he had a manila envelope clenched in his hand.

"Is that your father's…?" she asked hesitantly.

"Yeah." His gray eyes held hers. "It's a shocker, Madison. I want you to read what he wrote."

Her heart was hammering. He sounded so serious. Not only as if he'd had a shock, but also as if whatever was in that envelope would affect *her*. The only reason it could was if it had to do with her father.

"All right." She was proud of her steady voice.

He opened the envelope and half rose to hand her a single sheet of paper. His storm-cloud eyes held something powerful—she had the odd sense that it might be grief. Then he sat down and watched her, impassive but for the spasm of a muscle in his jaw.

Stiff with apprehension, she bent her head and began to read.

I've kept a secret that I probably shouldn't have.

"This is a lie!" Madison threw the piece of paper away. It fluttered to the surface of the coffee table. "It can't possibly be Dad he saw. If he saw anybody. Has it occurred to you this could be fiction? Some kind of practical joke on my dad?"

She saw nothing but pity on his face.

"No. That's—" Troy nodded at the paper "—my father's voice. There's nothing self-conscious about what he wrote. He's too miserable, too obviously battling his conscience. If that was a successful joke, it was written by a master, not a college kid."

Frantic as she was, Madison heard the truth in what he said.

I don't want to make trouble for a friend. And I keep telling myself what I'm thinking is all in my head. Guy of all people wouldn't do something like this—

There was nothing slyly humorous about his language, nothing that said sardonically, *Gotcha!*

She pressed on. "He admits he barely caught a glimpse of Dad's face. He mistook him for someone else. That has to be it."

"Of course it's possible. Dad could have been wrong

and your father really did fall asleep and never showed up."
Troy paused, that disturbing gaze never leaving her face.
"It's also possible your father was there and had nothing
to do with the murder but had some other reason for lying.
By morning, he might have found out about King's death
and was afraid he'd be suspected, especially if it was commonly known he didn't like the guy."

Madison absorbed what he said. His voice, low, reso-
nant and soothing, had calmed her somewhat. At least
he wasn't automatically accusing Dad of murder. He was
saying, *I acknowledge there are alternative explanations*.
Thank God.

"But if that's the case," she heard herself say reluctantly,
"and it really was Dad, why would he have 'rushed away'
and then not come back to meet your father, the way he'd
promised?"

"I don't know."

The pity wasn't soft. Instead it glinted, she thought in
alarm, like the steel barrel of a gun.

"You're not going to let this go, are you?"

"How can I?" Troy's face had never looked harder. "I
wear a badge every day, Madison. Today, for the first
time in my life, I'm ashamed of my father. But at least he
was a private citizen. I'm not. My job is to catch killers."

She shot to her feet. "My father is not a killer! He's…
You don't know him, or you wouldn't even say that!"

He rose, too, more slowly. "Somebody murdered Mitchell King. Bludgeoned him to death." He paused to give
emphasis to the brutal reality. "And odds are, it was somebody who knew him. Who wasn't even noticed in the gym
because he belonged there by rights. He damn near *had*
to be a member of the college community, Madison." His
head cocked slightly to one side. "Of course you don't

want to think your father could have done something like that. Nobody would want to."

Her legs gave out and she collapsed back onto the sofa. She was trying to be furious on her father's behalf, but mostly she felt scared. She understood Troy's point, but somehow, she had to make him understand that Dad, of all men, *couldn't* have done this. It was simply impossible.

"Dad doesn't cheat on his taxes," she said. "If a restaurant bill leaves an item off, he draws the waiter's attention to it. Dad is unrelentingly honest. He held me to standards as high as his own. If I tried to lie even to myself, he called me on it. As a businessman, he has a tough reputation because he can be ruthless and maybe hard, but he's also known to live up to his promises. I have spent my entire life…" Her voice caught. She couldn't finish.

"Trying to live up to his standards?" Troy circled the coffee table and sat down on the cushion beside her, taking her hand in a warm grip. "I've tried to live up to my dad's, too. And I've just discovered he made one hell of a mistake. He didn't live up to his own standards."

"Murder is a much bigger mistake." If her father had committed murder, her entire world was undercut. "No," she said aloud, strongly. "Not Dad."

Troy shook his head. "I can't ignore this, Madison. That's all I came to tell you. I have to go to my police chief."

She pulled her hand from his. "Do you know what this would do to my father's reputation?"

He grunted. "It won't do much for my father's either."

"That's not the same!" she cried.

His jaw tightened and he shook his head. "I have no choice."

"Please," Madison begged.

"What kind of cop would I be if I shrugged and decided I could let this guy off because, hey, I don't want to get my girlfriend's dad in trouble?" His eyes bored into hers. "Tell me that."

Girlfriend? Was that how he thought of her already? Inexplicably, her heart warmed. Even so, she couldn't quit fighting.

"Can't we, I don't know, investigate quietly instead? I could ask Dad about the murder, even tell him I knew somebody had seen him at the gym that night. Then, if he has a good explanation, nobody would have to know." While she meant to sound reasonable, she knew she was coming off as pathetic. Her voice was even shaking, and she despised herself for it.

"This isn't only about me being a cop, Madison." Troy sighed, expression troubled. "Dad wrote down every detail and put it in that damn time capsule because he knew it all had to come to light. He isn't here to do what should be done, but I am. It feels like something he handed to me. A trust."

"But he never did report what he saw to the police," she said quickly. "Are you so sure he wouldn't have burned that piece of paper the minute he got it back?"

His eyes burned with pain. "I hope to hell he wouldn't have done that."

Madison felt cruel for having said what she did. Troy was already living with the knowledge that his father had fallen short when faced with a tough decision. Of course it would have occurred to him that Joe Troyer might have destroyed this last evidence of his shame.

They sat in silence, Troy seemingly staring blindly at the brick fireplace. She doubted he saw the framed photos on the mantel; several of them included her father. She squeezed her hands together so hard they hurt, and gave Troy the time and space to think.

"All right," he said suddenly, harshly. "We'll play it your way." He turned that stare, now fierce, on her. "But you do know I could lose my job over this. If I get caught suppressing evidence, it could be the end of my career."

The hope that had momentarily swelled within her collapsed like a balloon pricked by a pin. *Oh, dear God.* Her throat closed and she struggled to speak. "No," she finally said. "No, I didn't think. I was wrong to ask," she said with difficulty. "It wasn't fair. I don't want you to make that kind of sacrifice."

Some of the tension visibly left Troy's body. One side of his mouth crooked up. "I've been known to break the rules before."

"But not for the sake of a man you don't even know."

"Actually, sometimes it was." The smile became more genuine. "In this case, I'm not willing to take the chance for your father's sake. I'm doing it for you."

Her breath rushed out. "Oh, Troy." Her eyes burned, but she refused to let tears fall. She never cried. Tears had disgusted Dad.

"Don't look like that," he said gently. His big hand covered her still-knotted fists. "I've got a stake, too, remember. If we can get your father off the hook, mine will be, too. Then *I* can burn that damn thing."

She swallowed and nodded, blinking several times. "Did you show it to your mother?" she asked, her voice a little scratchy.

"No." Troy stared at the sheet of paper, lying askew on her coffee table, with a repulsion that almost equaled hers. "She hasn't been herself since Dad died. I want to believe she'd ask me to do the right thing, but I don't know."

That made Madison's throat close up again. She had to struggle to get words out. "So instead *I* pleaded with you to pretend you hadn't seen it, to defy the oath you took as a police officer."

Troy's smile crinkled the skin beside his eyes. "I don't remember you asking anything like that. You just want me to sneak around and investigate on the sly."

"That's bad enough," she mumbled.

"No. We'll still get at the truth, Madison, if you'll help me."

She squared her shoulders. "If you mean it… Of course I'll help."

"Good." Abruptly, he laughed. "You look like you're braving yourself to walk over hot coals."

Madison's mouth curved in irresistible response. "Did you read about that inspirational speaker who gets participants in his workshops worked up enough to do exactly that?"

"After which they all make a quick trip to the local E.R.?" Troy grinned. "Yeah, I read about it."

She made a face at him. "Okay, I do feel a little nervous. For one thing, I've never investigated anything."

"Sure you have. What's an investigation but research? You've dug into records before, maybe taped some interviews, put together what you learned."

"Well…of course. But when I interviewed people, I didn't have reason to think one of them was a killer!" More softly, she added, "I wasn't investigating my own father."

"Let's start by getting something straight." Now he sounded stern. "*I'll* be doing the investigating here. You'll be my silent partner. I'm counting on you to provide the resources."

Her eyes widened. "But you won't be able to take anything you learn to court, will you? Not when what you know was learned illegally."

He was sprawled comfortably on her sofa now, one arm

lying along the back behind her. The relaxed pose didn't make her any less aware of his sheer size. "That's not the way we'll be doing it. I'm going to ask for permission to reopen the case." When she stiffened, he lifted a hand. "I'll claim I heard enough talk this weekend to stir my curiosity. That you're intrigued and want to help. What I won't do yet is show anyone what my father wrote. I'll get a warrant and, with a little luck, the college will decide not to fight it in return for our promise to do this as quietly as possible. You'll be politely ordered to cooperate. Then, if we discover nothing—" He shrugged. "No harm, no foul. If we do get somewhere, the arrest will be clean. Got that?"

By the end of his speech, the face she saw was all cop and she realized that the relaxed pose wasn't quite what it appeared to be. *This isn't fun and games,* he was saying.

But she had no real choice, did she? If she said no, he *would* take his father's confession to the Frenchman Lake Police chief, just as he'd said he would. And the investigation would be opened anyway, with a greater chance her father would be immediately targeted and that word would somehow get out. Her only hope of protecting his reputation was to help.

A choice? Sure. Right. She could either help voluntarily…or do it involuntarily, after that polite order had been issued.

"I understand," she said steadily. "No one should get away with murder." She had to say this. "Not even my father."

"Good." Troy's smile was warm with approval. Madison felt it as palpably as the strong sunlight coming through the window. He squeezed her shoulder and she was bothered by how much she wanted to turn and nestle against that broad chest, even at a moment like this.

"So…where do we start?" she asked to distract herself.

"I talk to my lieutenant tomorrow morning. We hope no big crime happens to suck up my time so I can't justify opening a cold case."

Nothing *big*. She stared at him, realizing he meant a new murder. Or a rape, or who knew what. Something unimaginably awful. The kind of thing, in fact, she'd convinced herself didn't happen in Frenchman Lake. By burying her head in the sand, she had felt safe and even smug in her belief that this small college town was perfect.

Suddenly, Madison didn't like herself very much.

"No," she said. "I'll hope nothing big happens."

Troy's eyes searched hers, and she had the sense he was looking deep inside her. The thought, on top of her self-reflection, made her cringe. She was suddenly struck by how much she'd learned about herself since she read her father's short story last night. *No deep revelations,* she'd told herself, but she now knew she'd been wrong. The insight she'd gained hadn't been so much into her father's behavior as into her own.

Too bad that she had to be dismayed by most of what she'd discovered about herself.

"Hey." Troy stroked her cheek with his knuckles. "Where'd you go?"

She shook her head. "Just thinking."

"How would you feel about some lunch? Me, the thinking I'm doing is about pizza."

Madison seized on the sheer normalcy of it. "Pizza sounds really good," she agreed. "Let me put on shoes."

He smiled. "I sort of like your bare toes, but okay."

"You'll still see my bare toes," she assured him. "If not for work, I'd wear flip-flops most of the time."

"Even in the snow?"

"I've been known to," she admitted.

She loved his laugh, deep and slow. "Go find a pair," he said. "I'm starving."

WHEN HE ANNOUNCED he wanted to reopen the Mitchell King homicide, Troy's lieutenant didn't say a word for a long time. Without ever taking his eyes off Troy's face, he reached for a peppermint from the bowl on his desk, tore off the wrapping and popped it into his mouth. Instead of sucking on it, he bit down on the hard candy with his molars. *Crunch, crunch, crunch.* Troy kept his composure, only waiting instead of picturing his bones being crunched instead.

"Why?" Davidson finally asked. But before Troy could so much as get his mouth open, he shook his head. "No, this one is going to have to get approval from the top, anyway. You can tell the chief and me at the same time." He reached for the phone.

Ten minutes later, Troy found himself in the police chief's office for only the third or fourth time since he'd arrived on the job. He'd expected this, and fortunately he liked Chief Jim Helmer. The guy was young for the job—maybe early forties. He'd risen in the ranks of Pierce County Sheriff's Department on the west side of the state, which gave them a lot in common. Pierce County was a mix of rural, including some pretty damn poor areas, and urban that hung on the fringes of cities like Tacoma. With the joint Fort Lewis–McChord military base added to the mix, it was a tough county to police. Helmer was a cop, not a bureaucrat, and therefore had the respect of everyone in the department. Troy had never heard the story of how Helmer had ended up in a small town on this side of the state. It wasn't as if they were drinking buddies.

"Did you learn something new?" Helmer asked once Troy and the lieutenant were settled in chairs.

Troy generally tried not to lie and hated doing it now. He had to picture Madison's pleading eyes before he could unclench his jaw and get on with it.

"Only hints," he said. Lie number one. "I've been interested since I moved back to Frenchman Lake." Truth. "My father knew King and sometimes talked about his murder." Half lie. "I pulled out the book and skimmed it early on in my time here, but nothing jumped out to justify stirring the pot."

Both men nodded.

"It was this weekend reunion that got me thinking. There was a lot of talk, as you'd expect. I heard some suggestion that students—never named to the police— were seen in McKenna Center that night." One, anyway.

"A lot of years have passed. These aren't scared twenty-year-olds anymore. They're more likely to open up now." He hesitated. "I spent some time talking to the alumni affairs director, Madison Laclaire. Her father was a senior at Wakefield that year, too. Apparently he wasn't a real fan of King's, although she doesn't know why. I got a few hints from other alumni here this weekend that he wasn't much liked by anybody." Lie number three—or four? He'd lost track, he realized, his jaws flexing. *Goddamn it.*

Troy looked from one man to the other. "I'd like to interview Ms. Laclaire's father and everyone else who knew him well. I'd like to revisit the question of who saw what. Ms. Laclaire has expressed her willingness to help by digging out contact info, if she can get approval from the college president."

Helmer rubbed his jaw and scrutinized Troy with narrowed eyes. Keeping his body and face as composed and relaxed as he could, Troy hoped like hell he hadn't given away his discomfiture.

The police chief's gaze flicked to Lieutenant Davidson. Out of the corner of his eye, Troy saw an abbreviated nod. An instant later, he was under scrutiny again.

"No question, you're ideal for this investigation," Helmer said thoughtfully. "Considering these people knew your father, they might be more likely to open up to you."

"I'd like to think so." Troy called it the "snob reflex," that automatic Wakefield assumption that townies weren't as smart as the elite members of the college community. Growing up, Troy had gotten many automatic dismissals when a Wakefield student realized he was a local kid.

"When I was hired, I read that murder book cover to cover, too," the police chief said, surprising Troy. "Leaving a crime that ugly unsolved sticks in my craw. I don't know if it's possible to get anywhere after this many years— it's not as if we have a DNA sample we can pull out like a rabbit from a hat—but I can't see what it hurts to try." He nodded once, decisively. "Let's do it. Instead of going for a warrant, I'll try for voluntary cooperation from the college. They can't like having this clouding their reputation any better than we do." A grim smile stretched his mouth. "I'd like to exorcise Mitchell King's ghost. I'm betting the president, Lars Berglund, feels the same. I'll make some calls," he concluded.

Taking that as his dismissal, Troy thanked the chief and left the office along with Lieutenant Davidson.

Heading back to his desk, Troy considered calling Madison, but decided to wait. It would be interesting to hear about the uproar on her end after Helmer's calls. Itching to get started, he wondered how long it would take before he had the final go-ahead.

CHAPTER SIX

"ARE YOU READY?" Troy asked quietly.

Madison nodded even though she was consumed with guilt at the trap she was laying for her own father—and that's what this was, however much she wanted to believe she was doing the right thing. She closed her eyes briefly. This had been the deal. Troy had come up with a list of questions that now lay in front of her. His handwriting was bold and easy to read in case she panicked midway. They'd talked through every eventuality, too, including how far she should go with the claim that they had a witness who placed Guy at the gym within the same time frame as the murder.

Troy looked pointedly at the phone in her hand. Sucking in a deep breath, she found her father's number and, after only the briefest of pauses, pushed the call button.

He answered after the third ring. "Madison. Good to hear from you."

That was warm and fuzzy, for him. He'd never called her by any pet names. She had been about ten years old when she'd shyly told him that Mom had started calling her Maddie. Dad had snapped, "What's she trying to do to you? We named you Madison. That's a name with dignity and strength. Don't let her demean you, Madison."

Now, she understood a little of what he'd meant. Madison *was* stronger, Maddie softer, maybe more feminine. But at the time a pet name had translated into her mind as affection, and she had been desperate to feel loved by either of her parents. Nonetheless, the next time she saw her mother, she'd firmly told her that she preferred to be called by her full name.

"Dad," she said. "Listen, I'm going to put you on speakerphone. I've been teaching myself to quilt, and I thought I could do it while we're talking."

"Quilt? Good God, Madison."

There's the Dad I know and love, she thought wryly. "I'm enjoying it," she said simply, touching the speaker button on her phone and setting it down on the coffee table, halfway between her and Troy. "How was your trip to Japan?"

He told her, surprising her by being more expansive than usual. Very aware of Troy sitting across from her, his elbows braced on his knees and his eyes keen, she nonetheless asked questions in appropriate spots and even laughed a few times at her father's stories.

"How did the great time capsule weekend go?" he asked, surprising her again. He'd remembered. "Did you raise a lot of money?"

"I did." She smiled. "Even better than I expected. Did you know Rob Dayton?"

"Software," he said promptly. "He was a year or two behind me, I think. Can't say I really knew him, but I've followed his career recently."

"He wrote a check for a million dollars."

"He can afford it," her father said. "I put a check in the mail, by the way. Have you received it yet?"

"No. Thank you, Dad. I appreciate your support." She thought about asking how much the check was for, but stole a glance at Troy and closed her mouth. Dad wouldn't be stingy—he'd never bother with something like a fifty-dollar contribution, but she didn't suppose he would be supporting his alma mater to the tune of a million bucks, either. Dad's memories of his time at Wakefield didn't seem to be that fond.

Her eyes met Troy's, which a minute ago had glinted with amusement when she'd been so obviously indulging in the self-satisfaction of her success. Now his eyes were resolute.

"Dad, there was a lot of talk this weekend about that murder here on the campus your senior year. You never said much about it."

The silence was longer than it ought to have been. Madison caught herself leaning forward until she practically hung over the phone. Troy stared at it, too, lines deepening on his forehead.

"It didn't have anything to do with me," her father said, sounding abrupt. "Shook everybody up, of course. Sure as hell, nobody took a sauna by himself again the rest of that academic year. Having the police on campus day after day asking questions guaranteed one hell of a finals week, I can tell you."

"Did Mitchell King have a girlfriend?"

He made a humming sound as though he really was thinking back. "I seem to remember they'd broken up not that long before. The police must have looked in that direction, but word was she had a solid alibi. Some all-night study thing, I think."

"It doesn't sound like a woman's kind of crime," Madison suggested tentatively.

Troy nodded his approval at her.

"No, it doesn't, but if you make someone mad enough, who knows what can happen."

"The few times you've mentioned him, you didn't sound as if you liked Mitchell King."

"I don't remember ever talking about him." Clipped and

forbidding, this was her father's I'm-going-to-shut-down-this-whole-topic-of-conversation voice.

"After I took the job here, we talked a little bit about it."

Madison would never have believed the atmosphere could be felt so intensely through an open phone line. But during that silence, she changed her mind. Maybe it was so charged because they couldn't see each other's expressions. Or, gee, maybe it had something to do with her own gigantic omission, the words unsaid: *Dad, just so you know, there's a cop here next to me listening to everything you say.*

You think?

"I guess we did," her father said after the prolonged pause. "No, Mitch was a sly little asshole."

Surprised, Madison raised her eyebrows. Her father was always blunt, but rarely crude.

"I don't think anyone liked him," he continued, "except for the girlfriend, I guess. Temporarily."

Troy mouthed a question.

"Sly? What's that mean?" she asked, obedient to the prompting.

"We lived on the same hall freshman year. I caught him a couple of times listening at closed doors." Distaste tightened her father's voice. "He liked knowing things. Then he could make use of what he knew. Get jabs in."

"Into you?"

"Of course not," her father snapped. "He got a reputation, though."

"Do you think that's why he was killed? Because he learned something he shouldn't have about somebody?"

"What's with the questions, Madison?" He suddenly sounded very controlled and cold. "The investigation isn't being reopened, is it?"

She looked at Troy, who nodded.

"There are rumors it might be. I'm guessing the college would encourage it if the police decide to. You'd think people would have forgotten about it, but they haven't. Even the admissions officers still have to tap dance around questions when they're out promoting the college. Laying the whole thing to rest would be really good."

"There's not a chance in hell after this many years," her father said brusquely. "Take it from me."

Troy tilted his head in interest.

"Why do you say that, Dad?" Madison asked hastily.

"If anybody had seen anything or knew anything, it would have come out then. I thought the cops figured it was a transient. Maybe even that killer they arrested in Spokane a few years back."

She knew who he meant. "I'm pretty sure he killed only women, Dad. Anyway, once he'd been caught he confessed to some murders they hadn't known he committed. This wasn't one of them."

"Well, I wish anyone luck who thinks he's going to try, poor fool." She could all but see his dismissive shrug.

Troy sat up. "Go for it," he murmured, his compelling gaze holding hers.

She swallowed. "Dad, I'm partly asking because I heard someone say he saw *you* at the gym sometime in the right time period. He assumed the police had talked to you, but you never mentioned it so I was curious."

Oh, God—she didn't sound like herself at all. That had come off as canned, which it was.

"What?" His voice shimmered with fury, although he spoke barely above a whisper. "Who the hell said that, Madison?"

"I don't really know." She squeezed her hands together. "It was somebody in a group, you know, just talking about the murder. I couldn't tell who said it."

"If the police start investigating, then that's who they should talk to." Every word sounded bitten off. "The only reason to sling around that kind of accusation is to deflect attention."

Madison couldn't help noticing that her scrupulously honest father hadn't said, *I wasn't there.*

She closed her eyes, unable to look at Troy. "Did you go to the gym at all that night, Dad?"

There was another of those quivering silences, this one raising goose bumps on her arms.

"You know me better than that," he said harshly. "At least, I'd like to think you do. No, the police didn't talk to me. They had no reason to."

"I wasn't accusing you." The quaver in her voice made her mad. She had always quailed before her father's usually quiet, scathing anger, and she despised herself for it.

His anger *was* quiet, she reminded herself. Guy Laclaire had a biting tongue, but he had never been violent. Never even threatened violence. As Dad would put it, he might have chewed Mitch King a new one, but he certainly wouldn't have bludgeoned him.

Not my father.

"It's a mistake to reopen that case," he said with finality. "If anyone asks you, that's what you'll tell them. I have calls to make, Madison. Glad this thing went off well for you. I only hope it didn't stir up crap that had settled at the bottom where it belonged."

She barely had a chance to say goodbye before he ended the call. After a moment, she leaned forward and hung up her phone. Then, reluctantly, she raised her gaze to meet Troy's.

HE FELT LIKE an asshole. *Damn,* Troy thought. He should have followed his first instinct and taken his father's testimony-from-the-grave to Davidson. He should never have involved Madison, who looked miserable.

My doing.

Yeah, hindsight was a wonderful thing, he thought sardonically. Too little, too late.

"This is hard on you. I shouldn't have asked you to call him."

"I offered. I wanted to," she reminded him.

"Did you?"

"I wanted…" What she wanted died unspoken.

"To turn suspicion from your father. I know." He hesitated. *Say it.* "I'm not so sure we managed that."

Alarm flashed in her pretty brown eyes. "What do you mean?"

"You know what I mean," Troy said, as gently as he could. "Your dad worked around the question real hard. He never said, 'Hell no, I wasn't anywhere near McKenna Center that night.'" Troy held her eyes. "You were right. He is an honest man."

Madison gave a cry of despair and buried her face in her hands.

Moving swiftly, Troy left his chair and sat beside her, pulling her into his arms, though she stayed stiff and even briefly struggled.

"Hey," he murmured into her hair. "We knew it might not be easy. Don't panic."

She sagged against him, her face buried into the crook of his neck. While he was expecting tears from her, he didn't feel any. A couple of long shudders shook her body. Troy kept on with the reassurances, his hand making soothing circles on her back. At last he felt her take a deep breath, after which she carefully separated herself from him. However reluctant he was to let go, he didn't try to hold on to her.

JANICE KAY JOHNSON 95

Face set, eyes dark, she looked at him. "You're right. At least he didn't lie."

Troy wouldn't have put it quite like that; Guy had definitely tried to lie by omission and misdirection. But to give him his due, that was a step above the flat-out, direct lie he'd told his best friend the morning after the murder.

"Impressions?" he asked Madison.

She curved her mouth into a smile that fell flat. "He's utterly opposed to the investigation being reopened."

In turn, Troy grunted something like a laugh. "Yeah, I got that. Are you going to follow orders and tell me it's a mistake?"

"I think we can call it too late." She made a face at him. "Would you like a cup of coffee?"

Except for the one betraying moment, she was hiding what she was feeling well enough. She'd promised to help him get at the truth, and she was following through, however personally devastating the process was. And whatever the truth might turn out to be.

Madison Laclaire had guts. He hadn't realized until now how much he valued that particular quality in a woman. Somehow the issue had never arisen before. Probably because he'd never been really serious about any woman.

Or it could be that this surge of admiration and even relief came in response to his recent observation that his own mother lacked this brand of moral courage.

Nice thought.

He shook it off. "Coffee would be good."

He followed Madison to the kitchen and leaned one hip against the tiled edge of the countertop, watching as she poured from the carafe that sat ready. He liked the room even though, according to her, it was a work in process. The cupboards were old, dating from the 1940s or '50s, he guessed. Instead of replacing them, she'd laid on a new coat of paint—a dark, rich red—then tiled the counter and backsplash in a checkerboard of white and dark red. The floor had been stripped to the original oak planks and refinished.

After she handed him his cup, Troy carried it to the round oak table by a window that looked out on her small backyard.

She sat across from him, cradling her own mug.

"He was there that night, wasn't he?"

"Sounded like it to me." He hated seeing her distress. "Remember, he may have been there but saw nothing, and was only trying to stay off the police radar."

"But why would he care?"

Whatever her father had done wrong, Troy thought, *he'd done one thing very right. He had taught his daughter to face the truth without flinching. You have to admire that.*

She shook her head. "If he was there and didn't see anything, why wouldn't he have volunteered a statement? Kids that age like nothing better than being the center of attention."

Troy had been thinking about this. "You know," he said slowly, "another possibility is that he was in the same boat as my father. He *did* see something or someone—but he didn't want to tell tales, either."

Her eyes fastened hopefully on his. "You believe that?"

He had already decided he wouldn't lie to her. "I'm keeping an open mind." That was the best he could do.

The change in her expression was subtle but unmistakable. She pressed her lips together and nodded.

"One thing I couldn't help noticing," he said slowly. "When he insisted that if there'd been any witnesses, they would have spoken up back then."

She stared at him with a deer-in-the-headlights look.

"He sounded smug," Troy said flatly.

Madison winced. Yeah, she'd noticed that, too. The tone had been subtle, but unmistakable. Until his daughter's phone call, Guy had been real confident that no one had seen him that night. The passing years, all thirty-four plus of them, had given him faith that he was safe.

Guy Laclaire, Troy thought, was a powerful man accustomed to getting his way. If Guy had had any idea what his old buddy Joe Troyer had put in the time capsule, chances seemed good, Troy speculated, that the capsule would have disappeared from that foundation stone beneath Cheadle Hall. When she looked for it, Madison would have uncovered a gaping, empty hole, and been left without a clue who had taken the capsule or why.

Her mouth had stayed stubbornly closed when he said that about her dad sounding smug. Troy watched her, not wanting to push too much.

"Now what?" she asked finally, probably with the hope of diverting him, he suspected.

He let her get away with it. "Now I talk to other people. I'll start with the original witnesses—the students who admitted to being there at some point that night. What I need from you is current contact information."

"That won't be any problem for the alumni who have stayed in touch with the college. We do lose track of a certain percent along the way, though. I'll search old records so you at least know where they were at our last contact with them."

"Do your best."

She frowned. "Will you be getting in touch with men only?"

Troy shook his head. "Presumably women wouldn't have been in the men's locker room, but they could just as well have noticed who was at the pool, the gym, the indoor track or coming and going."

"Don't you think women would have been less likely to be there in the middle of the night?"

"Maybe," he agreed, "but some may have gone in pairs or groups."

"Yes." Her jaw firmed. "Okay."

"This is going to take time." Troy set down his mug and stretched his arms above his head. "I'd much prefer talking to every potential witness face-to-face, but I can't justify any kind of travel budget at this point."

"A surprising number do live in Washington. We work at attracting out-of-state and even foreign students, but still a substantial majority is from Washington, Oregon and Idaho."

He'd sort of known that, but hadn't thought through the logical corollary—that many of those same grads would stay in the Northwest.

"If that's the case, I can set up a bunch of appointments in the Seattle area. Or, worse come to worst, I have buddies with Seattle P.D. I can ask to do the interviews there." Seeing the strain on her face, he had the feeling he'd worn out his welcome for the evening. He hoped she had something to do besides worry once he left her alone. He stood and carried his mug to the kitchen sink. "So," he asked, "have you really taken up quilting?"

She followed him. "No, but I've been thinking about it. Heaven knows why. I was dangerous with my foot on the pedal of a sewing machine when I had to take Home Economics in high school."

Troy laughed at her. "Needle get away from you?"

"Yes!" She made a comical face and held up her right index finger. "Literally. I poked my finger in the wrong place and the needle went right through it. Missed the bone, thank goodness, but it *hurt*."

Troy winced. "I can imagine."

She wrinkled her nose. "Oh, sure. You've probably been shot or stabbed or something way more dramatic than a sewing accident."

"I have been shot." He rotated his arm, recalling the pain, then grinned. "It was a flesh wound, just like yours."

"Couldn't help one-upping me, could you?"

"Nope." He waited while she dumped out the remnants of her own coffee and placed the mug in the sink. When she turned to face him, he gathered her into his arms. Placing his chin on top of her head, he whispered, "I'm sorry."

Her lips moved against his throat. "You don't have to be."

She meant it, which blew him away. Even so, something had changed between them, and he didn't think it was all in his head. Madison rested against him, her arms around his torso, as if there was nowhere else she'd rather be. But her expressions were more guarded now; some reserve had created a wall that hadn't been there before.

Troy usually had a near-limitless store of patience. He wouldn't be good at his job if he didn't. Cops with a short fuse didn't last long, and they sure as hell didn't make it to detective. A long, involved investigation would drive an impatient man crazy. Talking to the same people over and over, listening for new shades of meaning and deviations from their original story. Sitting with the phone pressed to your ear, on hold, with nothing better to do than stare into space. Anyone in law enforcement spent a *lot* of time on hold. Then there was the rest: studying reports, poring over driver records, watching piss poor quality video recordings made by store and parking lot security cameras in hopes of one useful glimpse of a face or a vehicle or a license plate.

Troy was hanging on to that patience right now with a sweaty, tight grip. Madison must have mixed feelings about him. She might like him, she might be attracted to him, but he had become a major threat to the person she most loved and therefore he was a threat to her world as she knew it. He'd watched her closely as she talked to her father. Her hands had given away tension her expression didn't. Her fingers had knotted rhythmically into fists on her thighs. They would loosen, flatten, then squeeze tight again the next second.

He'd give anything to have met her weeks or months ago, to be able to *know* their relationship had roots deep enough to ensure they survived this. Some primitive male instinct insisted he ought to get her in bed *now,* as if he could bind her that way.

Troy suppressed a groan. Man, he wanted to take her to bed. He had since he set eyes on her, but then he'd had patience and common sense on his side. Now…shit, now he was battling panic.

Leave her alone and you'll lose her, the primitive side of him growled.

The modern man—yeah, he still kept his grip on the more evolved part of himself—knew that expecting her to choose sides too soon was asking for her to pick daddy. And why wouldn't she? The man had raised her. He was her rock. For God's sake, she'd gone to daddy's alma mater and now worked there, as if this was home because he had said so.

She'd known Troy for less than a week. They'd kissed half a dozen times. On the surface, whatever they had was new and tentative, even if it didn't feel that way to him.

Holding her close, breathing in her scent, he told himself not to be an idiot. Madison wasn't rejecting him. Yeah, she had some major internal conflict—and who wouldn't in her position. She was handling it well.

And she's leaning against me as if she trusts me.

A smart man would take what he was offered and not screw up by demanding more.

I can be smart.

He pulled back enough to let her look up at him. The wariness on her face was a hammer blow. All he could do was pretend not to see it.

"You okay?"

"Of course." Her lips formed a smile he recognized as the one she trotted out on the job, if a little weak— practiced and not necessarily reflecting what she felt. He didn't like it.

"Can I come by your office in the morning?"

"Yes, of course." Without making it obvious, she had backed away. Now, arms crossed, she rubbed her hands up and down them. "I'll have the class lists from those years and all the available contact information ready for you."

"Good." He frowned. "I didn't ask. Does everyone know you've been asked to do this?"

Madison shook her head. "Lars asked me to keep it quiet for now. Word will eventually spread, but we prefer that current students don't hear rumors."

"You must have alumni email loops and chat groups and what have you. They're going to light up by the time I've talked to three or four people."

"Probably," she agreed with a sigh.

They walked to the front door, but he didn't reach for the knob. Instead, he faced Madison. Her eyes met his shyly. "I'd like to kiss you," he said, his voice low and rough.

Her mouth trembled. "Please."

At the exact same moment he reached out, she launched herself at him with a cry. Troy took her mouth with starving intensity, driven by the fear that he'd found her only to lose her. Rising on tiptoe, pressing herself against him, she kissed him with as much passion and desperation.

She's afraid, too, he realized with the small sliver of his brain that was still functioning.

Her fear, her need, eased his and allowed him to gradually gentle the kiss. His hands stroked her from the delicate nape of her neck to the lush curve of her hips, savoring the womanly contrast. She turned him on, big time—but now was not the moment, however painful it was going to be to take his hands off her.

He let his lips travel from her mouth across her cheek to the complex whorl of her ear and the tiny gold hoop she wore. He nibbled it, flicked it with his tongue then traveled upward to her temple. Then he kissed her closed eyelids, feeling the quiver of movement beneath the thin, delicate skin.

Reluctantly, Troy lifted his head, looking down at her uplifted face. For a long moment, she stayed like that, her eyes closed, her lips parted and slightly swollen. This time he did groan.

"I'd better go while I still can."

Her lashes fluttered before lifting. The brown of her eyes was melted into a soft chocolate. "Part of me wants to ask you to stay."

God. Every muscle in his body seemed to clench. "But the other part of you?"

"Isn't quite ready." She looked apologetic.

He kissed her forehead and tried to smile. "The timing isn't the best."

Gathering herself seemed to include taking a step back. She crossed her arms as if to hug herself. "I know he sounded strange tonight," she said in a sudden burst, "but you're wrong about my father. He wouldn't murder anyone. He wouldn't."

Troy had never heard a plainer warning. She might have kissed him fiercely one minute, but she was defending her father with equal strength the next.

Yeah, the timing completely sucks.

He nodded, accepting what she'd said. "I'll do my damnedest to find out the truth," he promised.

His reward was a shaky smile. "Thank you."

Troy didn't try to kiss her again, didn't dare. "See you in the morning."

He thought she said "Good night" just before she closed the door behind him. He got in his SUV and slammed the door before he let himself swear, a long litany that didn't come close to being the release valve he needed.

CHAPTER SEVEN

TROY FROWNED AT the ream of paper Madison had just handed him. "Can you email me this file?"

"Yes, of course."

He watched as she did so in front of him. "All employees are allowed to use the facilities, right?" he asked. "It occurs to me that I'm going to want the names of Wakefield College employees during that year, too." He glanced up.

Madison was dressed down today. In deference to the continuing heat wave, she was wearing calf-length chinos and a tiny T-shirt with a deep scooped neck and sleeves that barely qualified. His body had responded the instant he saw her. He was having a hell of a time lifting his eyes from her cleavage, especially since a bead of sweat was even now trickling in slow motion from her chest into the valley. He couldn't decide if he wanted to follow it, or lick it.

Damn it, concentrate!

Her eyes widened at his question. "Yes, of course all employees have full access, but in the middle of the night?"

"Not likely," he agreed, "but the faces would be familiar. A student wouldn't think twice if he saw someone who, sure, is usually out mowing the lawn, but is always around. Young, hip professors might keep the same hours as students do. And in this case, the killer wasn't there to swim a few laps. He was there because Mitchell King was." If he suddenly sounded grim, Troy thought—so be it.

Her head bobbed. "Yes, okay." She seemed to think about what he'd said—and his request. "I'll have to clear it."

"Understood." While reluctant to leave, he stood nonetheless. "This gives me a good start. Thanks, Madison."

She rose to her feet as well, more slowly. "You'll keep me informed?"

"Daily updates," he promised. "Preferably given over dinner."

She relaxed enough to smile. "Deal. Although I don't want you feeling obligated...."

He took a step toward her and slid his hand beneath the silky bob of her ponytail. She was sweating there, too, but sweat, he had discovered, could be sexy. "You haven't noticed that I want to spend time with you?"

Her eyes sparkled. "Actually, I had."

He was about to bend his head when boisterous voices announced the arrival of somebody—at least two somebodies—in the outer office. Troy almost groaned.

"Another time and place," he conceded. Releasing her, he stepped back. "Damn, it's hot up here. Haven't you complained?"

"Believe it or not, this *is* air-conditioned. Just not very effectively. I whine, maintenance shows up and I hear some bangs and clangs but the temperature never drops. Fortunately, the heat only lasts for a few weeks after school starts. By December, it's the people on the first couple of floors who have to come to work wearing wool socks, scarves and gloves while my office is completely comfortable. And spring is lovely for all of us."

"We do have nice springs." Even a hard-bitten cop occasionally paused to smell the lilacs once they came into bloom in every shade from white to the deepest plum. The old bushes crowded damn near every porch in town and branches weighted with blooms hung over sidewalks.

He settled for a quick, light kiss and let Madison escort him out of the office, past the curious stares of the two students who apparently were her helpers today. He'd have to ask what her next big project was. Maybe one of those—what had she called them? Those get-togethers that happened across the country? On the Road? He thought that was it. That got him wondering, as he descended the stairs, how much time she spent on the road herself.

He found the police station to be relatively quiet today. After spending some time highlighting the names of people he wanted to start with, he went to talk to Davidson.

He outlined his plan of attack, starting with his hope to meet with as many potential witnesses as possible in person.

"Several of the students who were interviewed still live in eastern Washington, two right here in town. From there on, I intend to focus first on the senior class."

His lieutenant nodded, as he'd anticipated; as a senior in college, King would have known his classmates better than younger students. A freshman might have been a witness, sure, but probably not the killer.

"I'll begin with the ones I can talk to face-to-face. I'm expecting to make a trip to the Seattle area in the next week."

"We can swing that," Davidson agreed gruffly.

Troy told him his intention to speak to as many professors and other employees who'd been here at the time, too. "I'm not sure investigators at the time did."

"It'll be interesting to see what you learn about the victim." Davidson ran a hand over his crew-cut, graying hair. "Like every other cop in Frenchman Lake, I've read that whole damn murder book. Students who knew King were pretty reticent, as you'd expect, but between the lines…"

Troy nodded. "He wasn't well liked. Hard to miss."

"I'm betting people who knew him will be more willing to open up now. Why wouldn't they?"

Troy pushed himself to his feet. "Here's hoping."

"I won't swear you'll be able to give this all your time," he was warned.

"I know." With a nod, he left.

He'd counted himself lucky when he saw that two students who had admitted to being at McKenna Sports Center on the night in question still lived in Frenchman Lake. If Madison's records were complete, Karen Blair Wardell was currently unemployed although remaining an active volunteer in the schools, and Bob Schuler was an attorney. When he called, both were available to see him today.

Turned out, Karen Wardell's husband had inherited one of the few wheat farms large enough to survive the trend toward conglomeration. Troy actually enjoyed the twenty-minute drive through the rolling countryside, mostly covered by curving rows of grapevines. Eventually a rocky gully formed a sort of demarcation, and golden fields of wheat, familiar from his childhood, took the place of the grapes. He turned into a long driveway bordered by tall poplars that dead-ended at a good-sized rambler surrounded by farm outbuildings.

Ms. Wardell was a still-trim woman with curly brown hair captured in a bun and a friendly smile. She invited him in.

"Detective Troyer. Any relation to Joe Troyer?"

"My father." He accepted her condolences, and then an offer of lunch. While they ate sandwiches and a fruit salad, he asked how well she'd known Mitchell King.

"Not well," she said frankly. "You're wasting your time

talking to me. I had a roommate who dated him for a few months back in—oh, I don't know, our sophomore year? If not for the murder, I doubt I'd even have remembered him. As it is…"

She didn't finish the sentence and didn't have to. Nobody attending Wakefield College at the time would ever have forgotten Mitchell King's name.

"Any impressions of him?"

"I couldn't see the appeal." She wrinkled her nose. "But the roommate and I didn't stay friends either, so…"

He smiled. "Would you mind telling me her name?"

She did, and he jotted it down in a spiral notebook.

"Was your, er, distaste physical, or did you not like him in general?" he asked.

She paused with the sandwich halfway to her mouth. Wrinkles formed on her forehead as she thought. "A little of both," she finally said. "I mean, he wasn't my type, but mostly there was something about him…" That required more thought. "He had a really unpleasant sense of humor," she concluded, her expression troubled. "Somebody was always the butt of it. Someone not present to defend him or herself. You know?"

"I've met the type."

"Like I said, I didn't see enough of him to tell you if my impression was accurate."

He asked about the night of the murder, and she told him that she and one of her housemates—by then she was living in a rental off-campus with three other women—had gone to McKenna for a swim. "I wonder if those all-nighters actually helped when we sat down to take the exam, or hurt," she said wryly, her smile reminiscent.

He smiled, too. "It's tradition."

"More like the perennial tendency of kids to put off until the last possible second what they don't want to do today. So I guess we can call it human nature." She poked a strawberry with her fork but he had the impression she didn't see it. Her gaze was fixed on the past. "I actually saw Mitch that night. I think Becca and I were the only two who did."

Or the only ones who admitted to seeing him, Troy thought.

"He was pushing open the door to the men's locker room just as we arrived. We were quite a ways down the hall, of course. I guess we were talking, because he turned his head and looked at us. He sort of nodded and I didn't give it another thought." A pained smile told Troy how often in the days following the murder she'd remembered that nod, that moment.

Back then she'd said King was carrying a duffel bag, which in fact was found in a locker along with his clothes. She struggled now to remember the few other people she'd seen. He was dismayed to note the list didn't include anyone new—or two of the names she'd given to the police at the time. He knew what had happened—her memory of the night had gotten trapped in that last glimpse of Mitch King himself, in the realization that within an hour, max, he'd died horribly. For her, it would be like a scratch on a record album, replaying over and over while what came after never replayed.

She and her friend Becca had stayed together, she said, which meant she was unlikely to have seen anything Ms. Wardell hadn't.

He thanked her sincerely, appreciating both her cordiality and the lunch that saved him from a fast-food stop once he got back to town. When he told her he was on his way to talk to Bob Schuler, she smiled.

"Bob and his wife are good friends. I know he'll help you as much as he can."

As he drove away from the farmhouse, a golden tail of dust rising behind his Tahoe, Troy reflected on how much happier he'd be to talk to someone who *wasn't* thrilled to cooperate. Someone who maybe had secrets, or at least bad memories.

You already did, he reminded himself. Madison's father. *Hell.*

So, okay, what he really wanted was to find someone *else,* someone with an even bigger secret. He couldn't say he'd much liked Guy Laclaire after listening in on the one phone conversation. But he knew this much: he surely didn't want to have to arrest the man.

MADISON SPENT PART of her day on a teleconference call with Jasmine Miller, a 1995 grad who was serving as liaison for the Alumni Admission program. An assistant director of admissions, Marco Quiroz, had joined her. Last year, nearly a hundred alumni across the country had volunteered to interview kids who'd applied to the college. The program had taken on increasing importance, as the impressions conveyed by the alumni interviewers had more of an impact on an applicant's admittance than most people would have guessed. Inevitably, some of those interviewers wouldn't be available to do it again this year. Jasmine had ideas for recruiting more alumni to help and for offering guidance to the volunteers, all of which had Marco and Madison nodding and offering their support.

Alone again in her office, she tried to concentrate on the column she was supposed to be writing for the upcoming college magazine that went primarily to alumni but was also used by admissions officers in recruitment. She kept an eye out year round for alumni who did something exciting enough to merit a feature article. This particular magazine included an interview with a fifty-eight-year-old woman who, after her husband died, decided to fulfill her dream of becoming a Peace Corps volunteer. She'd been accepted with enthusiasm and sent to Ghana.

Madison realized she'd been staring at her computer monitor for a good ten minutes, her fingers resting, unmoving, on the keyboard. Not a single sentence had formed in her mind, much less appeared on the blank screen. She made a sound of disgust and sat back.

The column wasn't due for a couple of weeks. She might as well give up. The truth was, all she could think about was Troy's quest. So why not do something useful? Maybe she could descend into the basement, where paper records were stored. She'd been mildly surprised to discover how many classmates of Mitchell King had dropped off the college's radar at some time in the past thirty-five years.

And, hey! It was bound to be cool down there.

It was so much cooler that she moaned with pleasure, then sneaked a surreptitious look out into the hall to be sure no one had heard her.

The pleasure fled when she got a look at the banks of old metal filing cabinets and tall metal shelving units packed with dusty cardboard banker's boxes. If she had to open every drawer and box…! But it turned out labeling was adequate for her to find a good starting place, saving her from perusing records that dated to the 1930s or who knew when. Eventually Madison plunked one of the boxes on the single library table and pulled out the first file.

Nope—these graduates were seven years ahead of her father. She checked a couple of other files then replaced the lid and heaved the box back onto a top shelf, taking down the one next to it.

She was already tired by the time she found the first records from her father's year of graduation. They'd been tidily put away in alphabetical order. Jennifer Abhold was the first student.

Jennifer, Madison discovered, had dropped out before the end of her freshman year.

Gerald Ackerman had graduated. There were a couple of brief communications from him—he was working toward a Ph.D. in Biochemistry at an East Coast school, he'd gotten married... And then at the back of his slim file was a note from his wife, saying that Gerry had been killed by a drunk driver.

Feeling sad, Madison jotted down the widow's name and last contact information. Her husband might have talked to her about the murder.

And so it went. Madison was only halfway through the Cs when she realized the basement had grown silent. She glanced at her watch in surprise to find it was 5:30. Troy was to pick her up in not much over an hour. Time had flown. Looking down at herself, she made a face. Between the sweat and the dust, she *so* needed a shower.

The hour before she saw him was enough for her to work up a case of nerves. Silly, since she'd been seeing him daily, but their meeting that morning in her office had been a smack of reality for her. Except for that moment at the end, Troy had been back in his cop persona. The badge glinting at his waist was enough to remind her what he was, without the unavoidable additional sight of an alarmingly large black handgun holstered at his side.

She had looked at him and had the shocked thought, *This man is investigating my father.* Wow. He suspected Dad of murder. She had yet to succeed in wrapping her mind around the bizarre concept. Maybe that mental resistance explained why she'd been able to keep falling for Troy even as she accepted that he was determined to do his job—which, at the moment, involved patiently hunting down a killer who he fully expected to be her dad.

In the interest of protecting herself, shouldn't she pull back a little? Maybe suspend the dating side of this relationship?

Yeah, but if she did that, would he continue being as open with her?

Maybe not. Probably not.

Her uneasy reflections continued. Did he want to see her daily because he had the hots for her...or because she was potentially useful? Plus, oh yeah, it would be a good idea to ensure she didn't warn her father.

So maybe we're using each other.

Great if she could be appropriately cynical and accepting, and actually believe that, but Madison knew better. Her stomach was full of sparkling fireflies because Troy would be knocking on her door any minute, then those gray eyes would survey her, head to foot, after which he'd give a slow smile, step forward and kiss her, one big hand at her neck or waist, holding her firm.

She huffed out a breath. Maybe she should have sex with him *now.* All illusions might be ripped from her. Her knees could quit going weak. He'd be just another guy, crude, over-muscled and ultimately nobody she'd want to keep around. And *then* she could think with real clarity.

Good plan, but what if he turned out to be a fabulous lover? What if he made her feel things she never had before?

This is such a mess, she thought unhappily. She'd felt... safe—she guessed that was the right word—once Troy had agreed to keep quiet about what his father had seen. The fact that he was doing something he considered unethical because she'd asked it of him was amazing enough that she'd let it obscure the bigger truth. Troy had every intention of finding the killer, no matter who he was.

The doorbell rang and her heart did a dizzying spin worthy of an Olympic gymnast.

Madison walked from the kitchen to the front door, disturbed by the realization that regaining her emotional equilibrium wasn't actually an option anymore. She was afraid it hadn't been since the big man with sun-streaked brown hair had walked into her office and looked at her with an arrested expression, as if without so much as moving or speaking she'd shaken him.

She knew something else, too. If she went to bed with him now, baring herself physically and emotionally, she'd feel as if she was betraying her father.

Again.

She was having enough trouble living with herself after making that phone call. After she'd set Dad up to say things he wouldn't have if he'd known a cop was listening in and cold-bloodedly analyzing every word.

As she turned the doorknob, the last thing Madison felt was a surge of anger, this one directed at her father—who almost had to have done something wrong.

But not murder. It couldn't have been murder.

TROY DIDN'T SEE Madison the following night. Dinner for him was grabbed at a restaurant in Walla Walla, a college town that looked a lot like Frenchman Lake.

He had made a good-sized swing around eastern Washington, talking to two people in the Yakima area, one up in Moses Lake, another in Pullman—now teaching at Washington State University, and finally yet another professor, this one at Whitman College in Walla Walla. He'd leave Spokane for another day—there was a fair cluster of alumni up there.

Swallowing iced tea while he waited for his entrée, Troy brooded about his day. He was beginning to think his whole strategy needed rethinking.

Karen Wardell had laid down the pattern for what he was hearing. Not a single soul had remembered seeing anyone at the gym that night they hadn't mentioned to the investigator in the days following the murder—and most, like her, didn't remember everyone they claimed then to have seen.

The one exception was the guy in Moses Lake, who had given a recitation of what and who he saw that was as methodical as if he'd practiced it like a speech to his local chamber of commerce. Of course, it happened that he was a CPA, so maybe methodical was part of his blood makeup.

The WSU professor had been distinctly annoyed to be cornered by a cop. If he was into social media, he'd probably been tweeting by the time Troy reached the stairwell twenty feet from his office. If he was too old-fashioned for social media, he'd likely picked up the phone and placed a call to Wakefield College president Lars Berglund.

That was something Troy expected to happen sooner or later, but he'd been hoping for later. Just as he'd been hoping it was a while before anyone he talked to felt compelled to phone every former classmate to tell them the investigation had been reopened and some cop would be around to ask questions. He'd really prefer to catch them by surprise, to watch their faces as they ground the rusty gears of memory into motion. He especially didn't want potential witnesses chatting to each other, embellishing their own memory with patches and sparkles from someone else's.

But that's the way it goes, he thought in resignation, nodding his thanks to the waiter who brought him a sizzling steak and an enormous baked potato. And, damn, was he starving.

If Madison had been here, she'd have ordered one of the more interesting vegetarian items on the menu, and he might have done the same. But what the hell.

Damn it, Dad, why didn't you follow your conscience?

Had it ever occurred to his father, once Troy came home to Frenchman Lake, that *he* might be the one who would have no choice but to investigate—drum roll, please—the grand prize winner of the Most Shocking Revelation to Come Out of the Time Capsule award?

He grimaced as he cut a piece of the tender meat. No, Dad had still been relaxed, because the thing wasn't supposed to be opened for another fifteen years.

Troy had to come to terms with the fact that, if Dad had been there to accept the envelope with his name on it, he most likely *would* have taken it home and shredded or burned it. If guilt or twinges on his conscience had any impact on him in the intervening years, nothing would have stopped him from walking into the downtown police station and saying, "There's something I need to tell you."

Why, Dad? Goddamn it, why?

Knowing he'd never get an answer felt a lot like the acid, gnawing beginning of an ulcer in his belly.

WHEN HER PHONE rang midevening, Madison pounced, thinking Troy had called. Seeing her father's number on the screen took her aback.

"Dad?" she said cautiously.

"Madison." He started most calls that way, with her name gravely spoken. "How are you?"

Um...not any different than I was three days ago?

"I'm good," she said. "Busy." She started chatting about a couple of new alumni networking groups, one all

women, one gay/lesbian, and of the eagerness to partici-
pate that had really pleased her. Her father listened in silence, which inexplicably drove her to keep talking. All
the while, she knew she was really trying to keep him
from telling her why he'd phoned her. Finally, however,
she ran out of things to say. "Sorry," she said, abashed. "I
don't suppose you are that interested."

"I'm always interested in your accomplishments."

Just not in her failures or doubts or the impulses he considered silly. This resentment was new to her, even as she
knew she wasn't being entirely fair. In his own way, he'd
been an attentive parent, certainly not neglectful. What
she was really having trouble with was the knowledge that
he'd cared more about whether she measured up to his ex-
pectations than he did about *her*. Did he even know who
she was aside from those accomplishments?

Probably not, but some of that was her own fault, she
admitted privately. Feeling abandoned by her mother, she
had been so insecure, *she* was as focused as he was on
achieving successes that would please him. That would
earn her one of his rare genuine smiles. She'd never had
the nerve to lift her chin and say, "Dad, I had a great day
without getting an A or being told I was being moved to
an accelerated class. In fact, I got a B on a quiz in algebra,
but who cares? I don't like math, anyway. What *really* matters is, this guy who is *so* cute stopped at my locker and
talked to me, and I like him, Dad, I really do." Or, "Oh,
and it felt so good to dive into the pool today, like I was
weightless and free! That's why it was a good day." Nope,
she'd never said anything like that to her father.

"So what's up, Dad?" she made herself say now.

"I can't call you without a reason?"

You never do. But that was another of the things she
didn't say to him.

Feeling stubborn, instead she said nothing.

He cleared his throat, a rare indication of discomfiture.

"I admit, I keep thinking about you overhearing some-one claim he saw me at the gym the night King was killed." He paused. "Or was it a she? You didn't say."

Oh, boy. Madison thought frantically before deciding to go with some semblance of truth. "It was a man."

"What the hell would get into someone to say that now? He sure didn't thirty-five years ago when the police were asking questions."

"Maybe…could it have been a friend of yours who didn't want to get you in trouble?" Breathless, she waited.

The silence was just a little too long. "Some friend," her father muttered at last.

"Well…he might have been trying to be."

"I could have cleared it up then."

"You could talk to the police now."

"For God's sake, none of this has anything to do with me," he snapped.

"It does if somebody saw you there." Her voice shook slightly at her audacity. Usually she would have backed down by now.

I'm acting like I'm afraid of him.

Of course she wasn't, she told herself hastily, and knew that what she feared wasn't her father, it was the possibil-ity of losing him. No matter how judgmental he was, he had always been her security.

"I could sue whatever idiot claims he saw me there," he grumbled.

Madison kept her mouth shut.

"Mitch King made plenty of enemies," her father said in a hard voice. He either hadn't noticed her lack of com-ment, or he'd fallen into the trap of needing to fill a silence. "The police won't have any problem finding people who hated his guts."

Oh, dear God, she thought in horror. Would she have to tell Troy what her father told her? She closed her eyes.

"Dad, I don't understand. He was a college student. A kid! I mean, being unpopular is one thing, but what could he have done to make people actually hate him? That's a really strong word." Madison realized she was all but begging. *Tell me* you *weren't one of the people who hated Mitchell King's guts, rather than merely disliking him.*

"Other students' screwups were his wine and song." There was a startling knife-edge of bitterness in her father's voice Madison had never heard before.

"Dad?"

"Enough about him," he said brusquely. "Hell, I hadn't so much as thought his name in twenty-five, thirty years. I'm sorry to have to remember him now. Don't let yourself get sucked into this, Madison. He's not part of your job."

She made a noncommittal sound that seemed to satisfy her father, because after a few general remarks he ended the call. It was strange, though, because inside a part of her was protesting that last statement. Whatever else could be said about him, Mitchell King had been a Wakefield college student, and barely a semester from being an alumnus. Didn't that make him, in a way, legitimately her responsibility?

Thinking about the conversation with her father, Madison stared down at the now blank screen on her phone. Suddenly she felt as if the air was being squeezed from her lungs, and, afraid her phone would ring, she turned it off in a rush. She couldn't talk to Troy now. She needed time to decide whether she would even tell him she'd talked to Dad, and if so what she would say. She wasn't a very good liar.

Anguish filled her. What could Mitchell King have done to her father? Madison desperately wanted to believe it was something relatively normal and innocent. They'd fought over a girl, maybe. Or Mitch had bad-mouthed Dad around campus. Dad had told Madison on more than one occasion that he considered his reputation to be all-important.

But...*hate?*

She couldn't escape the terrifying realization that her father had been telling her he understood why somebody would want to murder Mitch King. No, not only murder— the savagery of the attack hadn't been any secret. Who-ever had hit him over and over again until his face was unrecognizable had wanted to wipe him out of existence.

Had hated him.

Not you, Dad. Please, please, don't let it have been you.

CHAPTER EIGHT

MAYBE A CHANGE of tactic was in order.

Brooding and oblivious to the noise and activity around him at the station, Troy sat with his chair tilted back precariously and his feet propped on his desk.

Starting with the original witnesses was a waste of his time, if the ones he'd already spoken to were representative. Unless he hit on one of them who was flat-out lying, they'd already said their piece.

No, what he needed were witnesses who hadn't been identified at the time.

Back to the original murder book. He took his feet off the desk and put them back on the floor, in the same motion reaching for the binder that held the sum total of what investigators had learned thirty-five years ago. Opening it, he tried to remember whether those investigators put out a general appeal on campus for witnesses, or focused on King's classmates as Troy's first impulse had been.

It took him a while to figure out that a general appeal *had* been issued—but not until students had come back after Christmas break for second semester. In other words, weeks later. *Big mistake,* he thought clinically. Two or three weeks was long enough for memories to blur or, maybe worse yet, get corrupted after too much chitchat with friends who'd heard *this,* or knew for a *fact* that so-and-so had been there that night. He could imagine panic spreading along with rumors that police were looking at anyone who admitted being at McKenna Center that night as a suspect.

In fact, when he contemplated the list of students interviewed, he discovered the vast majority were seniors. Was that because seniors took finals most seriously and were therefore more likely to be awake in the middle of the night—or because investigators had looked with immediate suspicion on classmates?

Troy was torn. He could learn more about Mitchell King by talking to people who'd known him best. On the other hand, his best chance of locating a witness nobody had talked to back then was to start with the freshmen on up.

Maybe some of each, he mused, flipping through the list he'd gotten from Madison. A number of the alumni on the list lived in eastern Washington. He'd set up appointments.

He filled his afternoon with local appointments, and, left with an hour or so before he had to set out, he started calling graduates he was unlikely to ever get a chance to interview in person.

He left a lot of messages, but also spoke to three people. All remembered the excitement around the murder, but hadn't even known who Mitchell King was until they read about him in the local newspaper and heard the talk. He thanked them politely, shut down his computer and left for the first appointment.

During the short drive, he called Madison at work and suggested dinner. She sounded guarded, which made him suspect she wasn't alone, but agreed. He'd pick her up at seven.

His first two appointments proved to be as disappointing as the morning's phone calls. Because they lived in Frenchman Lake, both women recalled details of the murder better than the more far-flung alumni did. The *French-*

man Lake Herald occasionally ran a retrospective on the most lurid crime ever seen in the small town. But neither had ever so much as met King, and at the time of the murder they'd apparently been tucked in their narrow beds in their dorm rooms sleeping the peaceful sleep of the student too well prepared to need to pull an all-nighter.

The third appointment was different. He hit on something—okay, not a nugget of gold, but a flake. A glimmer of hope.

Ben Gossett, a partner in a real estate brokerage, had betrayed himself with a few twitches as he listened to Troy explaining why he was asking questions about a crime committed so long ago.

"Yeah, I had a class with the guy, although I can't say I really knew him." He eyed Troy. "I heard things, though."

"If you'd be frank with me, it would be very helpful."

Gossett hesitated, running a hand over his thinning pate. "I only heard rumors," he said cautiously. "It may all be BS."

"That's okay, too." Troy smiled. "I'll be talking to a lot of people. Right now, I'm trying to build a picture of the guy. The original investigators got hints that Mr. King wasn't well liked, but they didn't learn anything that would suggest a motive for his murder. I'm hoping I can."

"Yeah, okay." The multi-line phone on his desk rang, but Gossett ignored it. "What I heard is that he was blackmailing some people. 'You pay me off, I keep my mouth shut.' That kind of shit."

Troy hid his elation. "Can you give me any names?"

Gossett shook his head. "If it would help, I can tell you who told me."

"That would help."

Gossett told him; Troy jotted down the name.

After further questions, the guy admitted that he'd

heard there was at least one student who had been at the gym that night and hadn't wanted to talk to police.

"He was a stoner. He didn't like police."

"What about now?" Troy asked.

"Don't know." Gossett shrugged. "He wasn't a friend of mine. I don't know what happened to him after he left Wakefield."

He seemed to have less compunction about giving Troy this second name. Troy thanked him cordially and they shook hands. Leaving a card, Troy walked out past a couple of desks staffed by agents who were all on the phone. He gathered from the photos and property descriptions covering one wall in the reception area that Gossett & Armstrong specialized in farms and acreage. With the growing wine grape business, arable land in the county was probably a hot commodity.

The minute he was behind the wheel of his Tahoe, Troy grabbed the file that lay on the passenger seat and searched for the two names. It took him a minute, but the stoner was there with address and phone number. He had been a sophomore that year. The second, the kid who might know who had been blackmailed, was there, too, but with no contact info. He'd been a junior, like Ben Gossett.

Unfortunately, the stoner lived in Maryland. Troy didn't recognize the name of the town. After thinking it over, he placed the call. It would be almost 8:00 p.m. on the east coast, which increased the odds of catching the guy at home.

A woman answered. When he asked for Curtis Tucker, she said, "Just a moment, please," and he heard her yell, "Curt! It's for you."

Troy waited a good minute before a man came on. "Yeah?"

"This is Detective John Troyer. I'm calling from Frenchman Lake, Washington. We've reopened the Mitchell King homicide and I'm contacting alumni all across the country in hopes of finding witnesses who didn't come forward then. I'm interested in talking to anyone who knew King well, too."

The silence had that bottomless feel that only happened during phone calls.

"So you just got to my name?" Tucker finally asked.

"Actually, I was steered to call you by someone who'd heard secondhand that you might have been at the gym that night but chose not to talk to police at the time."

"Who…?" He broke off. "Never mind. It doesn't matter. Yeah, I was there. If I'd seen someone kill the guy, I'd have come forward, but I didn't."

"I'm interested in what and who you did see," Troy explained patiently. "If you give me a new name who gives me a new name, eventually I may be able to learn something useful."

"Okay, I get that. The thing is, I'd been smoking weed that night." He half laughed. "I probably shouldn't be telling you that."

"It's of interest to me only if it affected your ability to remember what you saw."

"Yeah, well, I was relaxed, mostly. I spent some time in one of the small weight rooms lifting. After that I meant to take a sauna, but when I opened the door there were these two dudes in there, see. One of them was sitting, wearing only a towel. He was sweating like he'd been in there awhile. The other guy hadn't stripped down, which was weird. I mean, he even had street shoes and socks on. I could tell I was interrupting something intense. The dude in the towel glared at me and said, 'Do you mind?' so I backed out. I showered and left."

Troy questioned him further, and he remembered there

was a second towel in a heap on the bench next to him, like maybe he'd been lying down and had his head on it.

"Did you know either of the two guys in the sauna?" Troy asked.

"Not then. I mean, they were familiar because, hey, Wakefield isn't that big. You know?"

"Later?"

"The dude wearing the towel was Mitchell King. His picture was everywhere the next few days. Freaked me out, I can tell you."

Troy knew that, in fact, King had been nude when he was murdered. A blood-soaked white towel had fallen to the floor below his body, found on one of the slatted-wood benches in the sauna. One towel, not two. The killer had to have taken the second one, likely to have bundled some of his own clothes. He couldn't have inflicted that much damage without getting blood on himself. He'd avoided stepping in it, though; luminol had turned up no blood traces outside the sauna.

He worked hard to make his voice nonjudgmental. "And the other guy?"

"You're not going to think he killed King just because he was there talking to him, are you?"

"Did he have anything with him that could have been a weapon?"

Troy could have been wrong, but he thought this silence was a thoughtful one.

"He had his wallet in his hand, which I thought was weird. I don't think he had anything else with him. Not even a gym bag. I figured he knew King was in the sauna and stuck his head in to talk to him. You know?"

"That's a natural assumption. And chances are, that's exactly what was going on. But he might be another witness. He could have passed another person going in as he was leaving, for example."

"I guess that makes sense." Pause. "I recognized him the next year. We had a class together. His name made me think of politics. That's the only reason I remember it. It was Govern. Like government, or McGovern. Roy or Ray or something like that."

Troy flipped through his lists. There it was. Rafe Govern had been a junior the year of the murder.

"Did you hear any part of what Mitch King and this Govern were talking about?" he asked.

"Nah, they cut off what they were saying the minute I pushed the door open. I could tell they didn't want me to hear."

Upon further inquiry, Troy learned that Govern hadn't been wearing a jacket, only a T-shirt, jeans and athletic shoes.

"Do you know what time it was when you went into the sauna?"

Tucker was vague on that and admitted he'd been vague even back then. He hadn't paid attention. His best guess was around one o'clock to one-thirty. Which was as much as a half hour before the murder, although of course they couldn't be sure.

Troy talked him through the rest of his visit to the gym. The only other people he'd seen had given statements at the time. Finally Troy thanked him for his honesty and ended the call. The elation was huge. He had a witness who'd not only seen King, he could identify someone else who'd been in the sauna room talking to King—and by all indications, the two had been set on keeping their discussion private. There might even have been the suggestion of tension between King and this Rafe Govern.

Starting the engine, he was conscious of a fierce grin

pulling his lips back from his teeth. If he were fanciful, he'd think he had caught a whiff of the acrid scent of blood.

He knew this much: he was already a giant step ahead of the investigators who had failed to find a murderer.

MADISON HAD BARELY gotten as far as fastening the seat belt in Troy's SUV when she asked if he'd found out anything. She did not feel patient.

He slanted a glance at her. "Let's wait until we're sitting down for dinner. I have quite a bit to tell you."

What could she do but agree? During the five-minute drive, he made polite conversation by inquiring about the past couple of days, and as if by rote she found herself telling him the same things she'd told her dad. Troy made appropriate noises, but she could tell he was listening with only part of his attention.

He'd suggested a bistro on the main street in downtown, and they were seated at a wrought iron table outside. A few potted plants and checked tablecloths gave the patio some atmosphere. The evening was still sunny and warm, but she enjoyed the breeze playing over her skin. There were only a couple of other parties seated out here, and neither was nearby.

The minute the waiter took their orders, she leaned forward. "Tell all."

He smiled with what she took for cold satisfaction. "I talked to someone who heard that King was running a blackmail business. Apparently it paid better than waiting tables in the dining hall."

She heard a huff of air and knew it came from her. It was as if a passing car had jumped the curb and hit her, compressing her chest. As if he was standing behind her, Madison heard her father's bitter voice.

Other students' screwups were his wine and song.

And bank balance, too.

Oh, God—Dad had *known*. And if he knew…wasn't it likely he'd been paying blackmail himself?

Troy was watching her strangely. Madison had no idea what her expression was giving away.

"The person who told you." She licked dry lips. "Was he being blackmailed?"

"No, or if he was he didn't admit it." Troy rolled his shoulders while apparently mulling over the idea. "No, I don't think so. He'd heard it secondhand, and I believe him. He was too casual about the whole thing. He did remember who told him, but I have no contact info for this guy. I'm hoping you can find something."

She nodded, almost numb now. "Yes, of course. What's the name?"

"Frank Claybo."

"Oh. I hadn't gotten far into the Cs yet." Realizing they hadn't talked since she started her project, she explained about going through old records. "I was too busy today to continue."

"Can you look for Claybo in the morning?"

"First thing," she promised, even as she wondered whether this Claybo would know who had been being blackmailed. Of course, if it turned out there was a whole list of victims, it wouldn't matter so much if her father was on it. Because then there would be a whole lot of other people who'd had reason to hate Mitchell King.

Dad had said that, too, she remembered. So he must have been aware he wasn't alone.

"You said you had a lot to tell me."

"I also located a witness who walked into the sauna that night and saw King and another student talking. The other student wore street clothes and had a wallet in his hand."

Madison jumped to the obvious conclusion. "He was making a payment."

"That's a possibility." Troy glanced up and she realized the waiter had brought their drinks. White wine for her and lemonade for him. He nodded his thanks and waited until they were alone again. "There are probably a dozen other explanations, though. He might have been paying him back a few bucks he'd borrowed the week before…"

"In the middle of the night in the sauna?"

A smile lifted one corner of Troy's mouth. "I didn't say it was likely, only possible. He could have been pulling out a slip of paper with someone's phone number to give to King, he could have been loaning *him* a few bucks, he could have been…"

She rolled her eyes.

Troy grinned, but he also had a steely glint in his eyes that reminded her that he was, in his own way, a hunter. One closing in on prey. His prey just happened to be human.

And one of the people he intended to cut out of the herd could easily be her father.

"Do you believe the guy who told you this? How come he didn't talk to police back then?" she asked.

"He was apparently high that night. I gather he smoked a lot of weed, which may explain what sounds like a chronic distrust of law enforcement. He said he'd have come forward if he'd seen anybody get hurt, but he didn't. He didn't actually know either guy in the sauna until he heard about the murder the next day and saw pictures of King on the news."

"What about this Claybo?"

"The witness was in a class with Claybo the next year and recognized him. Claybo was a junior the year of the murder, and the stoner was a sophomore."

Their salads came and then their entrées. Madison ate without tasting. Troy told her about some of the other people he'd talked to and his conclusion that he'd started in the wrong place. All the while, Madison desperately searched her conscience.

He was being open with her, exactly as he'd promised. What's more, even as he'd reopened the case Troy had started with a handicap because he'd promised not to tell anybody about his own father's accusation. She owed him for that. They had agreed to investigate together…

No, Madison reminded herself, he'd been quite firm about saying that *he* was doing the investigating. She was only providing research support. Still, fair was fair.

Also, he was already suspicious of her father. Would she really be making things any worse for him if she told Troy what Dad had said? And it did seem to confirm some of what Troy had learned, which might be helpful.

She roused from her brooding to realize Troy was watching her with a faint smile. He had the glass of lemonade in his hand and was rocking it slightly, enough to clink ice cubes off each other.

"Deep thoughts?" he asked, in a voice husky enough to make her wonder if he was thinking about murder anymore.

Her heart cramped, both at the look in his eyes and at the conclusion to her inner battle. *Oh, God. I have to tell him,* she realized. *He's done something amazing for me. I can't lie.*

"I talked to my father last night," she said, and saw the slow change of Troy's expression. His very features seemed to harden.

"You called him?"

His tone was so careful, Madison realized in outrage that he thought she might have broken her promise.

"No!" she exclaimed. "I said I wouldn't tell him anything, and I didn't."

"Okay." Troy set down the glass of lemonade. The hard line of his mouth had eased and small lines creased his forehead. "I'm sorry. I didn't mean to accuse you, but I can't lie. It crossed my mind that you got to feeling guilty and decided you had to tell your dad everything." He grimaced. "I'm not sure I'd even blame you."

"Well, *I'd* blame me." She frowned at him. "I made a promise."

"Okay," he said again. "So if you didn't call him, that means he called you. Is that usual?"

She hesitated, hating the feeling of having her loyalty ripped jaggedly down the middle like a piece of fabric. "No," she finally admitted. "We often go a month or more between calls. At first he made conversation. I could tell that's all he was doing. And then I asked why he'd phoned and he admitted that Mitchell King had been on his mind. I think what he most wanted to know was who it was who claimed to have seen him that night."

"What did you say?"

"I admitted it was a man, but that's all."

"Good."

"Dad wondered why the person hadn't told the police then, and insisted he could have cleared up any questions. I suggested he contact you now and he said the whole thing didn't have anything to do with him."

"Because he wasn't anywhere near McKenna Center?"

"He didn't say that," she admitted reluctantly. She drew a deep breath. This was the hard part, she thought, but squared her shoulders. "He told me that lots of people had reason to hate Mitch King's guts."

Troy had gone very still. "He said it in those words."

"Yes. I asked him why, and Dad said because other

students' screwups were Mitch's wine and song. That's a quote."

Troy's eyes narrowed slightly. "That jibes with what I was told today."

"Yes. That's…why I thought you should know what Dad said."

"You didn't want to tell me."

She felt ridiculously close to tears for someone who didn't cry. "No."

"I do understand, Madison." His voice was gentle and he reached across the table for her hand. "You're in a really lousy situation."

She made a face at him even as she relished the warm, enveloping clasp of his hand. "Yes, I am. It sucks. I feel like a traitor."

"Do you want to stay out of this from now on?"

She didn't even have to think about her answer. "No. It would be worse being kept in the dark. And I know I owe you."

He shook his head. "No. I offered to keep quiet about what Dad wrote for my own reasons, too. Don't forget that. I don't want you to help because you think you have to."

"I'm curious now. I can't let go of it."

"Then we're two of a kind," he said softly.

The night had cooled enough that when the waiter brought coffee, Madison welcomed it. Neither she nor Troy wanted dessert, but she was glad to continue sitting here as dusk settled. There was very little traffic on the street, and all businesses except for restaurants were closed. She and Troy were alone out here.

After the waiter left them alone, Troy scooted his chair partway around the small round table. He took her hand again, as if that was the most natural thing in the world, and seemed comfortable lifting his coffee cup with his left hand.

They sipped in silence for a few minutes, Madison, for one, grateful for the release of tension. She actually felt a little bit limp—maybe the aftereffect of the wine, although that wasn't fair since she'd only had the one glass.

"I've been wondering," Troy said. "There's a lot you haven't said."

Apprehension balling in her stomach, Madison looked at him. "You mean about Dad."

"No. Well, I guess I don't understand your relationship with him, either, but it's actually your mother I was thinking about. What happened there?"

"You haven't said much about your mother, either," she countered.

He half smiled. "True enough. The way I feel about my mother these days is…complicated. Hard to talk about something you haven't yet worked out yourself."

Madison nodded her understanding. "I'm not sure how much of what went wrong was Mom's fault and how much was mine."

He looked at her, his gaze compassionate. "How old were you when your parents split up?"

"Seven. And they fought a lot before."

His hand tightened, but he didn't say anything.

"It started because Mom left me with Dad. She said it was only temporary, until she figured out where she was going to live and what she was going to do, but I didn't believe her." It wasn't hard to remember the child's shock and hurt and bewilderment.

"What kid would?"

"Dad didn't talk to me much about what was happening, but I heard enough to know he canceled a few business trips in the next couple of months because he didn't want to leave me even though we had a housekeeper and he could have gone. I think maybe he did more things with me than he had before. You know?"

Troy's expression was so kind, it melted something deep inside Madison. She wasn't sure she'd ever had anybody listen to her in quite the same way. In fact, she'd never talked to anyone the same way, not even college roommates and later friends. She had never until now been tempted to open the lid to expose emotions she hadn't quite come to terms with.

My own Pandora's box.

"Then one day Mom was there, saying I was to go live with her. Part of me wanted to, part of me didn't."

"Did you have to change schools?"

She nodded. "That didn't help, of course. But the worse thing was that I found out she'd already remarried. She hadn't told me or invited me to the wedding. On the drive to her house she talked about how much I was going to like my new stepfather. She also admitted she was pregnant and that I'd have a new baby sister or brother in a few months." She gave Troy a shy glance. "I thought she'd gotten fat."

He laughed, a deep, rich sound that improved her mood.

Even so, resuming her tale plunged her back into the utter misery her then eight-year-old self had felt. "Probably no surprise, I hated her husband. The baby was born only a few months later. Even at that age, I figured out she'd gotten pregnant not very long after she left Dad. I still suspect she was already involved with Thomas before the separation. Not that it matters anymore." She sighed. "They were excited about the baby and consumed by her. A girl."

"Direct competition," Troy murmured.

Madison ignored that, although it was undoubtedly a

truthful observation. "Abby was blonde and blue-eyed like Thomas. In comparison, I felt like the ugly duckling. I thought they were relieved when school let out and I went to stay with Dad for the summer. When fall came I had to go back. I threw some major temper tantrums, which neither of my parents appreciated. I was so miserable that year, though, that when I begged to stay with Dad after the next summer they let me. I still went to Mom's for holidays and for a couple of summers, but by that time I had a half brother, too, and I was eleven, I think, and already starting to get breasts and I felt like this hideous, ungainly, unwanted, ugly *thing* compared to my mother's two perfect children."

Troy's chuckle and hug were the responses she needed. "You're beautiful."

"Thank you." She smiled at him. "Anyway, that's the story. I suspect my mother loved me as much as ever, but I was so suspicious and angry I probably frustrated her and I'm sure I gave them good reason to be happier when I wasn't around. Dad isn't the warmest guy in the world, but I think he actually did want me with him. I convinced myself he loved me in a way Mom didn't really."

Again Troy was quiet for a minute, but this time his eyebrows had drawn together and she thought he looked disturbed. "The screwed-up modern family" was all he said.

"Yup. Mine's classic." She managed a smile. "Could be worse, though. I had a friend in college whose father remarried three times and her mother once after their divorce. She had so many half siblings and stepsiblings, she wasn't sure she'd recognize all of them if she ran into them by chance. At least Mom stayed with Thomas." She gave a jerky shrug. "And Dad never remarried. He dated and I suppose had relationships, but he was never serious enough about any of them to bring them home to meet me."

"You friends with your sister and brother?"

"Friendly acquaintances is probably a closer description. There is a pretty big age difference between us. They're in their twenties now, of course, and we have more in common when I see them than we did as kids."

"Have you and your mother ever talked about any of this?"

"She tried. I deflected." Madison wrinkled her nose. "I can be stubborn."

"Never noticed." Smiling, Troy kissed her cheek, ending with a nuzzle that made her nerve endings sizzle. "Once again, I think we've outstayed our welcome at a restaurant."

"What?" As she turned her head, she realized night had fallen and even the interior of the restaurant seemed to be deserted. "Oh, dear. I suppose they close at nine on weeknights."

"Looks that way." Troy stood easily and held out his hand. "How about we save my family history for another night?"

"That's reasonable." She realized she hadn't even noticed him paying, but he put an arm around her and steered her out to the sidewalk without going back into the bistro.

On her front doorstep at home, he kissed her good-night with what felt more like tenderness than passion, although Madison noticed that he was fully aroused.

He'd decided not to act on it, she thought, surprised and touched and feeling a stew of emotions that made her entire chest ache. Troy thought he'd upset her when he really hadn't. Telling him about Mom had actually been liberating, Madison decided. As an adult, she could see that she'd probably hurt her mother's feelings almost as much as Mom had hurt her. Of course Mom had been overwhelmed with a baby and then a toddler as well as her sullen older child. And no, maybe she *hadn't* loved Madison enough to dig in her heels and say, *You're my daughter and you will live with me.*

But I had Dad, and he tried. He wasn't perfect, but he was enough.

Which, of course, circled Madison back to the beginning: he deserved his daughter's faith and, yes, her loyalty.

Only…he had also taught her right and wrong and how crisp the line between them was. He'd emphasized the absolute importance of never letting her ethics become mushy.

She was steadied, remembering his many lectures and his acute disappointment with her the few times he thought she'd failed to uphold the values he had taught her.

He couldn't be a murderer. That's all there was to it. In fact, she couldn't imagine him ever doing anything bad enough that he'd pay to hide it. The idea was so ridiculous, when she looked at it head-on, that Madison felt sure she'd misinterpreted everything in those two phone conversations.

If Dad had been at the gym the night of the murder, of course he'd have gone to the police, she thought in relief. Troy's father was wrong, that's all there was to it. Dad would be appalled if he ever learned she had felt she had to protect him.

Buoyed by her new confidence, she turned off lights and got ready for bed. It was only after she was in bed, tired but weirdly not sleepy, that a niggle of uneasiness made itself felt.

She'd heard the acute dislike in her father's voice when he said *Mitch was a sly little asshole* in that first conversation. *He liked knowing things. Then he could make use of what he knew.*

To blackmail.

Oh, yes, Dad knew.

Sickness rose in her throat and she blocked out all the things she didn't want to think about by remembering how it felt sitting on the restaurant patio in the near dark with Troy's arm around her. The gentleness in a voice that could often be harsh, the controlled strength of his hand holding hers, a good-night kiss so soft it felt…loving.

Madison was beginning to think she wanted nothing more in the world than for Detective John Troyer to love her.

Her stomach quivered with the force of her conflicting needs, her father on one side, Troy on the other. It was a long time before she slept.

CHAPTER NINE

TROY HADN'T BEEN exactly dodging his mother, but the past couple of weeks he hadn't gone out of his way to see her, either. He'd continued his usual brief, nightly phone calls, during which she told him, as usual, that she was fine, just fine. While a few old friends made the effort to stay in touch with her, she still wasn't going out.

A man could only push the kind of worries he had about her to the back of his mind for so long. He phoned her the next morning and suggested he take her out to dinner that evening. "We haven't done that in a while."

"Oh, you know how much fun it is for me to cook for you," she said in that vivacious tone he knew to be fake. "It's hardly worth cooking when it's only me. When shall I expect you? Six?"

Suddenly, in his mind three red cherries lined up. *Ding!* How could he have been so oblivious? He shook his head. Man. He'd been putting off labeling his mother's condition, but now he was being slapped in the face.

Agoraphobic.

She never left the house and yard anymore. He didn't know how it had happened or why, but it had. Troy tried to remember whether she'd had any tendencies that way before Dad died, and had no idea. Mostly when he'd seen his parents it *was* at their house. He'd had dinner there a lot of Sundays, when he had the day off. He and Dad met for lunch sometimes, which had seemed natural with the bank only four blocks from the city hall/police station complex. But Mom? He drew a blank. She must have at least gone shopping in those days.

Hell, I've enabled her, Troy realized, disgusted with himself. He thought of how helpful he'd been in the months after Dad died, doing all Mom's errands for her because he could see how hard grief had hit her.

Yeah, and I just kept doing them. He did her household repairs, picked up any little things she needed like fertilizer and mulch— "Whenever you happen to be at the garden center," she'd say.

He sat back in his chair and pinched the bridge of his nose hard enough to make the cartilage creak. Damn it, now what? He had a feeling she was too far gone for him to simply start declining to do her errands. Those friends and neighbors would probably pick up the slack, not realizing she had a real problem.

Talk to her. Get her to admit that she *had* a problem.

He grimaced. Dinner tonight was going to be good fun.

His cell phone rang and he checked to see who was calling. Madison. Even the sight of her name lifted his mood.

"Hey," he said.

"Hi."

She'd complained to him once that she didn't like her voice. She thought it was too sweet and light, that it got in the way of her being taken seriously. Troy loved her voice and especially the hint of a laugh that often ran through it, like the faint burble of a distant stream. It occurred to him that he hadn't heard that extra lightness in her voice recently, which was a dead giveaway: she was living under a lot of stress.

He glanced around to be sure he was relatively alone in the bustle of the busy squad room. "How's your day?"

When she said, "Fine," Troy winced. Not his favorite

word at the moment. "Actually," Madison continued, "I found the file for Frank Claybo."

He leaned forward and grabbed a pen. "And?"

"He was one of those grads who left Wakefield and never bothered to stay in touch. We have no information on what he did after graduating. I have his parents' address and phone number, but…"

"They'd likely be in their eighties."

"Yes." Something smug in her voice told him she was holding out on him. "Turns out, though, that he has a younger sister who also graduated from Wakefield. And she has stayed in touch."

"Now you're talking." There'd been no other Claybo on his list, so presumably the little sister had yet to arrive on campus.

"She didn't pop up even when I did a quick computer search because she had a different last name. Thank goodness there was a note in his file about sending information to her when she was in high school. She's a half sister, I guess, who has since married and changed her name yet again." Madison gave him that name, her current phone number and address. She was in southern California— Newport Hills, which he vaguely thought might be a ritzy area.

"You just saved me a hell of a lot of work," he told Madison. "Thank you."

"You're welcome." That sounded sincere enough, but also solemn and…something else.

Of course she had to have mixed feelings. When Troy found him, Frank Claybo might name her father as one of the blackmail victims. At this point, Troy thought it was certain that Guy Laclaire had forked over bucks to King in return for silence. The big question was why. Some secrets might be worth paying an irritating little worm like

King to keep quiet; the kind of thing that would get you in trouble with a girlfriend, or the college administration, or even parents. But a secret worth killing over—that was another story.

"I'm having dinner with my mother tonight," he said. "I'll let you know if I learn anything significant. Otherwise, can we plan for tomorrow night?"

Since this was Friday and she wouldn't be working tomorrow, Madison offered to cook for him. He accepted with a lot more pleasure than he had felt when his mother made the same offer. Troy felt a sudden urge to tell Madison his worries, but capped it; this was the middle of a working day for both of them. And he needed to find out what Mom had to say anyway.

After hanging up, he muttered an obscenity. He knew what she'd say. He was being silly, she was fine. Just fine.

"TROY!" MOM GREETED him at the door with such delight that he was stabbed by guilt.

Well, damn. He should have managed to spend more time with her, rather than letting himself get so preoccupied with work and with Madison.

He hugged her, then stood back. His mother had been a pretty girl and was an attractive woman who made sure she stayed that way.

"You're still losing weight," he said, perturbed. But her makeup was carefully applied and her hair stylishly cut and streaked. Then with a gleam of hope he thought, hey, maybe he was wrong and she did go out. He knew those pale streaks weren't natural and he doubted if she spent that much time in the sun. Didn't that mean she was visiting a salon?

Mom kept beaming. "Thank you."

"That wasn't a compliment." He immediately felt like a jerk. "I worry about you."

Her smile dimmed, but she continued to clutch his hand. "I could afford to lose a little. Honestly, John. All you do is fuss."

Fuss. He kissed her cheek, thinking she wasn't going to like anything he had to say tonight.

She'd made one of his favorite casseroles and he spotted an apple pie cooling on the counter. With a little luck, she'd send a few slices home with him. Seeing what a small portion of dinner she dished up for herself, he suspected she'd send the entire remainder of the pie with him. She couldn't be eating a lot of desserts these days.

"Your hair looks good. Do you still go to that same salon?" He frowned as if trying to remember. "What was it called? Shear something."

"Shear Beauty. No, I've found a woman I like better. She either works out of her own home or goes to her clients. It's so handy having her come here."

Well, shit.

"So tell me what's up with you," she said brightly.

"Uh." Momentarily he went blank. Did he plunge right in with a demand for her to start going to counseling? Or tell her what Dad had put into the time capsule? *Eenie meenie.* "I'm seeing a woman" was what came out of his mouth. "I'd like you to meet her one of these days."

That lit her up. "How wonderful! You haven't brought a woman home since…" She had to reach way down in the memory banks. "You were barely out of college."

He hadn't thought of Shari in years. They'd lived together for about a year. He'd never kidded himself that he was madly in love with her, but moving in together had seemed like the thing to do at the time. Under the circumstances, he hadn't felt able to go home for Thanksgiving without inviting her. He remembered hoping she'd have other plans, but no, she hadn't.

Shari was the first and last woman he'd cohabited with. As she got more and more demanding, he'd increasingly felt trapped. He'd been careful ever since to avoid getting cornered like that.

Madison, though...

He shook off the thought that was closer to a moment of yearning.

"Madison's father went to school with Dad," he said. "Guy Laclaire. They knew each other."

Mom's expression changed. It was subtle enough he wouldn't have noticed if he hadn't been paying close attention. "Oh, my," she said. "How did you happen to meet? Her father doesn't live here in Frenchman Lake, does he?"

Why did he suspect she knew a great deal about Guy Laclaire?

"No, Portland. Madison came to Wakefield because her dad had, and she now works for the college. She's director of alumni relations. We met because she organized the event when the time capsule was opened."

"Oh, my," Mom said again, as if she had to say *something*. But he thought she was frightened.

"I like her."

"Well...of course I'll be glad to meet her." Mom's hand fluttered over the basket that held rolls, then away again.

"I read what Dad put into the time capsule."

Her eyes, wide and—yes—frightened, first met his then skittered away.

"You know what he wrote, don't you?" Troy had tried to keep his tone calm, but her reaction suggested he hadn't totally succeeded.

Mom touched her throat. "Yes," she said finally. "He

told me a long time ago what he'd seen. He regretted ever writing it down."

Not what he'd wanted to hear. "Why?" Troy asked.

"He couldn't believe that Guy could have done anything awful like that. Joe couldn't understand why Guy didn't speak with authorities, but he was sure he had good reasons."

"And that's it." He shouldn't be staggered, but he was. "Dad saw someone running away from the scene of an ugly murder, with what could have been the weapon in his hand, and he decided Laclaire was too nice to have hurt anyone."

"Well…yes," his mother said timidly.

Troy swore in a way that had her eyes so wide, the whites showed like a spooked horse. "Son of a bitch," he said finally. "You and Dad taught me everything I know about integrity, and the two of you were keeping a secret like this all these years."

She ducked her head, but too late. He'd seen the tears spilling in huge rivulets down her cheeks, carrying mascara with them. She snatched her cloth napkin from her lap and balled it against her mouth as if to stifle sobs. Troy was too angry to feel the guilt he probably should.

"I'm surprised you didn't insist on attending the opening to make sure I never saw what Dad wrote." He waited until her alarmed gaze lifted. "But then," he said softly, "you'd have had to leave the house to do that, and you can't, can you?"

"Don't be ridiculous," she gasped. "Why are you being so hateful?"

With an almost violent movement, he pushed his plate away. "Am I being hateful because I pointed out that you have a problem?"

"Your father was a good man." His mother scrubbed

wildly at her wet cheeks, further smearing the mascara. "How can you say he wasn't?"

"I'm a cop, Mom. How do you think I felt to discover my own father had impeded an investigation into the most brutal crime that's ever happened in this town?"

"He was a boy...."

"Sure he was. Then." He let the word thud down like a rock. "What was his excuse ten years later? Twenty? He sure as hell didn't retain enough faith in Guy Laclaire's *goodness* to stay friends with him, did he?"

His mother sat frozen, a small creature afraid to draw notice.

His belly was knotted up tighter than a fist preparing for a blow. "You know what he was thinking. Tell me."

"I don't know!" Her face crumpled. "Why are you yelling at me?"

"God." He pushed back from the table. "I can't believe you knew, too."

She stared past him, her face ravaged. "It wasn't my place to say anything. The decision was Joe's to make."

He swung away, unable to look at her. When he reached up to massage the muscles on the back of his neck, his fingers dug in with a painful will. "All right," he said at last. "You're right. You were respecting his wishes. I can understand that."

There was a long enough silence that he almost turned around to be sure she hadn't crept like a mouse from the room.

"Why are you making so much of this?" Mom asked, while his back was still to her.

"Because I've reopened the investigation based on what Dad said." He did turn finally, to see her still sitting in her place but now staring at him in shock.

"You've...*what?*" she whispered.

"You heard me."

"But…he didn't want…"

"That's not what he said." Troy clenched his teeth, then had to work to unclench them. "He started by saying he knew he shouldn't have kept the secret. That at least by writing down what he'd seen and putting it in the time capsule, he could be sure it would all come out someday. He admitted it was his way of absolving himself of guilt." He looked steadily at his mother. "I'd like to think I'm following my father's wishes."

"You're wrong."

"What I know," Troy said grimly, interrupting her with no compunction, "is that I'm doing what Dad *should* have done. I intend to find out who beat a twenty-one-year-old kid so viciously he didn't have a face left. I plan to find out who has gotten away with the crime for thirty-five goddamn years. And if Dad wouldn't have approved, I'd be even more disappointed in him than I already am."

She seemed dazed. "You'll destroy his reputation."

He could have, should have, told her that no one but he and Madison knew what Dad had written. He was too enraged, too stunned, to feel like soothing his mother's fears. "Got to say, when I put Dad's reputation on one side of the scale, it seems pretty light compared to the hideous, unsolved murder weighing down the other side."

She kept staring.

Churning with frustration and too many other unresolved emotions, Troy shook his head. "I think I'll skip dessert, Mom. Thanks for dinner."

She was stuttering a protest while he kissed her on one cheek and strode to the front door. He got out of there quick, before he could say anything he would regret more than what had already passed between them.

Pulling away from the curb, Troy didn't look back. He

didn't want to see that his mother had followed him to the front door and was watching him go. He didn't want to see his mother, period. Right this second, he couldn't imagine when he would want to see her again.

MADISON WAS SURPRISED when her doorbell rang just after eight that evening. Even friends didn't often drop by at this time of night without having called first.

She peeked through the small square of leaded glass panes to see Troy, half turned away, his hands shoved in his pockets. She hurried to undo the dead bolt and flung open the door. "Troy?"

"Hey." He offered her a smile that didn't quite come off. "You busy?"

"Of course not. Come in." She stepped back. "I was watching a dumb comedy. I've hardly turned the TV on for the past month, but someone told me this show was good. Apparently we don't share the same sense of humor."

He followed when Madison led the way into her living room and used her remote to darken the television set. "Would you like coffee?" she asked.

"Yeah…no. Hell, I don't know. Sure. Maybe."

Although disquieted by his indecision, she smiled. "Coffee it is. Why don't you come with me?"

He propped a hip against the kitchen counter while she put on a pot.

"You went to your mom's," Madison ventured.

"Yeah, and stormed out." He grimaced. "I was probably an SOB, but goddamn it!"

"There's a reason you haven't talked about her."

"You could say that." He sighed. "Don't get me wrong, I love her. She was a great mom. I was closer to Dad as I got older, probably only because I was a boy. Mom was never much into sports, although she came to my games and cheered me on."

"What kind of games?" Madison asked, momentarily diverted.

"The usual. Little League, Pop Warner football. Then I played high school football and baseball."

Madison nodded, leaning back against the cupboard and crossing her arms.

"My parents were really in love." He frowned. "Sometimes the way they looked at each other made me uncomfortable. You know?" His eyes sought hers. He seemed satisfied when she nodded again. "Mom hasn't dealt very well with losing Dad. It hit me hard, too, but I didn't live with him. Sometimes I still think, I'll have to tell Dad… And then I remember." He fell silent for a moment. "At first I thought my mother's grief was natural. Sometimes she pretended for my sake, but mostly she's turned inward. She doesn't even want to see friends. Until she discovered delivery, I did her grocery shopping for her. That kind of thing."

Madison had the uneasy feeling she knew where this was going.

"She found a lawn service, so I didn't have to mow anymore. I've kept doing home repairs, picking up the odd thing at the hardware store or the plant nursery for her." His mouth curved into an utterly humorless smile. "Funny how easy it is not to notice that a person never leaves her home."

"Does she not go outside at all?"

"To her yard, yes. She's always been a gardener and still is. Far as I know, she grabs her mail and newspaper from the boxes outside the front gate. I'd been thinking she still did things like go to the salon. But today she told me breezily that she's found a nice hairdresser who comes

to her house. It didn't go so well when I told her she had
a problem."

"If she's scared, it's not surprising she'd be resistant
to admitting it."

His eyes, she saw when they met hers, were like storm
clouds. "It might've helped if I hadn't said that in the middle of an argument about Dad. Turns out she's known all
these years that Dad didn't go to the police when he should
have. I mentioned you and then your father. You should
have seen her face."

Oh, wonderful. She was falling in love with a man
whose mother had a major aversion to her family. An aversion that would become something much worse if Dad really *had* murdered Mitch King.

Which he didn't. You know he didn't. Madison hid her
expression by turning to reach into the upper cupboard
for mugs. Pouring gave her something to do.

"I said I bet she wished she could have gone to the time
capsule opening so she could make Dad's little confession disappear. Except she couldn't make herself leave
the house, could she?"

Madison winced. She could only imagine the tumult
of emotions both Troy and his mother had been feeling.

She cleared her throat slightly and turned back to face
him. "No, that probably wasn't the best way you could
have raised the agoraphobia issue with her."

"Tell me about it," he muttered, reaching for the mug
she extended to him.

"Let's go sit down," she suggested.

In the living room he sank down on one end of the sofa
and held out his hand, drawing her with him. Madison,
who hadn't especially wanted coffee anyway, set her mug
down on the table, curled her feet under her and cuddled
into Troy's embrace.

He took a swallow of his coffee and then set it down, too. His arm tightened and she felt his cheek gently rubbing the top of her head.

"Short girl," he said.

"Tall man."

She loved the vibration of his chuckle under her ear and the knowledge that talking to her had been enough to allow him to let some of his frustration and anger and fear for his mother go. In fact, she felt squishy and warm inside at the realization that he must have driven straight here from her house.

"I needed you." His mind had obviously been working on a similar track.

"I'm glad," she whispered, shifting so she could see his face.

His kiss came swiftly. It metamorphosed from soft into urgent with stunning speed. Within moments, she was plastered against him and his hands gripped her butt, lifting and fitting her to him. Little sounds escaped her, and her own hands squeezed the taut muscles in his shoulders. She was desperate to climb a little higher onto him, to feel the ridge in his pants where it would do the most good....

It might have been the desperation that triggered an internal warning. *You're not going to do this, remember?*

She so didn't want to listen. Didn't care why making love with Troy had once seemed like a bad idea.

But remembrance slipped into her head, anyway. *Dad.* It had to do with Dad.

Troy thought her father was a murderer. He might end up arresting him, and she didn't know if she could bear that.

She had gone still in his arms. The rhythmic kneading of his hands slowed. He lifted his head and looked at her, his eyes heavy-lidded and dark.

"Madison?"

"I'm sorry. This is, um, a little fast for me." She flushed at her own lie. She'd revved every bit as quickly as he had. In fact, she'd been frighteningly close to launch, and they were both still fully dressed.

Muscles hardened under her hands. He searched her face for the longest time. "Okay," he said finally, voice rough and deep. He lifted her, wincing as she scrambled to get off his lap and planted a knee close to his groin. "Maybe I should go."

"No!" She was as startled by her own cry as he looked. "Please don't." Madison looked down at her hands. "To be honest, I'm a little mixed up because of Dad and…and my fear of what might happen. But…I really like you. I'm hoping you can be patient with me." She hesitated. "I don't want you to leave," she finished, her voice smaller.

His chest rose and fell with a long breath. She couldn't help seeing how aroused he was. But all he did was rest his head against the back of the sofa, close his eyes and say, "Yeah, okay."

"You understand?"

He groaned and opened his eyes. "I don't want to, but I do."

"Really?" *Oh, that was pathetic.*

"I know how hard this is for you, Madison." He reached out and took her hand in his. "Don't worry."

She gulped. "Thank you."

His expression was half amused, half…not. "We haven't known each other that long. What kind of creep would I be to throw a fit because you said 'Whoa, slow down, buddy'?"

A smile crept onto her face. "When you put it that way…"

The beginnings of his answering smile made her heart

do some peculiar gyrations. "I do," he said in that husky voice. They sat and looked at each other, Troy still with his head resting against the back of the sofa, Madison half turning to face him, one foot under her. For what seemed like a long time, all they did was look. Deeply, without any defenses. *Adults never simply stare at each other like this,* she realized in some remote corner of her mind, but this felt…right.

Troy's lashes finally swept down, veiling his eyes, and Madison blinked. She hadn't in ages. When he looked at her again, he was smiling crookedly.

"I told my mother I wanted her to meet you."

Madison's stomach did a cartwheel. Or maybe it was her heart. "This might not be the best time."

"No." His smile became more crooked and less happy. "It seemed…meant to be that our fathers knew each other."

"Maybe it was meant to be."

"Maybe." Lines gathered on his forehead. "But if so, not in the way I thought."

"No." She felt light-headed. "What are you going to do about your mother?"

"God," he groaned. "I don't know."

"Do you have any other family?"

"No. I guess Mom had some kind of female problem and had to have a hysterectomy when I was only three or four. They talked about trying to adopt another kid but never did. They originally wanted to have a big family, maybe three or four kids, because they were both onlys. Weirdly, one of the things they had in common was that their parents were in their forties when they had them. I don't know if they were an afterthought, or their parents had trouble getting pregnant, or what."

"That might have been a big thing to have in common," Madison said thoughtfully. "I mean, the fact that their parents were so much older than everyone else's. Although it depends what kind of people they were."

He was frowning into space. "Mom's father was kind of a bastard, from what she's said, and her mom timid and quiet. Dad never said that much about his parents, which probably means something."

"Maybe they were both lonely."

"And held on tight when they found somebody." He grunted. "Now Mom's alone again."

"No, she isn't," Madison said stoutly. "She has you."

"Not the same."

"She's not too old to remarry."

Troy gave her a "get real" look.

"Would you mind?"

He had to think about that. "No," he said finally. "Of course not. But I can't see it."

"I guess the first challenge is getting her out of the house."

He grunted again.

"Why are you so angry at her?"

"You can ask that?" he asked incredulously.

"You're mad she didn't tell you." Madison was the one to do some thinking this time. "Is that because you're disappointed in her—I don't know, her ethics? Or because she's holding on to her loyalty to your dad at your expense?"

The moment the question was out, she regretted it. Too late.

Troy swore, jackknifing to an upright position. "You don't pull any punches, do you?"

Madison bit her lip. "I shouldn't have said that. I'm sorry." Would he leave now? She'd understand if he was seriously pissed. She didn't even know his mother, and she hadn't known *him* that long. And here she was, psychoanalyzing him.

"No," he said, a little hoarse. "I want you always to say what you think. The hell of it is, you might be right. Partly right. Yeah, she probably hurt my feelings and I didn't even realize that's what was going on."

"That's probably natural," she said tentatively.

He mumbled another curse. "Yeah? I thought I was all grown up, past getting my feelings hurt because Mommy allied herself with Daddy instead of me."

Madison giggled.

Troy laughed, too, low and rueful. "On that note, I probably should leave."

"Before I say something else we'll both be sorry for?"

"Before I kiss you again while we're both so conveniently on the couch. I can manage a polite good-night kiss at the door, though."

"Oh, good." She let him tug her to her feet. "I do love kissing you."

"I'm glad." He had that heavy-lidded look again, but he kept moving, towing her toward the front door. Where the kiss got a little heated, but not out of control. "Tomorrow," he promised, and left.

She stood without moving for too long. To her silent house, she said finally, "I am in serious trouble."

CHAPTER TEN

"You're looking for my brother?" Janet Short sounded surprised. "May I ask why?"

Troy hesitated. It had taken him two days to get this woman on the phone, and he didn't want to lose her. On the other hand, he was wary that she might call her brother to alert him.

"I'd rather not say, ma'am," he said. "I can only tell you that he's not in trouble. I'm hoping he can give me some information, that's all."

She dithered, but finally gave him the number. Frank, she said, lived in Texas but worked on an oil drilling platform, so sometimes he could be reached and sometimes not.

Hell, Troy thought. *It would be a bitch if good ol' Frank turned out to be unavailable for the next month.* Wasn't this still hurricane season in the Gulf, too? Storms couldn't be good for phone reception.

He dialed as quick as he could, though, wanting to beat Frank's sister to the punch.

On the fourth ring, a gruff male voice answered.

Troy identified himself and asked if he was speaking to Frank Claybo, who had graduated from Wakefield College.

Silence.

"I haven't been back to Frenchman Lake since the day after I graduated. What's this about?"

The spiel was well-practiced now. Police had reopened

the investigation into Mitchell King's murder. New information had been received. Detectives were trying to speak to any potential witnesses and also students who might have known King well.

Claybo did not leap to offer observations or remembrances. Troy could hear him breathing, and that was all.

"Your name was given to me as someone who might have significant information regarding Mr. King," Troy said. "I was told that you identified him as a blackmailer."

More silence. He didn't hang up, which was something.

"I guess it doesn't much matter anymore, does it?" Frank said finally, sounding resigned.

"The murder?"

"No, any stupid thing I did."

"Not unless that stupid thing included bashing in Mr. King's head," Troy agreed.

"Oh, hell, I wasn't that desperate. The asshole was blackmailing me, though. I'm pretty sure he was blackmailing a bunch of people."

"Do you mind telling me what he was holding over you?"

"Why not? Like I said, it doesn't matter anymore. I stole some marijuana from—" He stopped as if belatedly nervous. Not wanting to tattle? "This guy who was dealing. I'd have gotten the shit kicked out of me if the guy found out. I always wondered if Mitch was blackmailing him, too, but that might have taken more balls than he had."

"What made you suspect you weren't his only victim?"

Now that he'd gotten started, Frank seemed happy to open up. He thought King's approach was too slick; this wasn't someone freaking himself out because he'd seen an opportunity and dared to blackmail a fellow student for the first time. The demand wasn't unreasonable—fifty bucks a month until the end of the school year. Like most students, Frank held a part-time job and all it meant was that he couldn't always afford to do stuff with friends.

"So he had a good idea what you could afford. Maybe guessed your breaking point," Troy said thoughtfully.

"He got it right on. Much more and I'd have been in trouble. As it was, I kind of viewed it as penitence. I shouldn't have ripped off that baggie. So I was paying for it. You know?"

It occurred to Troy that the psychology might have been familiar to King. Calculating how much pressure to bear, how much money to demand, how much risk he was taking—all that required skill. The cost if he screwed up was high. All it took was one victim saying "I don't think so" and going straight to the administration to end Mitch King's career as blackmailer *and* his stint in academia.

"He kept a ledger," Frank continued. "That's what made me think there were a bunch of us. He always had me hand the money over in person and he'd note down my 'payment'—that's what he called it—in his ledger. Real businesslike. My entries weren't on the opening pages. He'd have to leaf a ways into that book to find me. He'd turn over..." There was a pause. "Maybe ten, twelve pages."

"Can you describe this ledger?"

"It was black, I think a wire or plastic spiral binding, nothing fancy. Pretty thin. You can buy things like that at any office supply store. Maybe even grocery stores. He kept a pen clipped on it."

"Where did you generally meet with him?"

"I'd only made three payments when he was killed. Uh...once he told me he'd be sitting out on Allquist Field, like he was studying. After that I'd watch him sometimes and see people come and go, but he was real good at whisking that money out of my hand. It was hard to tell who was making payments and who was stopping to talk."

"Your other meetings with him?"

"He had me stop by his room once. The other time, uh, it was the locker room at McKenna Center. He was wearing sweats, like he'd been working out. I don't know if he really had. I remember a towel was lying on the bench beside him. As I was walking away, I looked back and saw that he'd moved it and that damn ledger was under it."

Troy's eyebrows rose. The second towel in the sauna had been covering the ledger, and that made its disappearance more complicated than he'd thought. Probably if it had been blood-soaked, it would have been left behind. No, chances were the towel had been used to wrap the ledger so no one saw it. Which suggested the killer wasn't wearing a jacket, or he could have tucked the ledger inside it.

He grimaced. The guy might only have been rattled. Not thinking at all, only desperate to get away.

Running away into the dark, something clutched in his hand. Lying the next day about whether he'd ever made it to McKenna Sports Center the night before.

He cleared his throat. "Did it cross your mind, when you heard about the murder, that Mr. King might have been conducting business in the sauna that night?"

This silence was answer enough. "Yeah," Frank said finally, to his credit. "But I talked myself out of believing it. I mean, the middle of the night? And he was nude? Plus, if it was hot and steamy in there, the ink would have run, wouldn't it? So I figured he was pulling an all-nighter like the rest of us. He presumably had to get the grades, too. Somebody was paying his tuition, right?"

"He had parents," Troy confirmed. Divorced, but both had kicked in to pay the bill. They presumably had expected passing grades at a minimum. Troy found himself hoping neither was alive to learn that their son had been killed because he'd gone into business as a blackmailer. "Mr. King didn't ask you to come to the sauna, then?"

"No, I'd made my December payment a week or two before. I think that was the time I went to his room." This recollection came out as rueful.

He proved willing to dredge his memory for the names of everyone he could remember seeing with King. Troy took a lot of notes. A part of him was relieved that Madison's father's name wasn't on the list. One particularly interesting name was Gordon Haywood's, the senator. Troy remembered again Haywood's hasty departure once he had his time capsule contribution back in his hot little hand.

"You going to have to tell anyone about my part?" Frank finally ventured.

"Who would care, except maybe your sister or parents?" Troy asked. "It doesn't sound as if you did anything that terrible."

"Only time I ever stole anything. I still don't know what I was thinking. But, man, finding out someone had seen me and then getting blackmailed really worked to deter any repeat, I've got to tell you."

After he'd thanked Claybo and ended the call, Troy found himself chuckling low in his throat. Gee, gosh, maybe they should fit a halo on Mitch King's memory. Could it be that *all* his victims had thereafter seen the light and lived virtuously?

Guy Laclaire, for example, who set such uncompromisingly high standards for his young daughter and who was a man who believed in honesty with fervor. Had he, like Frank Claybo, learned his lesson from Mitchell King, the worm who was getting rich at everyone else's expense?

There was some irony there, Troy was sure.

HE WAS SO DAMN EAGER, driving to Madison's house, Troy
didn't recognize himself. There wasn't even any special
reason; clearly, he wasn't getting her into bed until this
was all over. He was having dinner there. Full stop. But
he felt as excited as he had as a kid on his way to the fair,
or when he was eighteen and his parents had driven him
to Seattle to leave him at the UW the first time. He was
yearning to be there.

Even more disturbing was realizing how much of a refuge Madison had become for him.

Not until the evening he'd gone straight from his mother's house to hers had he suspected how much Madison
was coming to mean to him. Before that, he'd known he
was sexually riveted by her, a fancy way of saying he
wanted her more than he'd wanted a woman in a long time,
if ever. He knew he liked her, that she was easy to talk to,
that he was happy listening to her and felt unexpectedly
protective. There were times when she was talking about
her father or mother that he'd have given damn near anything to erase the more hurtful memories and make her
feel secure in a way he sensed she never had.

Loved. Madison had never believed herself to be
loved—unshakably, bedrock-deep, no-matter-what loved.

And yeah, the very word was unsettling. He'd had relationships that got pretty intense. But not once had Troy
ever thought he was in love with one of them. He figured
maybe that was because of his parents. In them, he'd seen
love in action—the expression on their faces when they
looked at each other, the brief touches, the care they took
of each other. They occasionally squabbled; they never
fought. He didn't remember his parents ever raising their
voices, either at each other or him. He'd never seen his father check out another woman, not even in that automatic
way most men did.

Troy had never consciously thought, *That's what I want*. But he realized now he'd decided exactly that, probably when he was quite young.

He needed a woman who would never bore him, who made him laugh. A woman he could trust, yeah, unshakably, bedrock-deep, to keep liking and loving him even through the tough times in their lives. On top of all that, there had to be an explosive attraction between them, the feeling when he touched her that only she would do, that he would never want to touch another woman.

With Madison, it was all there.

Her face was beautiful to him, from her gently rounded chin to the forehead that was high and had a curve that struck him as childlike. The tiny dimple beside her mouth, Troy found irresistible. She had a cute nose with a small bump on the bridge, fine-textured skin with a golden tone and those warm, melting eyes. Damn, he loved her hair, from the hint of a widow's peak to the soft new hairs that tickled his mouth at her nape.

Even thinking about her lush body was enough to arouse him.

But *needing* a woman on a level that had nothing to do with sex—that was something he'd never experienced before.

A man *should* want the woman he was falling in love with. And Troy had been okay with the desire to keep her safe and happy. He guessed that fit with his nature, although he'd never analyzed himself that way before. When he did now, he discovered he held some probably old-fashioned beliefs about a man being ready to stand between his family and the world in all its violence and cruelty. Some of that was a natural offshoot of being a cop.

He wanted her to turn to him with good news and bad,

to share a laugh, for comfort. For everything. Because she needed him.

The part he hadn't expected was *his* need to turn to her. He had this hunger to talk over every problem with her, personal and work-related. To bounce ideas off her, to share the weird shit he saw and the funny moments. She never seemed to leave his head, which was more than a little disconcerting.

And he had to face the fact that, after only two weeks, he couldn't imagine his life without her.

What he had no idea of was whether she felt anything close to the same for him. He thought she did...but he also thought what she felt scared her. Troy understood why that would be so. He had the advantage of having grown up knowing he was loved, and with the ever-present example of his parents' love for each other. If Madison felt with anything like the intensity he did, she probably couldn't begin to understand it. Or maybe she did, but didn't trust what she felt or that *he* could feel the same.

They had some major obstacles facing them, and he had a bad feeling they couldn't begin to overcome any of them until the elephant wasn't lumbering along at their side anymore: until he could be certain Laclaire hadn't committed a brutal murder. Until both could know that he wouldn't have to arrest her father.

Troy didn't see that happening real soon, given his ever-growing list of suspects. He could spend months interviewing every student who'd attended Wakefield College back then, and never arrive at an answer.

Then what? he asked himself bleakly. Would the uncertainty eat at Madison's relationship with her dad...and with him? Or could they put it behind them?

Could he accept having a father-in-law he seriously suspected of having murdered someone?

And…what if Madison had to choose between the father who had been her only security, and this guy she'd only met a few weeks before?

Troy didn't even like to think about that last question.

He pulled into her driveway, set the emergency brake and silenced the engine.

Disconcerted, he discovered that his brooding hadn't in any way lessened his eagerness to see her.

To Madison, Troy's mood seemed strange. Was it because she'd put the brakes on their physical relationship? But he'd seemed to understand, so she had trouble believing that now he was sulking. Then it occurred to her that, given his job, he must have some really bad days.

She finally set down her fork and propped her elbows on the table. "Did something happen today?"

"Something?"

"A horrible, bloody car accident? A child was murdered? Or…?" Her imagination failed her. She was disconcerted to find she half *hoped* his mood had to do with something unrelated to her. She crossed her fingers under the table. *I don't want anyone to have suffered or died. Really.*

Troy laughed, his body language loosening. "None of the above. So far, my lieutenant has dropped me from the rotation and is letting me focus a hundred percent on the King investigation. I've been lucky. He won't be able to do that forever."

"You seem withdrawn tonight," she observed.

"I'm sorry." He smiled, but she couldn't help noticing that his eyes were still shadowed. "I'm getting somewhere, and it hit me on the way over here that every bit of new information opens yet more avenues. We're talking literally *hundreds* of people I may have to interview." He shrugged. "It's big. Made even bigger by the intervening years, the fact that those people have spread out across the country and even the world."

"You're feeling daunted," she said.

"Yeah, I guess that's it." His eyes met hers. "I'd have liked to clear your dad right away."

"So you never had to show anyone else what your father wrote."

He grunted. His jaw muscles knotted. "And so *your* father would quit standing between us, glaring at me and staring reproachfully at you."

Madison blinked at the image. "Is that what he's doing?" she asked after a minute.

"In my head."

"In mine…" She had to stop; she closed her eyes, then opened them again, unable to be less than honest with Troy. "In mine he's looking angry and scared at the same time." She hesitated again. "The way he sounds," she said, even more softly. "And then I think I'm betraying him, and I picture his face when he finds out."

Troy swore and started to push back his chair. "I shouldn't have raised the subject."

"No." She held up her hand and even smiled. "Don't be silly. Sit down and eat. I'm fine. I just…have my moments."

"I'll bet."

She traced the condensation on her glass. "You think Dad is between us."

He put down his fork again. "I guess I do."

Why was she even poking at this? *She'd* been the one to tell him to slow down because of the complications. "I'm not, um, real quick to leap into bed with a guy, anyway."

He looked at her gravely. "Is that what I am? A guy?"

Shame heated her cheeks. "You know you're more than

that. And it's not that I'm blaming you for having to investigate Dad. I understand you do, okay?"

"I offered before, but if your involvement is getting to
you, I can track people down another way."

"And I said no." She jutted her chin at him to be sure
he knew how determined she was. "I meant it."

Troy smiled faintly. "Okay." This conversation hadn't
reduced the shadows in his eyes at all. "We'll get through
this."

She wanted to, with startling desperation. Troy was different. How she felt about him was different. Which made
him frightening, too, but she longed to find out where a relationship with him would take her. Being haunted by her
father—the ghost of past, present *and* future, she thought
with a twinge of humor—was definitely getting in her way.

"Dad hasn't called again," she blurted.

He didn't say anything.

"You haven't told me if you ever got in touch with Frank
Claybo's sister."

He had. What's more, he'd talked with Frank, who had
been, well, frank about having been blackmailed. Appalled, she listened as Troy told her about the ledger and
Frank's suspicion that there had been multiple victims.

"Then…if Dad *was* being blackmailed, it means he
wasn't the only one."

"That's what it means."

Apprehension squeezed her throat. "Did…did he have
any idea who any of the other people were?" Her voice
had come out too high and squeaky.

"He gave me a list of students he'd seen talking to
Frank. I doubt he remembered everyone—think about
how many years have passed!—but I suspect he was pissed
enough to be paying close attention." Troy frowned at the

expression on her face. "Your dad isn't on the list, Madison. Don't look at me like that."

"I'm sorry." She was proud of herself for her ability to curve her mouth into an almost reassuring smile. "I have serious daddy issues, don't I?"

Troy grunted a laugh. "You and me both. You'd think we'd have outgrown it, wouldn't you?"

"I'm not so sure you have issues. You've been disillusioned, which is different." She stood and picked up dirty dishes with both hands. "Coffee? I picked up cookies at the bakery today, too."

His smile verged on rakish. "I haven't outgrown cookies."

When she returned with the plate of cookies, Madison continued as if she had never left off. "You're really angry at your dad, aren't you?"

Lines deepened on his face, although he wasn't exactly frowning. "You think I shouldn't be?"

"I don't have an opinion. I suppose I'm being nosy."

His eyes warmed. "I want you to be nosy where I'm concerned."

Breathing was suddenly a challenge. "I want you to be curious about me, too," she finally managed to say.

"Good." He said it the way he always did, with solid satisfaction. Possibly a hint of smugness, which she found she didn't mind.

As she watched, he added cream to his coffee. She'd noticed before that he drank it black in the morning. Only in the evening did he dilute it.

"Does your stomach bother you?" she asked, nodding at the small jug of cream in his hand.

He glanced down. "Ah...yeah. Sometimes. Mostly when I go to bed."

"You probably shouldn't drink coffee at all in the evening. I wished you'd told me. I could have made herbal tea."

Troy grinned, a vivid flash of humor. "Please don't. I might have to start making my excuses the minute I finish the last bite of dinner."

Madison chuckled. "Oh, fine." She dumped plenty of cream *and* sugar in her own coffee. Truthfully, she didn't drink it in the evening at all when she was alone.

"Back to Dad," he said abruptly. "I keep wondering why this whole thing has rattled my perception of him so much. I haven't totally figured it out yet." Troy's face and voice both had tightened. "Maybe I'm afraid I didn't know him as well as I thought I did. I always felt lucky. I don't know many guys who are really close to their fathers. I guess I thought I was privileged, and now I have to wonder if that relationship went as deep as I thought it did."

"Has it occurred to you," she said gently, "that he never told you because he was ashamed? Because measuring up in your eyes really mattered to him?"

He ground his teeth together. "If he was ashamed, why the hell didn't he do the right thing?" Troy asked, sounding angry again. "Tell me that." He closed his eyes. "Oh, damn, I'm sorry, Madison. It's not your fault. And you're right, that is a possibility. But it's one that means Dad wasn't the man I believed him to be."

The shadow of her own father seemed to fall over her. She was chilled enough to pull her arms close in to her sides. "Are you so sure? You've also described a man who was completely loyal to the people he loved. Maybe he was to friends, too. He sounded as if he considered my father to be a good friend. Your dad's certainty got shaken and he typed up that witness statement, but maybe as soon as the time capsule was closed up he realized he'd been an idiot and that he *believed* in my father. The ability to be that kind of friend is admirable, too, isn't it?"

He considered her for a minute that stretched into two. Those furrows still aged his face, but somehow made him no less sexy. Madison had the sudden, panicky realization that, if anything, a troubled Troy trying to untangle a complicated emotional dilemma was even more appealing than the straightforward man she'd first met, the one who'd gone into instant hunting mode where she was concerned. *He* was a lot more complex than he'd first seemed, which also gave her hope that he wouldn't decide she was a flake because of all her confusion and give up on her.

"Yeah," Troy said gruffly. "You're right. I'd find that picture of him a lot more convincing, though, if he and your dad had stayed friends, at least until the end of the school year."

"Do you know that they didn't reconcile?" she challenged.

He stared at her, his expression sharply arrested. "No," he said slowly, "I guess I don't. But when did that happen? The time capsule was closed up and put in the building— when?—in April. Months after the murder. Plus, I'm going on the fact that Dad told Mom about what he'd seen and written. It sounded like it ate at him. You know?"

"Maybe what ate at him was having put that stupid, impulsive thing in the one place he couldn't recover it from."

"You really think they got to be buddies again in the last month and half, two months before graduation?"

"The capsule was put in the foundation in April, but what if it was closed up earlier than that? Construction on Cheadle Hall might have gotten delayed."

"You're reaching," Troy said flatly.

She sat stubbornly silent.

Troy let out a gusty sigh and shoved his fingers through

his hair. "I'm being a jackass. You're right. There are a lot
of possible answers. The truth is, I keep remembering all
these talks Dad and I had. In law enforcement and bank-
ing both, you sometimes stumble on this mushy, gray ter-
ritory. Dad would be frustrated because the bank would
come down like a hammer on some poor schmuck who
was running late on his loan payments under pitiable circumstances, but then give second, third and fourth chances
to someone else who had the right family or political connections. It can be hard to arrest someone you sympathize
with, or see the resources of the department focus on one
crime while another one—say, the murder of some poor
black woman or a homeless guy—gets short shrift. Not
that long before he died, Dad and I sat out on the patio in
the dark and hashed out some of those issues. Right versus practicalities. And now I'm thinking, had he put out
of his mind that he saw your dad that night? Or was it always simmering inside him?"

The unhappiness and frustration she heard jolted Madison. She'd been ridiculously defensive when Troy had only
been trying to tell her why he'd been hurt by the picture of
his father, suddenly skewed. He'd made it clear that he understood her mixed feelings. He respected them. In doing
so, he'd given her something she hadn't reciprocated. As
confused as she was, Madison knew she wanted to be a
person who deserved Troy's love.

"I wonder," she said, "whether he started being more
bothered by the choice he made once you became a cop.
Maybe those talks you had were part of his process of…
oh, I don't know, coming to terms with a decision he could
never quite make himself undo."

Troy breathed out a sound that might have been "Huh."
He seemed to be staring into space rather than at her.
"When I was a kid—maybe twelve—I saw a friend shop-

lift. I told Dad. At first I wouldn't say who." He briefly focused on her and waited for her to nod her understanding. Of course he hadn't. "We talked for a long time about the obligation any of us owe to a friend. About how much we can expect to influence another person, about being honest about how we feel about someone else's behavior. About when speaking out is right and isn't tattling. And about when we should cut ties with someone whose choices we don't like." He shook his head, seemingly absorbed in his memory of that talk with his father. "Funny, I'd forgotten the whole conversation."

"What did you do?" she asked.

Once more she had his attention. "About the friend? I told him I didn't think stealing was cool, and if I saw him do it again I'd quit hanging out with him." His mouth curved. "He did, and I did. We actually got to be buddies again later. I was first baseman on our high school team, he was shortstop. He told me he was really pissed when I ditched him, and he went out and stole some stuff and got caught. It freaked his mother out, and he admitted that's what he'd wanted all along. His parents had gotten divorced, Mom was seeing a new guy and he felt invisible."

Madison laughed. "A self-aware high school boy? I didn't know there was such a thing."

He clapped a hand over his chest, his own laugh transforming his face. "*I* was a self-aware high school boy. Give me some credit."

"But two of you." She shook her head. "I don't know. That stretches credulity."

"I confess, it was probably a momentary aberration. I have no doubt we were crude and sexist again in no time." His smile became wry. "That talk Dad and I had. He came down pretty hard on the side of friendship. You've got a point."

Some instinct made her stand up and go around the table. Troy pushed his chair back and held out an encircling arm. She sat on his thighs and pressed a kiss against his jaw, prickly with evening stubble. "Your father sounds like a good man, Troy. You *were* lucky."

He cupped her cheek and lifted her face so he could see her. His expression disquieted her. "You're pretty convinced your father was, too."

Her stomach took a sickening dip. There was a difference, she suddenly saw, between having an inflexible standard of conduct and being good. *Good* suggested something more than not doing wrong—like kindness, understanding and accepting other people's weaknesses, caring about them anyway.

She was not at all sure her father really was good. And she had a very bad feeling Troy knew exactly what she was thinking.

"You want to talk about it?" he asked, in a gentle voice.

She shook her head hard.

He stilled the movement with his big hand. "Okay," he murmured, pulling her closer so she could bury her face against his neck. They sat there for a long time, either not needing to talk or unable to, but soaking in something from each other.

The entire experience was new to Madison. She'd never known it was possible to gain strength from someone else's touch. Anger sparked in her. *Why* didn't *I know? Why didn't Mom or Dad ever hold me this way?*

Her nose against his skin, she breathed in Troy's scent, distinctive to him even when it was overlaid by coffee or whatever he'd eaten for dinner, and she thought, with aching need, *I want this.*

CHAPTER ELEVEN

PLEASE, WILL YOU TELL ME anything you learn about my dad?

As he listened to what Don Mayer had to say, Troy winced at the recollection of a promise he'd been foolish enough to make to Madison. Mayer had thought Guy Laclaire was a prick.

He wasn't the first person to tell Troy that.

Did he have to pass along what he was learning to her?

Now that Troy's list of potential blackmail victims was growing, he'd started asking more general questions of each person he talked to, trying to get a sense of personalities, relationships, tension. Which of these victims got heated up easily? Buried anger until it exploded? Thought so highly of himself that he'd do anything to avoid shame or humiliation?

Troy grimaced at the last thought. There was no getting around the fact that Madison's dad was still his best suspect.

His impression of Frank Claybo had been confirmed by a couple of people.

"Frank? Nice guy. Not very competitive."

"Always broke," someone else said. "His dad had died, I remember that, and his mom was a secretary. He had great scholarships at Wakefield, or he wouldn't have been able to go. He worried because his mom had to take on some loans. Most of us got money from home, but all Frank had was whatever he made."

Troy had confirmed blackmail victim number two. Randy Pearson hadn't even hesitated when Troy reached him.

"Yeah, I paid the son of a bitch for almost a year. I broke into a professor's office to take a look at the test he'd prepared the night before he was going to give it to us. Mitch took a Polaroid of me climbing in the window. I'd have told him where he could go and then made up some story, except the professor happened to be my major advisor." A certain amount of anger still bubbled just beneath the surface, but also the same rueful self-knowledge Troy had heard from Claybo. It said, *He was an asshole squeezing blood from me, but I'm the one who screwed up. Made my own bed.*

The killer, Troy thought, was someone who *didn't* think whatever he'd done was wrong. Or, if he knew on some level that it was, he also believed he was justified, that he had a *right* to break whatever rule he'd broken, steal whatever he'd stolen. His rage would have all been directed at Mitch King, not at himself.

Troy also doubted the killer was someone who'd been making monthly payments for that long. Unless...

"Did Mr. King ever try to up your payments?" he asked.

"No." There was a pause. "I used to worry about that. What would I do if he suddenly decided to double what I was supposed to give him? Triple it? But it never happened. The whole thing was surreal. When I stopped to slip him the money, he'd laugh and joke or complain about a paper he had due like we were friends."

He added a couple of other names to Troy's list, one of whom was Laclaire.

"Laclaire was so full of himself, I really wanted to know what he'd done. I'd have liked to tarnish some of his shine. You know?"

"You had classes with him?"

"I roomed with him freshman year. Can you believe it? Even then, he had his nose in the air. The rest of us were on financial aid, the great anonymous pool of money for good students whose parents weren't loaded. Guy, though, he'd won one of those prestigious *named* scholarships. He'd been valedictorian of his high school class. He made sure everyone knew he'd been accepted at Stanford, but decided he wanted to attend a smaller school. I discovered my high school biology class had been grossly inadequate and got a C first semester at Wakefield. Guy breezed through with a four point. He played varsity tennis even as a freshman. He was awesome at debate. The frats all wanted him. The *girls* all wanted him."

"You wanted him to stumble."

Randy Pearson laughed, sounding good humored. "Yeah, who wouldn't? But that wasn't it. You can like a guy even if you envy him. Guy's problem was, he was sure he was better than all of us and didn't bother to hide it."

"Great way to make friends."

"Yeah, but he did, anyway. He could be wickedly funny, and even when you didn't like him, you were flattered if he asked you to be on his intramural rugby team or whatever."

Troy didn't get a lot more that was useful out of him.

He met with several employees at the college who'd worked there at the time of the murder, ending with a professor in the English department.

Herbert Wilson was a stooped, slightly built man who couldn't have been more than five foot seven or eight when he was young and had stood straight. His scanty gray hair was cut short, doing nothing to hide a bulky hearing aid.

When Troy stepped into his office and introduced himself, Wilson bellowed, "Who?" then reached up and fiddled with the hearing aid, which squawked, making him jump. "Damn thing buzzes," he muttered. "I turn it off when I'm alone." He focused exceedingly intelligent blue eyes on Troy. "What can I do for you, young man?"

Once he understood the purpose of the visit, he settled quite happily in for a bout of reminiscence. He hadn't personally had Mitchell King in a class, but recalled at least two other professors remarking that they weren't impressed with him.

"He was a shallow thinker," he proclaimed. "His work was geared to earning good grades. No fire inside."

Troy had begun to believe that King was actually a rather creative thinker. How many college students kept up in class while also running a small business that brought in what Troy was preliminarily estimating to be one to two thousand dollars a month? He was utterly without conscience, of course, but that was another matter.

Three of the possible blackmail victims had been English majors. Dr. Wilson didn't recall one of them at all. One was only a distant memory. He brightened at the mention of Guy Laclaire.

"Fine, analytical mind." He nodded. "I understand he turned it to business. His daughter works here at Wakefield, you know."

"Yes, actually I do know. I suppose you're aware Madison organized the time capsule opening."

He chuckled. "So she did, so she did. Pretty young woman, too. Not surprising—Guy was a good-looking boy. Have you met him?"

"Not yet."

"If you do, you say hello to him from me."

"I'll do that, sir."

Dr. Wilson had not been Guy's major advisor. No, no, that had been... "Adams!" he declared in triumph. "Dr. Adams. She left the college, oh, twenty years ago. She's considerably younger than I am. I believe she's at Tufts in Boston, if I'm not mistaken."

Troy thanked him cordially and gave him a card, in case he thought of anything of interest.

"You believe it was another student who killed that boy."

"I think that's a possibility."

He shook his head. "Hard to conceive, but then the suggestion that the killer was a drifter never held water. When the gymnasium is open, even in the middle of the night like that, there's always someone on duty, you know. Of course, that would have been a student who probably had his head buried in his books, but I'm betting he still glanced up and made note of everyone who came and went."

"The student on duty was an excellent witness at the time," Troy agreed. "However, he apparently left the counter a few times to help students with equipment. There was a shower in the women's locker room that wouldn't turn off, too, and he probably needed to use the john. He either forgot or missed seeing a number of students who have since been identified as having been at McKenna Center within the hour or two before the murder."

Those blue eyes were still bright and curious. "Can't see how you'd get anywhere with this after so many years."

"It may prove impossible, but I've already learned quite a bit that eluded investigators at the time. I'm hopeful. Er, I have one more question, if you don't mind, sir."

Exceptionally bushy eyebrows rose. "Not at all."

"I'm wondering how likely it is that any employees of the college would have used the gym in the middle of the night finals week. I assume many, if not most, professors and probably classified employees did use both the gym and library."

"Certainly. I still swim laps in the pool." His eyes twinkled. "Slower than I used to, and fewer of 'em, but it's part of my routine."

Troy smiled his appreciation. He was rather enjoying Dr. Wilson.

"Middle of the night, though..." He shook his head. "Unless someone had insomnia and knew the gym was open longer than usual hours..."

"Everyone would know that, wouldn't they?"

"I suppose they would." He was speaking slower now, looking perturbed. He hadn't liked the idea that a student could have been a murderer, but obviously liked the possibility of an employee—God forbid a professor—being one even less. Troy couldn't say he blamed him. "We've always had some exceptionally *athletic* men and women on the faculty, I'll admit. Often the young ones. Perhaps more inclined to be lifting weights or using the swimming pool at odd hours."

"Can you think of any who were at Wakefield at the time?" Seeing the professor's discomfort, Troy added, "Please understand that at this point I'm looking primarily for witnesses. I can see why a professor might have been reluctant to come forward at the time and name students. But perhaps he or she would be willing to speak with me now."

The professor's concerns allayed, he turned to his bookshelves and produced a college catalog of classes for the relevant year. It appeared he'd kept the catalogs since arriving at Wakefield in 1969. Troy wanted to snatch it from his hand. Would Madison be able to find him one? he wondered. Or could he persuade Dr. Wilson to loan out his copy?

The elderly man paged slowly through the class listings, mumbling to himself. At last he suggested several names. "Antoinette Perry—Biology—was quite dedicated to her swimming. She competed at a masters level. Jay Aldrich—now *he* was an interesting fellow, he was actually an Olympian, a long distance runner—ran marathons as I recall. Not sure how much he used the gym, though. Stephen Coleman I remember as being a dedicated weight lifter. He was a Psychology professor, bearded, quite popular with the female students. I believe he left Wakefield only a year or two later. Hadn't thought of him in years."

Troy's patience deteriorated at the slow pace of the recollections, each page being turned deliberately with a finger moistened by the tip of Dr. Martin's tongue. He ended up, however, with a list of seven faculty members who had been frequent users of the college athletic facilities, from one who had, according to Dr. Wilson, tended to "hog" the racquetball courts when he really ought to have given way to students to a female sociology professor who had had polio as a child and regained surprising mobility by swimming as much as a couple of hours a day.

The visit might have taken more time than he'd allotted, but Troy had acquired some new information. He emerged from the basement of Welk Hall, where the English department had set up their offices until Cheadle was replaced, a process that was taking longer than expected. It would be at least the middle of October before it came down, at best estimate. Troy had never heard of a construction or remodeling timeline that *didn't* elongate.

He could just see the bell tower of Memorial from here, above a cluster of maple trees. Without having made a conscious decision, he started across the lawn toward Mem. He couldn't be this close and *not* stop to see Madison.

Both outer and inner office doors stood open. He found her alone at her desk, frowning with intense concentration at her monitor. She'd dressed up more today, wearing black slacks and a loosely knit, short-sleeved black cardigan over a red camisole. Remembering the red suit she was wearing when he first met her, he smiled. He was amused to see her shoes, which had at least three-inch spike heels, lying on their sides where she'd discarded them.

"Hey," he said from the doorway.

Madison jumped six inches. "Troy!" Her hand whisked to the computer mouse, closing whatever file she'd had open.

As if she didn't want him to see whatever she'd been looking at? As he wondered, his mood shifted to disturbed.

"Wow," Madison said. "I didn't hear you coming."

"Sorry." He ambled in, Mr. Casual. "I happened to be on campus and decided to drop by."

"Oh." Her smile didn't quite hide how flustered she was. "I'm glad." She lifted her face to his when he bent to kiss her lightly.

Despite himself, he was distracted by the plush feel of her mouth under his, the quiver of her lips and the soft sigh she made.

Even so, as he straightened, his gaze slid sidelong to her computer monitor, which showed only a college logo. He nodded that way. "Did I interrupt anything?"

"Heavens, no!" she exclaimed brightly. "I was only..." Her toffee-brown eyes met his and she faltered. "You can always tell when I'm trying to hide something, can't you?"

He propped one hip on the edge of her desk, resting his weight warily. Those pretty Queen Anne–style legs were kind of spindly. It felt solid, though, so he relaxed. "You're not a very good liar," he told her with a tinge of humor.

Madison scrunched up her nose. "I know I'm not. I have one of those faces. I'll bet *you* could get away with anything."

Troy grinned. "I'm a cop. How could I do my job if I couldn't hide what I'm thinking?"

No way was he going to ask again what she'd been up to. She was clearly uncomfortable about it, and he'd pushed her too much already. Whether what she'd been doing was related or unrelated to his investigation, she was entitled to some secrets.

He'd opened his mouth to ask if she wanted to take a break when she blurted, "I'm researching my father."

His back straightened. "What?"

"You heard me." She crossed her arms defensively in front of herself. "I called up all the college records, and then I searched him online."

To buttress her belief in the man who loomed so large in her life Troy was chilled by the shadow? Or because she really wanted to know the truth of who her father was?

"You have time to get away? We could go out for coffee."

She stood with alacrity. "Please. I'd suggest a walk, except—ugh. I wore heels today."

He waited while she righted her shoes and slid her feet into them. Her feet were dainty, but relatively speaking her toes were intriguingly long, as were her fingers. Troy had no trouble imagining some things she could do with fingers and toes both.

And, shit, that was enough to stir his libido.

In deference to her heels, they took the elevator down, a creaky, slow-moving relic of a midcentury remodel. It stirred some mild claustrophobia in Troy, who was glad when the damn thing finally chose to cast open its doors.

They strolled over to the Student Union, bought cold drinks and carried them back to the duck pond—and the same bench—where they'd sat before. About the time they left the SUB, students poured out of buildings like ants, rushing down the sidewalk or across the field. Troy glanced at his watch. Apparently they were between classes. He wasn't surprised when, a minute later, the flood of bodies ebbed and Madison and he were virtually alone. They sipped in contemplative silence for a few minutes.

"So?" he said at last.

Madison sighed. "I'm sort of getting the feeling Dad has a lot of enemies."

Troy watched her, wanting to catch every shift of emotion. "The kind of enemy who would assassinate him if he thought he could get away with it? Or the 'I wish a mud pie would hit him in the face' kind?"

This sigh was even gustier. "Oh, probably the second. I mean, nothing is overt. Most people aren't stupid enough to tweet about how they despise this businessman they're going to have to keep dealing with."

"Don't kid yourself," he said sardonically.

A quick smile lit her face. "Well, you have a point. But you know what I mean."

"Why did you start this, Madison? Did you talk to him again? Did something happen?"

She sneaked a peek at him, and he thought he saw shame in her eyes. "No. It's me. That's all. It suddenly occurred to me how I see him may not be how other people see him. And yes, I know I sound dumb. I mean, how obvious is that?"

Troy shifted his cup to his other hand and slid an arm around her shoulders. He was relieved when she immediately leaned into him as if her body couldn't conceive of doing anything else.

"Obvious if you stand back and think about it that way," he said, "but most of us don't. Especially not about someone we've known all our lives unless it is impossible *not* to see other viewpoints. I mean, if I'd had a sister who had been at war with Mom for years, no matter how well I got along with Mom I'd have to reconcile my opinion with my sister's. But…no sister. You're in the same boat. Nobody to say, 'Wow, Dad may be nice to you but *I* think he's a major jerk.'"

"He wasn't always nice to me. Why didn't *I* see?"

Wrung by pity, he kissed the top of her head. "Don't you mean, why didn't you let yourself see?"

"Oh, God. That is what I mean."

Troy grunted. "I sure as hell never questioned my faith in my parents. For both of us, outside events have forced us to take another look. We probably never would have otherwise."

She didn't say anything for a long time. With her head tucked into the curve of his shoulder, he couldn't see her face. "I think maybe I needed to," she finally said.

Aching for her and reminded, disturbingly, of his own shifting feelings for his parents, he frowned at the pond and a couple of students sunbathing and studying at the same time on the far shore. "I hope you know it's not necessarily a bad thing," he said, and realized he meant it. Not only for her, but for him, as well.

She straightened and smiled at him, although she couldn't totally hide sadness. "You're right. You asked what got me started this morning. It came to me that I wanted to know how other people feel about my father." Her forehead crinkled. "I always knew Mom was trying to stay positive. She'd never say anything bad about Dad. I was never even sure what split them up, except for the yelling. Now that I think about it, I'm in awe that she kept her mouth shut even when I chose him over her."

"You ever think the divorce was her fault and not his?" Troy wasn't sure why he'd made a suggestion that might upset Madison, but her mother's behavior struck him as odd. "You had your suspicions. What if she had an affair? She'd have felt guilty because she wronged your dad. Maybe so guilty she thought she had to let you go, that she couldn't take his daughter away from him, too. That he deserved you and she didn't."

Madison stared at him in apparent shock. After a minute she straightened away from him, as if she had to be self-contained to deal with what he'd said. "I did think… But I never…" She swallowed and looked away. "Another weird thing. He was my rock and I was so *mad* at her, but…in my heart I always believed the breakup was *his* fault. Dad is…easy to admire, but hard to like. Mom sparkles. She loves to entertain, and to laugh, and to be surrounded by friends. I suppose I thought his coldness had driven her away."

What would it be like to desperately love someone you also found hard to like? Troy wondered.

"Could be a little of one, a dash of the other," he pointed out. "Your dad's level of fault, for lack of a better word, might not reduce her guilt if she met someone else. Ultimately, *she's* the one who left. You were a little kid. She not only walked out, she abandoned you. She may have meant it to be temporary, but what does a word like that mean to a kid when mommy is gone with no more than an undefined promise to come back for you eventually?"

"Yes!"

The single, hissed word held pain that cramped Troy's chest as he watched her. He set his cup down on the ground and reached for her. "Come here, sweetheart."

She did, burrowing against him and clutching so tight to his shirt her knuckles dug into the muscles around his spine. He was vaguely aware of a few students passing, glancing at them with curiosity and the discomfort most people feel when they see distress they don't understand.

Madison didn't cry, though, which didn't surprise Troy. He didn't like to think what it would take to make her cry.

God, he thought. *Her mother leaving would do it.* How could Madison help but have cried then? He could see her waiting until she was alone, tucked into bed, and then sobbing into her pillow because she was being brave for her daddy, who didn't sound like the kind of man who would have understood a grieving little girl. Oh, yeah, Madison would have cried herself out, and maybe never let herself do it again.

Frowning, he held her and was a little shocked to realize his sinuses burned. Crap. He hadn't thought he could ever hurt for another person like this. Especially not when the pain was such an old one. There was nothing he could fix. Madison had mostly fixed herself.

She let out a long, ragged breath that he felt on his throat, and then eased herself back. Her eyes were too bright, but a rueful smile curved her mouth.

"Wow. It's really disconcerting to discover how much I never really dealt with."

He shook his head. "You grew up into an amazing woman. So you had to bury some pain and disappointment in your parents. As a kid, we're so dependent on them—we can't afford to doubt them."

Her throat moved as she swallowed. The smile shook and she gave up on it. "I'm not sure I really want to revisit all this."

"I know what you mean." He wasn't much enjoying his own experience trying to reconcile the Mom and Dad he'd thought he knew with the reality.

"I think I need to concentrate on Dad. And what I learned today is that he's admired, feared, but not much liked. I should probably be surprised, but...I'm not."

It took real courage for her to untangle how she felt

about her father. There was no therapist to help her on
the path, only him, and he wasn't exactly unbiased. No,
he was the man who suspected her father of murder. It
would have been easier for her to remain defensive, to
keep insisting that her dad was honorable and incapable
of making mistakes. Instead, she really and truly seemed
to want the truth.

Again, Troy had the fleeting, if disconcerting, thought
that he liked Guy Laclaire better than he should because
he had something to do with Madison's utter honesty, her
willingness to face even an unpalatable truth. Parents had
a lot to do with how their kids came out.

*Yeah, then shouldn't you cut your dad a break? And
maybe your mother, too?*

Something to think about later.

Troy had made a decision sometime in the middle of
Madison's speech to be truthful with her. How could he
do any less, after what she'd told him?

"A lot of people didn't like your dad when he was a
student, either."

Madison went utterly still. All she did was stare at him,
as if she were in a state of suspended animation. God, he
hoped this wasn't a mistake.

But he'd started, and still couldn't argue with his decision. Troy went ahead and offered an edited version of
what had been said to him.

"Some of it is clearly envy," he said. "Your dad was the
golden boy. Athletic, handsome, smart, quick-tongued.
Hard to see how he couldn't have known it. What he could
have done better was hide his sense of superiority." He
grinned crookedly. "In other words, he was cocky. Not
the world's greatest sin, especially given his age when he
was at Wakefield."

Her relaxation was subtle, but it was there. "Yes. You're

right. I had a couple of classmates like that in college. And one in grad school." Her nose wrinkled in distaste—she still didn't like whatever idiot she was thinking about. "Some people learn, some don't."

He hated to ask, but couldn't help himself. "Your dad?"

Madison gave his question real thought. "I actually think he did. Isn't that funny, after what I was telling you about him? Mostly I think he's disliked now because he's so aloof. He's hard to know. That comes across as arrogant, and maybe he is to some extent, but…" She shook her head. "He's more complicated than that. An arrogant man might think he's above the rules. My father has never thought that. Some of what makes him rigid and, well, unlikable is his complete refusal to cut himself any slack." More of that sadness, and a whole lot else, passed over her face. "Or me. Or probably Mom, or his employees or colleagues. It was really intimidating to me. I wish I could be more impulsive, but instead I'm totally conditioned to think, 'Wait—is this wrong? Will I regret whatever's about to come out of my mouth?'" Her shoulders slumped. "It's why I suck at lying, no matter how hard I try."

He gave her a squeeze. "*Not* a bad quality."

Her lower lip got sulky. "I suppose not, but it's aggravating sometimes."

Troy laughed at her. "I can just see you someday, trying to teach your kid to lie so she won't be as lousy at it as you are."

Madison's giggle satisfied him. But damn! He'd barely stopped himself from saying *our* kid. In that moment, he'd even seen her, small, perched on a chair, earnestly listening to her mommy, her chin gently rounded, her forehead a high, curving arch, her eyes big and brown. A little Madison. Not only Madison's little girl, but his, too.

Maybe he should be freaked, but he wasn't. Looking

at the woman beside him, he wanted her to be his future, his family.

The words *I love you* almost came out, but somehow he stopped them. He had to be sure all this emotion having to do with their respective parents wasn't skewing how he felt about her. And then there was the threat that hung over them both.

This wasn't the first time the fear that he might end up arresting her father for murder and putting him away for years had interfered with the function of his heart muscle. The pain, he suspected, felt a lot like angina, but was untreatable.

"I'd better get back to work," he said abruptly, hearing harshness in his voice as he bent to grab the cup on the ground in order to miss seeing surprise or hurt in Madison's eyes.

"Me, too." Her tone held only dignity as she rose to her feet.

Repentant, he straightened and met her steady gaze.

"Have you talked to your mother yet?" she asked.

He came close to squirming. "Uh…I left her a message the other day."

"Troy."

"I'll stop by tonight to see her. Is that good enough?"

A tiny smile flickered on her mouth as she started out beside him. "Your mother, your conscience."

"Oh, thanks," he muttered, disgruntled and feeling guilty that he'd needed a prod.

She laughed, which meant that after they parted at the foot of the wide granite step in front of Mem, he was smiling, but also feeling some more of those twinges in his chest.

CHAPTER TWELVE

BY THE TIME he got out of his vehicle in front of his mother's house, Troy had added several new layers onto his guilt.

His father would have expected him to take care of his mother. Dad would be disappointed in him, Troy knew. Even shocked because his adult son, the cop, had been too busy sulking to think about what Mom was feeling. *Suffering.*

Troy was ashamed to admit it had been all about him. His way of handling grief was to ignore it. But she'd become lost in it. He had to wonder, in retrospect, if he hadn't been oblivious to what was happening with Mom because he'd become impatient with her. *She's getting groceries delivered now? Great. One less thing I have to do.* How else could he have missed seeing something so obvious?

How long had it been since she'd stepped foot off her property? Three months? Six? Since Dad's funeral? Troy didn't know.

He rang the doorbell and waited on the doorstep, uneasy. How often did Mom even *see* other people? Talk to them? She could have a heart attack herself—*she could kill herself*—and no one would notice for one hell of a long time.

He grabbed his key ring and was about to let himself in when he heard her fumbling with the lock and then the door opened.

"Troy!" His mother's hair was disheveled and she looked older than he was used to seeing her. Because he hadn't given her warning, and therefore she hadn't fussed with makeup. "I didn't expect you."

"Sorry, I should have called," he said, without meaning it. "Are you okay, Mom?"

"Of course I am. I was just waking up from a nap." She hesitated then smiled tentatively. "Would you like to come in?"

"Thanks." Scraping clean soles on the mat and stepping over the threshold, he felt uncomfortably like a guest. This was *home*. Why did he ring the doorbell in the first place instead of letting himself in?

No easy answer came to him. It had something to do with losing Dad, but he couldn't delve into any more emotional crap of his own right now. This visit was about Mom. He thought about Madison, her clear-eyed truth and compassion, to give himself confidence. Troy was a little surprised to find it worked.

"I haven't started dinner yet," his mother began.

"Why don't I order a pizza? We haven't done that in a long time."

Her face brightened. "I could put together a salad."

"Excellent." He smiled, took a long stride to her and kissed her cheek. "I was a jerk last week. I'm sorry," he added simply.

Tears filled her eyes. "You had reason to be upset with your dad and me. I understood."

He nodded. "No reason to talk about that anymore."

Her eyes narrowed on him, and he was reminded that she *was* his mom. "That doesn't sound like you. When you think you're right, you never quit."

Troy laughed. "I'm not quitting. By God, I'm going to find out who killed Mitchell King." Until he heard his own unyielding voice, he hadn't realized how determined he was, although he shouldn't be surprised. Stubborn was his middle name. In this case, though, he'd been so focused on his initial goal—finding out whether Madison's dad had anything to do with the crime—that he'd missed the moment he shifted to a larger goal. He didn't even know why he was so damn determined. King wasn't likable, as far as victims went. In fact, he was a sleaze. The killer had reason to be enraged.

In general, the crime wasn't so different from most urban murders involving drug dealing or gangs. Nobody was sympathetic. A detective didn't need to like anyone to do his job.

This one was different, though, and Troy knew why without digging deep. It was his father's involvement. Dad had known the victim. Been good friends with Laclaire. As a senior, he'd have known almost everyone with whom Troy had so far spoken.

More than that, Troy wanted to know that Dad's choice of friendship over citizenship hadn't allowed a murderer to walk free. Too many people had been haunted by the unsolved murder. It was time to lay it to rest.

He ordered the pizza and watched as Mom made a salad that was fancier than anything he would have bothered with at home. He got out a soda for her and a beer for himself, because it was there, the brand he bought on the rare occasions when he drank, and he realized she'd been keeping it in the refrigerator for him.

They started on the salads while they waited for the pizza. Mom asked about Madison, and he told her more than he'd actually intended, about the sad girl she'd been and the charming, brave, smart woman she was.

"I can show you a picture," he offered. "I took one with my phone the other day without her noticing."

He pulled it up and handed his phone over the table so his mother could see. He'd gotten lucky, capturing Madison smiling at someone else. She was in profile, her dark hair tucked behind her ears, that tiny dimple beside her mouth in evidence.

"Oh, she's lovely," his mother said softly.

"Yeah." He had to clear his throat. "She is."

"Does she know…?"

"That I'm investigating her dad? Yeah. She understands. If I have to arrest him, though…" He discovered he was hunching his shoulders and had to consciously relax them. "That wouldn't be so good."

Mom nodded. "I'd like to meet her."

"Soon," he promised. "Mom…"

The doorbell rang.

When she started to rise, he shook his head at her and went to pay. He brought the box back, opening it in the middle of the table. Mom, of course, had produced plates and napkins and even forks and knives, although he was pleased to see that after watching his example—grab and eat—she didn't bother with fork and knife, either.

He wondered if she was bracing herself for the conversation they both knew they had to have, or whether she was in deep denial. Despite that underlying tension, talking to her felt easier than it had in some time. Maybe the blowup had unlocked something. At the very least, it had revealed to him anger and frustration with her he hadn't let himself admit he felt.

When she declared she'd eaten enough, he flipped the lid of the pizza box closed and sat back.

"You know you need counseling," he said flatly, but with an effort at gentleness.

Rebellion flared on her face. "You're creating a problem where there isn't one."

"When's the last time you left the house?"

Her mouth pinched.

"Drove yourself anywhere?" he continued inexorably. "Even took a real walk?"

"I'm managing nicely."

"Holed up here at home."

"Why does that offend you?" she asked tightly.

Troy leaned forward and rested his elbows on the table. "It doesn't. It worries me. That's not the same thing. How often do you see friends, Mom? At first they're okay dropping by the house, but eventually they'll be insulted if you aren't willing to come over for dinner or meet them downtown for lunch. Remember the walks you and Dad took almost every evening? He's not here, but a part of him would still be walking beside you if you'd only go."

Her face began to crumple. He felt cruel, but made himself keep going.

"You're living half a life, stuck on one city lot. You're a reader—when's the last time you went to the library? And—" These words caught in his throat. "What about me, Mom? Are you not going to come to my wedding? To be there for my wife if she needs you when our children are born?"

His mother was openly crying.

He swore and pushed back his chair, circling the table to bend and wrap his arms around her. "God, I'm sorry, Mom." His voice was hoarse. "But this had to be said. You know it did."

She wept, and he held her.

MADISON HAD LISTENED in silence. "It was a start," she said finally, when he'd wound down.

"I don't know. All she said was that she would think about counseling."

She laughed a little, shaking her head. "You wanted her to pick up the phone and make an appointment, preferably for 8:00 a.m. this morning."

"You're making fun of me," Troy accused her, suppressing his own smile.

"Yes, I am. Give your mother time to, er, work up her nerve."

"Or chicken out," he muttered.

They sat on the flat rim of the fountain in the courtyard outside McKenna Sports Center. The same fountain where Joe Troyer had waited, irritation growing, thirty-five years ago for Guy to show up.

Troy was not here as part of his investigation. When he'd suggested dinner tonight, Madison had persuaded him to go swimming with her.

"I haven't been getting enough exercise," she'd said firmly. "All you and I do together is eat."

He wasn't a great swimmer. She scoffed at his suggestion he meet her here after she swam. He might have persisted except for one thing she said.

"You sound like my father. You don't want to do anything you're not really good at."

It wasn't even the words so much as her tone of voice that convinced him. Troy knew one thing, no ambivalence: he didn't want to be like her father in any way that made her sound like that.

So he sat there, gym bag at his feet, prepared to make a fool of himself if necessary to prove that he was man enough to display his incompetence in front of the woman he loved.

"You'll feel better after a swim," Madison informed him, and stood up.

Reluctant, he followed her. Inside, she signed them in at the counter and pointed out the door to the men's locker room before looking chagrined when she presumably remembered he was well acquainted with this building.

It actually felt kind of strange to walk in, choose a locker and open it with a metallic clang, then start to undress in the middle of what he thought of as a crime scene. He could see the showers at the end of the aisle; the sauna was barely out of his line of sight. The place was, at least temporarily, deserted, which gave it that hollow, echoing feel. He had to keep reminding himself the crime was a very old one. He knew for a fact that investigators at the time had all but gutted the sauna in their search for trace evidence and blood that wasn't Mitch King's. The college would have finished gutting the room and built it fresh. No one would have wanted to look at the bench and wonder whether those boards had only been scrubbed clean. Troy wondered how often the sauna had been used until a crop of new students arrived the following year.

Wearing swim trunks, he reluctantly went into the pool area. The water lay placid; the only other person in here was a bored lifeguard sitting on a bench to one side of the pool, a textbook open on his lap. He barely glanced up before returning to his reading. This was dinnertime in the residence halls, Troy realized. No wonder he and Madison had the place to themselves.

He dropped his towel on a bench and even more reluctantly approached the edge. Behind him he heard the creak of a door and turned to see Madison walking across the deck toward him. The sight of her sucked the air right out of his lungs.

Her suit was her favorite fire-engine red, thin and as formfitting as a second skin. So snug, in fact, that the fabric tried, not very successfully, to flatten her generous breasts. It was a one-piece, high in front and leaving her shoulders free. The legs were cut well up on her luscious hips.

Troy was almost struck dumb.

"You're beautiful," he blurted hoarsely when she got close enough.

"I…um… Thank you."

He finally dragged his gaze up to see that her face was pink and *she* was either being shy and not meeting his eyes—or was fixated on his chest. Which she had yet to see bare, he realized.

"Um…shall we?" Madison fluttered a hand toward the pool.

He pulled himself together with an enormous effort. "We could call it good and just go to dinner," he suggested.

Madison giggled. "Not a chance."

She took the couple of steps to the pool ahead of him, giving him a too-brief opportunity to ogle her spectacular ass. Then, without pausing, she dove in, cutting the water's surface smoothly.

Well, shit, he thought, reminded how desperately he'd hated having to dive during those long-ago, torturous swim lessons his mother had insisted on. Since he'd panicked every time, he had mostly belly-flopped. He'd gotten his certificate as an Intermediate swimmer, but barely. On the skill level chart, the check for "Diving" had been in the "Needs Improvement" box. Troy persuaded his mother thereafter that he swam well enough to be safe in the water and she'd surrendered, agreeing that he didn't need to take any more lessons.

At the moment, he kind of wished she'd subjected him to another summer of them.

Madison had surfaced halfway down the pool and turned to look at him. Her dark hair, captured in a pony-

tail, was slicked to her head, making the curve of her forehead more obvious and letting her eyes dominate her face.

He jumped in. Not quite a cannonball, but there was
plenty of splashing. Damn it, he still didn't much like
water in his eyes.

Laughing, she swam back to him with an easy head-
up crawl stroke. "Doesn't the water feel good?" she called
before she reached him.

"Sure. Great." Then he grinned. Actually, it did feel
good. He'd been overheated all day, and the water was
cool without being cold as it slipped over his skin. He
bent forward and dunked his head then straightened and
flipped his hair back. "You can swim laps if you want,"
he said hopefully.

"Oh, I might do a few." She smiled at him. "But first I
want to see *you* swim."

"It's not a pretty sight," Troy warned her.

A smile played with her mouth. "How long since you've
been swimming?"

"I go to the lake most summers." Frenchman Lake was
deep and heart-stoppingly cold, but swimming out to the
floating dock could be exhilarating in the heat of July or
August. He could make it okay, and at the lake no one paid
attention to swimming form.

"Oh, good." She lay back and floated, her legs splayed
and her arms spread wide. She was still watching him,
and—damn it—he was suddenly, excruciatingly aroused.
He wanted her on his bed in exactly that pose—minus the
red swimsuit, however good it looked on her.

In self-defense, he made himself push forward and start
swimming. Floating wasn't an option. Maybe he had too
much muscle, he didn't know, but he tended to sink like
a rock if he wasn't in motion. So he turned his arms over,
kicked hard, held his breath and—to his mild surprise—

crashed into the other end of the pool before he ran out of air.

He grabbed hold, blinked chlorine-laden water from his eyes, and saw Madison's last couple of clean strokes before she reached his side and grinned at him.

"You're not that bad. Except...did you breathe?"

"Never was very good at that part."

She only laughed at him, but not in a way that made him feel as if she was making fun of him. Instead, she teased him until he chased her back and forth half a dozen times, talked him into cannonballing off the diving board, and played shark to his dumb, slow-moving human act. There was no way in hell he could catch her if she didn't let him. Water, he thought, was her element.

A couple of times he looked up to see the student life-guard watching them with an expression of disbelief. Apparently swimmers at McKenna Sports Center swam dutiful laps rather than playing in the water. When Troy finally did end up with an armful of wet, slippery woman in his arms, he thought, *Bet you're jealous now,* and planted a brief kiss on her mouth.

"Can we go have dinner now?" he asked hopefully.

She chuckled. "You sound like a kid. Are we there *yet?*" She had the whine down pat. "Come on, didn't you have fun?"

"Yeah," he said with a laugh. "I did. You know, it's still warm enough we could go to the lake this weekend. Take lunch."

Her utterly glorious smile rewarded the suggestion. "I would love to do that. And yes, Detective Troyer, we can get out now and go to dinner."

At the side of the pool, he gestured her ahead of him. "Ladies first."

The red suit looked even better wet. The action of

climbing the ladder did amazing things to Madison's figure. So amazing, Troy had to swim one more lap before he could get out and appear decent with his trunks clinging all too obviously to *his* body.

In the men's locker room, he heard voices at the other end, but was alone when he took a quick shower, toweled himself dry and dressed. Madison would take longer, he assumed. She had to put on a bra, after all, and would be bound to dry her hair, right?

Troy checked messages on his phone and found three. One was from a friend and fellow cop wondering if he wanted to go for a hike that weekend, and the other two were both from Wakefield College alums who had been fingered as possible blackmail victims.

The second of the two was from Senator Gordon Haywood. No over-the-top bonhomie in his voice, not the way he'd exuded it as he wooed classmates and potential future presidential voters—or while he was giving thought to climbing right into Madison's cleavage. Nope, he sounded tense and hushed.

"I can't imagine what questions you imagine I can answer for you, Detective, but please call in the evening when I'm at home. I'm too busy during the day." That was it.

He was definitely nervous, which pleased Troy more than it should. *Can't be prejudiced just because I don't like him.* But he couldn't help indulging in a brief, wistful fantasy of arresting the self-righteous senator for the long-ago murder. Possibly fun, he thought, but unlikely. Although…if Haywood had had political aspirations even back then, he would have had more to lose than most students if King had caught him in a peccadillo.

Food for thought.

Troy strolled out of the locker room and was joined only a minute later by Madison.

"What's with that expression on your face?"

"Suspicious woman."

"You look too pleased with yourself."

Troy laughed and kissed her, despite the presence of several other people in the corridor. "Maybe I'm just happy to be with you."

She wrinkled her nose. "It wasn't that kind of pleased."

He relented and told her he'd had a couple of messages from people he'd been trying to reach about the King murder. "One's been especially elusive." He held open the outer door and let Madison go ahead of him.

"Can you tell me who?"

This was a conversation he'd been avoiding having. He was well aware he had told her too much in the beginning stages of the investigation. He wanted to talk it all out with her, but he'd been keeping the names to himself.

"I'd better not say." He steered her toward the street where he'd parked his SUV and unlocked the doors.

"I suppose I understand," she said, then gave a heavy sigh. Half theatrical, half not, he suspected.

Once they were both seat-belted in the Tahoe and he was turning the key in the ignition, he said, "They're both people who may have been additional blackmail victims."

"There were a couple of stuffed shirts at that reunion I wouldn't mind finding out had feet of clay."

Troy shot her a startled look. Good God, had her mind leaped to the estimable Senator Haywood? He carefully composed his face to give nothing away if she mentioned the guy.

Instead she asked where they were eating.

"How about my place? I have a couple of chicken breasts I could grill." Having had an optimistic moment, he'd left them marinating in the refrigerator. The glass-half-empty part of him figured he had dinner ready to cook tomorrow night if she shied away from setting foot in his lair.

Her expression was a little surprised, a little wary, but she nodded. "If you're sure you want to cook."

"I want." After a glance over his shoulder, he accelerated away from the curb. "I'm only renting," he said after a minute.

"A house?"

"Town house. One of those places out on Narbonne." French Canadian trappers had left their legacy on French-man Lake in other ways than the obvious. The nearby creeks, mountains, canyons and streets had a confusing mix of English, Nez Perce and French names.

"You didn't want to buy?"

"I guess I was hedging my bets," he admitted. "I liked the idea of coming home, but, hell, I might've gotten so crazy bored, six months later I'd be ready to run screaming back to the big city."

"And yet, two years later—or is it three?—you're still here."

"Yeah." Momentarily, he brooded. Truth was, he hadn't at any time thought, *I guess I'm staying. Maybe I should buy a house.* The town house was okay, familiar. It served his needs. He hadn't needed a real home. *Because I had one,* he was surprised to realize. *Until Dad died.*

Since then… He hadn't thought about it. Hadn't cared. A man alone didn't tend to nest, not the way women did.

Now all he wanted was to pack up his things and move into Madison's cozy house. It already felt more like home than his place did. He'd even noted with interest that she had a good-sized shed in her backyard, plenty big enough to become a ceramic studio.

The drive was short, as pretty much any drive in Frenchman Lake was. Madison gazed with interest at the stretch of two-story town houses, each painted a distinctive color. Each had a single car garage in front and a patio in back screened by six-foot fencing on each side. The tiny yards, front and back, had been landscaped with bark and shrubs when he moved in. Someone came around and renewed the bark each spring. Troy cringed a little at how sterile his place looked compared to hers.

He parked in the driveway and let them both in the front door. The interior was one room wide—bottom floor had living room, dining area and, open to it, kitchen. Tucked under the stairs was a powder room. Translation: toilet and sink, with barely enough room to pull up your pants. Upstairs were two regular-sized bedrooms, a smaller one that was a home office, one bath, laundry room. The layout had more than a passing resemblance to the shotgun houses in New Orleans.

Troy winced again as Madison looked around with open interest, taking in his only decent furniture: a big leather sofa and leather recliner. Her gaze paused on the cheap bookshelves and even cheaper TV stand. He had one nice picture, a big framed photo of an autumnal forest scene, given to him by a girlfriend. He was ashamed that he couldn't remember which one.

"Very bachelor," Madison pronounced.

"I'm afraid so. No dirty socks or empty beer cans lying around, though," he pointed out.

"True enough." She smiled at him. "Did you clean up for me?"

Actually, he had, but mostly that consisted of running the vacuum cleaner around and mopping the kitchen floor, something he didn't often do. "I'm pretty neat," he said. He frowned, thinking about it. "I wasn't as a kid. I collected stuff. When I was little it was action figures, you know, whatever toy I was obsessed with. I went through a rocks and minerals phase that took over until my mother banned them to the garage."

"Speaking of, where's the ceramic studio?"

"That would be in the garage. You notice I didn't park in there." He started toward the kitchen. "Let me start the charcoal, and I'll show you if you want."

"I want," she said softly.

At her echo of what he'd said, Troy gave her a sharp look, but he couldn't tell if she'd meant it the way he had.

It only took him a minute to dump some charcoal in the grill and light it. Then he led the way to the garage.

Because of the lack of windows, he'd added some expensive lighting as well as heavy-duty wooden shelving units. The kiln sat at the back, near the door into the house, while he used a large, sturdy table planted by the garage door to knead the clay, glaze, do any other hand work. The wheel occupied the middle of the open space.

Delight lit Madison's face and she immediately began examining the pieces he'd thrown that were in various stages of completion on the slatted wooden shelves. Recently thrown and drying were in one area, footed and waiting to go in the kiln were in another. Fired but not yet glazed, glazed but not yet fired, and finally the completed pieces that he was satisfied with but hadn't yet sold or given away.

"I haven't done much these past few weeks," he said, feeling self-conscious. Much? How about nothing? Zero. Zilch. He'd spent as many evenings as possible with Madison rather than alone out here concentrating on his hobby, which he knew full well was more of a stress-buster than a calling to high art.

"These are amazing." Madison had reached the finished

pieces and picked up one of a set of cereal-sized bowls. She was delicately stroking the rim. He'd glazed them in a rich plum color that shaded into royal blue on the outside. The shape was pretty ordinary, but he'd been pleased with the glaze—something new he was trying.

"Would you like to have them?" He reached for a box and the bubble wrap he kept handy.

She gaped at him. "But…you can't just *give* them to me. Surely you could sell these."

"Maybe." He shrugged. "I told you I give away a lot of what I make. I'm not trying to make this a profession." He frowned then set back down the bowl he'd picked up. "I guess the colors don't go in your kitchen, though, do they?"

"I want them, anyway." She snatched up a sheet of bubble wrap. "You can't take them back."

Troy laughed and helped pack the four bowls. "You know," he said, "I made a vase that would look great on your kitchen windowsill." He turned. "It's here somewhere."

"There." She pounced. Sure enough, she'd spotted the exact piece he'd been looking for. It was a perfect column with the faintest flare to the lip, glazed in a dark cherry-red with a hint of a crackle. "Oh, my God, Troy! It's gorgeous!"

"And yours." He took it from her hand, wrapped it, too, and inserted it in the box beside the bowls.

Madison made him promise not to give her one of his teapots but begged to see them. He located the ones that were finished but that he hadn't yet taken to the gallery downtown. These were more whimsical than his other work, with lots of curves and glaze jobs that included polka dots and swirls in bright colors. They were selling as fast as he could turn them out. In fact, the gallery had left him a message a week or two ago asking for more. While he was thinking about it, he packed the two and tucked that box under his arm while Madison carried the one that held her goodies. Her head was swiveling all the way to the door.

"You ever tried throwing anything on a wheel?" he asked.

"No, I'm not very artistic." Her forehead puckered, as if she didn't like what she was thinking. "I didn't bother with art classes in high school or college."

Both set down their boxes on the kitchen counter. "Who says you aren't artistic?" Troy asked. "You've got great color combinations in your house. You've created a warm atmosphere with, I don't know, a good flow. That tells me you have an eye. If you'd like a lesson or to play around out there, just let me know."

She was quiet while he went and checked the coals, then came back in and got the chicken out of the refrigerator. He popped a couple of potatoes in the microwave. When he got out a cutting board and started pulling veggies out of the crisper drawer, Madison offered to help. He set her to work cutting chunks the right size for skewers, which he planned to grill, as well.

"Dad didn't think I was artistic," she said suddenly.

Troy turned, not liking her tone of voice.

"I sort of remember Mom putting my drawings and paintings on the refrigerator when I was little."

Troy nodded; his mom had done that, too.

"But once I overheard them talking. Dad said 'I guess we know one thing she won't be when she grows up.' Mom asked what, and Dad said an artist. We always had to do art projects at school." She glanced at him and he nodded. Every kid did. "When my teachers took them down and gave them back to us, I started throwing mine away.

Neither of my parents ever noticed. Although…" she hesitated "Mom might have been gone by then."

"Damn," Troy said. He crossed the kitchen in one long stride and gathered her into his arms. She let the knife fall with a clatter onto the cutting board. "Why do you love that son of a bitch?"

She stayed stiff. "He's not. It isn't wrong to encourage your kids to focus on the things they're good at. That's what he was doing."

Was it? Troy didn't see it that way, but he could tell he'd violated the unspoken pact. Her dad was off-limits to him.

He slid his hands up and down her upper arms. "Kids should be allowed to try everything and determine for themselves what pleases them, what they're good at, what's worth doing even if they'll never set the world on fire at it. That's what I'd do with my kids."

"You'd lie to them?"

"No." He nuzzled her face then let her go. "You can say, 'Wow, look at those colors.' Or 'You're getting a lot better at that.' You're proud they're trying and happy they're having fun."

Her head was bowed, but finally she raised her head and he saw the turmoil in her brown eyes. "That's what I'd do, too," she said quietly. "But…I do believe he loves me."

Troy barely hesitated. He'd heard the one phone call. He had also heard everything she had said about her father—and everything she hadn't said.

"Yeah," he agreed. "I think he does, too."

Her smile was pained but grateful. "Thank you, Troy." She rose on tiptoe and kissed his jaw, which had to be getting a little scratchy. "Hadn't you better turn the chicken?"

"Oh, hell!" As he raced for the barbecue grill, the laughter that followed him sounded happier, more like his Madison.

It didn't dissipate the ache in his chest or his fear. Because if it came down to her dad versus him, it would be no contest—Dad would be the winner hands-down.

CHAPTER THIRTEEN

MADISON ASKED HIM to take her home shortly after dinner. He couldn't tell if she was nervous he'd try to sweep her upstairs to his bed, or whether she really had things she needed to do. She had kissed him good-night with all her usual responsiveness and shy hunger though, so Troy didn't let himself brood about it even if she was pulling back a little.

A glance at his watch told him he could still make a couple of phone calls. He had a suspicion both Senator Haywood and Holly Cromer were waiting tensely for their phones to ring.

He waited until he'd gotten back to his place and poured himself another cup of coffee—with plenty of cream. Then he called Ms. Cromer first.

She answered, voice curt. "What is it you want, Detective Troyer?"

He'd explained in the message that he was investigating the murder of Mitchell King. No need to repeat that information. "Answers," he said simply.

She gave a laugh that was more of a gasp. "Do you need me to tell you what a creep he was?"

"You aren't the first to tell me that. Ms. Cromer, was Mr. King blackmailing you?"

"Yes. Yes, he was. Are you asking if I was glad to find out he was dead? I'm ashamed to say I was." Anguish transferred all too well over the airwaves. "I can't tell you how relieved I was."

"I'd appreciate it if you would share what he was blackmailing you for."

"It doesn't matter anymore. I've long since come out. I'm lesbian, Detective. I…hadn't altogether admitted it to myself back then, and the idea of telling my parents was beyond awful. They are quite conservative. I dated through high school and college and even giggled about boys when I called home and talked to Mom. But my junior year I fell for a woman. A senior. We became lovers, although we were very careful to be sure no one else knew."

Troy had heard that before. "Yet somehow Mr. King found out."

"Yes. I think he must have followed me, which means he suspected. We met… Well, it doesn't matter. He described what he'd seen in enough detail that I believed him. He threatened to let my parents know."

"Would they have believed him over you?"

"He'd seen a scar on my butt. The idea that he'd seen me naked at all would have horrified them beyond belief. I could have made up some story about him walking into the shower room or something, but I couldn't seem to think clearly, I was in such a panic. And he wasn't asking for that much money. I thought it was worth it, that there was no way he could pursue me after college. So I paid," she said bleakly.

She, too, had paid fifty dollars a month. She'd had enough in her account, she explained, that she had offered to pay the entire amount for the rest of the academic year right then, up front. She had wanted it to be over with.

"He turned me down. He said he thought it was better if I had a little, regular reminder of what I had at stake. Meeting him monthly was humiliating."

That, Troy guessed, had been the point. Maybe King had believed he could control his victims better if they had to present themselves with their payments at his summons, but mostly, Troy suspected, he had enjoyed seeing their helpless frustration and rage. However friendly that monthly exchange had been, he'd been needling them and they knew it.

Until the night he died, had it ever crossed his mind that, if you waved a red cape often enough, sooner or later you'd be gored?

Troy asked about the night in question, only to learn that Ms. Cromer had taken her only two finals for that semester early so that she could go home to attend her grandmother's funeral. A friend had called her the day after the murder, at which point she'd felt the knee-buckling relief.

"It's none of my business," he said, "but I hope your parents accepted you when you did come out."

"No," she said. "They didn't."

"I'm sorry." He thanked her for her frankness, ended the call and shook his head over the grief he'd heard in her voice there at the end.

It reminded him too much of Madison's and made him think again that he'd been even luckier with his parents than he'd known. Which made how he'd been treating his mother seem pretty damn childish, after she'd given him nothing but unfailing acceptance his entire life.

Frowning, he flipped to a new page in his notebook and dialed the phone.

The first words out of Senator Haywood's mouth were, "I met you at the college president's reception, didn't I?"

"Yes, sir. I was attending both as liaison for the police department and because my father, Joseph Troyer, was a Wakefield grad who had put something in the time capsule."

"If you had questions, why didn't you ask them then?"

He smiled grimly. "Because I hadn't yet overheard talk about several people who were at the gym that night and chose not to come forward to speak to the investigators. There was a lot of gossip that weekend, you know, some of it quite interesting."

"You're implying there was talk about me."

Troy straightened, finding the quiver of suppressed fury in the senator's voice interesting. More than interesting. So far, all the blackmail victims had talked about Mitch King and their own mistakes with an air of resignation. Some still felt shame, maybe, and the residue of dislike for the little worm who'd capitalized on their private actions. But flat-out anger and fear were long gone, maybe only because of the years, maybe because their long ago mistakes were now irrelevant.

A U.S. senator, though, was in a different place. Politicians could mostly shrug off the admissions that they'd smoked marijuana a time or two in college, had burned a U.S. flag, been unfaithful to their wives. But what if the young Gordon Haywood had done something different and less likely to evoke sympathy in his supporters? Cheating or stealing might not go over so well with the straight-laced far-right crowd. Given the way he ogled women, Troy didn't figure it was likely Haywood had flirted with homosexuality, but you never knew. *That* would go over even less well. Or drugs, something more serious than weed. His crowd wouldn't like that, either.

"We have become aware that Mr. King was blackmailing fellow students," he said flatly. "Your name has come up in that context, Senator Haywood."

"What an absurd accusation!" he snapped. "This sounds like a political attack to me."

"I can assure you that I have no political agenda, sir," Troy said in his best, expressionless cop voice. "As I said, you were seen having occasional conversations with Mr. King in a way that suggested you may have been making payments."

"I think I'm entitled to know who told you something so ridiculous."

"I can't tell you that, Senator. Let me assure you that my only interest in calling you is to gain a better picture of Mr. King's character and habits. Other Wakefield graduates have been honest with me about paying him off, and even told me why they felt compelled to do so. After thirty-five years, any lapses they made at the time have become irrelevant. I can assure you complete confidentiality."

"I scarcely knew Mitchell King," Haywood ground out, "and *I* can assure you I committed no offenses that I would have paid blackmail to keep secret. Good night, Detective Troyer."

He was gone. Troy ended the call himself and set down his phone. Once again, he had to do battle with the instinctive dislike he felt for the good senator. Even accounting for that, though… It was hard not to think Haywood had responded too vehemently to relatively mild questions.

Even more interestingly, he hadn't expressed any surprise at the information that King had been a blackmailer. No "What the hell?" Or "You're kidding. Really?" Troy's gut said Haywood *wasn't* surprised.

Oh, yeah, he'd been paying Mitch King off, just like all the others. Troy would have liked to know what his particular peccadillo had been, but really it didn't matter. No, what *did* matter was finding out where Gordon Haywood had been between 1:30 and 2:15, the window during which Mitchell King had been bludgeoned to death.

Apparently Guy Laclaire wasn't the only alum angry at any suggestion he had paid blackmail—or done anything worth hiding.

COME MORNING, TROY sat down with the chief and his lieutenant to update them on the investigation.

"The progress you've made is impressive," Chief Helmer said. "I want you to keep at this with everything you've got. I'm authorizing a travel budget that would allow you, for example, to sit down face-to-face with Senator Haywood if necessary." He hesitated. "I hope it goes without saying that I also have faith you won't cause a PR nightmare for this department."

"I'll be cautious, sir." A faint smile crooked Troy's mouth. "I think it's safe to say that the senator won't go to the press. The only danger from him comes if we go public regarding our desire to talk to him."

"And will that become necessary?"

"I don't think so." Troy explained his reasoning and belief that he might be able to pinpoint Haywood's whereabouts the night of the murder from other sources. "Normally too many students would have been asleep for that to be possible. But this was the second night of finals week and most were awake. Unlike many seniors, Haywood lived on campus. In a single, but it was part of a suite of other singles centered around a common sitting room and kitchen. I'll talk to the residents of other rooms."

He was dismissed with a nod. A couple of hours later, Troy had completed an ultimately useless interview with a long-time college employee—now retired—who lived only a couple of blocks from Troy's childhood home. On impulse, he decided to stop by for a quick visit with his mother. New guilt, he supposed, from last night's reflections.

He was still a block away when he saw her standing outside the gate on the sidewalk. Maybe the mail had just come. But in the length of time it took him to cover the short distance, Mom didn't move. She had her back to him, as if she was staring at something up the block. Disturbed, he saw how stiff her posture was and that her arms were crossed so tightly they'd pulled her shoulders into a hunch.

When he cruised to a stop at the curb and turned off the engine, she wheeled to face him, her face alight with alarm.

He jumped out. "Mom?"

"Troy?" Her voice shook. "What are you doing here?"

"Just thought I'd stop and say hi. What are you doing?" She sure wasn't grabbing the mail or newspaper, because her hands were empty.

She backed away, through her open gate beneath the white-painted arch covered by picture perfect roses, back into the safety of the yard. "I… Nothing. It doesn't matter."

She wore athletic shoes, not her rubber gardening clogs, and she radiated distress.

"Mom?" He stepped forward quickly enough that she couldn't escape him. He gently took her elbows in his hands. "Are you okay?"

"Of course I'm…!" Her mouth worked. "I'm…" And then she shuddered. Her face crumpled. "I'm…" Her last attempt came out as a despairing whisper, just before she began to sob.

He wrapped his arm around his mother and held her as she wept against his chest. God, she was so much more fragile than he'd remembered. When he ran his hands over her back, he felt her spine and ribs in a way he was sure he never had before.

His heart spasmed as she kept crying. He doubted she even heard his comforting, then bracing, words.

"You're making yourself sick," he finally said, gently shaking her. "You're scaring me, Mom."

She gradually pulled herself together, but it was a slow process, painful to watch. The worst was when his dignified, often reserved mom realized how awful she must look.

She tore herself away from him. "I need to... Oh!" She raced for the house and disappeared inside. The screen door slammed behind her.

Rueful, he climbed the porch steps and decided to wait outside. He settled on the glider and set it into motion. Staring at her front garden through the screen of some kind of vine—a clematis, he thought—gave him too much time to brood.

What had happened to set her off like that? Was it something to do with him showing up? Or—damn it to hell—was she having regular breakdowns she'd never admitted to him?

He remembered his conversation with Holly Cromer and her too-brief reply when he asked if her parents had accepted her. *No. They didn't.* Madison's expression when she talked about her mother rose in his mind's eye, the hurt and the knowledge that she hadn't mattered to her own mom as much as she should.

He groaned and bent his head back, closing his eyes.

Troy didn't open them until he heard the squeak of the screen door.

Mom's face was still blotchy, but she'd carefully reapplied her makeup and brushed her hair.

He rose to his feet.

"No, sit down." She joined him, sitting with her knees together and her hands clasped on her lap. Her back was very straight. "I'm sorry, Troy."

"Nothing to be sorry for," he said gruffly. "I know

you're still grieving. I hope you aren't still crying every day."

Mom shook her head. "No. This…wasn't about your father at all." As he'd done earlier, she stared straight ahead. For a moment he feared she was going to cry again, but she firmed her jaw. "This time, it was all me."

"What do you mean?"

"Since you…confronted me…" She swallowed. "I told myself I would start taking walks again, if only to prove you wrong."

Oh, hell. "That's what you were doing when I drove up. Trying to make yourself go for a walk."

"Yes." She was rocking slightly, clearly unconscious of the movement. "Every day, I've put on my walking shoes and told myself I was being silly. All I had to do was take one step and then another. I promised myself today I'd only walk to the corner and back. Of course I could do that!"

"But you couldn't," he said softly.

"I couldn't." Her face was breaking down again, becoming something—someone—unfamiliar. "I could not make myself take a single step farther. I…started to shake."

"Oh, Mom." Hurting for her, he scooted over enough to wrap his arm around her again. "I hope you know how brave you were to try."

"Brave? I'm a coward." Her smile was pitiful, but she was trying. "I have been…refusing to admit to myself how crippled I've become. I told myself it was natural to want to stay close to home. Why should I go to the hairdresser when she'd come to me? I never liked grocery shopping, anyway. Oh, I had a thousand excuses. I was mad when you accused me of something I told myself was completely ridiculous." She looked away from him. "Only, it wasn't."

"I didn't see it, either, Mom." He hesitated, then decided she deserved honesty from him, even if it showed him in a bad light. "I don't think I wanted to. I was impatient with the pace of your grief."

She met his eyes at last. "I could tell. And that's all right, John." She shook her head when he tried to speak. "No, listen. The part that I think *isn't* all right is that I can't help wondering if you've grieved at all. Have you let yourself, in your heart, accept that Dad is gone? Have you really cried?"

He opened his mouth to say an immediate and brusque *don't be ridiculous,* but even without hearing the words aloud was stunned by the echo. *How we lie to ourselves.*

"I don't know," he said finally, his voice having acquired a rasp. "Yeah, I've cried. I cried at the funeral." But instead of accepting that as natural, he had been embarrassed. What an idiot. "Not much since."

"Your father and I...weren't often apart." She examined his face, as if to be sure he understood. "I haven't been able to avoid knowing that he is utterly and forever gone. But you didn't see him as often. It would have been easier to think of him as temporarily absent instead."

"Yeah." Now he was hoarse. "I guess that's it. I think of things I want to say to him, and then it's a jolt when I remember I can't. Only——" He hunched his shoulders. "Hell, I guess I have a way of shoving that knowledge out of mind."

Wiser than he'd known she was, his mother nodded. "It's different for a son or daughter, anyway. You *expect* to lose your parents. It's part of the flow of your life. I suppose I'd hoped..." Her voice caught. "Hoped..."

"That you'd go first," Troy said gently. "Or together."

"Together," she whispered. "When I thought of it, that's always what I imagined. You read about the couples who die within a few weeks of each other when they're in their eighties or nineties. When one dies, the other lets go. But

I'm fifty-seven. It's too soon! I know that, but a part of me..." She choked again.

He took her in his arms again and she buried her face against his chest. His eyes stung. He felt unbelievably petty for having been hurt because she so obviously wanted to be with her husband, wherever he was, instead of her son.

But I don't need her, not the same way as a spouse does, and she's always known that. She's known the time would come when I'd find the woman I would need for a lifetime.

Madison's name sang in his head, softly, but he heard it and knew.

However much he loved his mother, it *wasn't* the same.

Mom, he realized, wasn't crying this time, only gathering strength from him. Without saying a word, he tried to give her as much as she needed.

After a minute, she straightened away from him. "Tomorrow I will call Dr. Drayton and ask for the name of a counselor." A tiny bit of mischief showed in her eyes. "One who *doesn't* come to the house."

Troy smiled at her. "Whenever I can, I'll drive you."

"I do still have friends." She patted his hand. "There's something else you could do for me, Troy."

"Anything," he said, and meant it.

"I believe, with you beside me, I could go for that walk. If you have time..."

"Yeah." He had to clear his throat. "I have time." He stood and crooked his elbow. "A walk sounds good to me."

His mother laid her hand on his arm. "Maybe we could talk about your father."

Crap. He didn't like the way his eyes still burned. "We can do that," he agreed.

"And your Madison. I'd like to hear more about her, too."

Talking about Madison was definitely something he

could do. "Sure," he said. He smiled. "Did I tell you she made me go swimming?"

Mom laughed. "What are you going to make her do in retaliation? Go fishing?"

They reached the sidewalk and turned onto it in tandem. "I was thinking mountain climbing."

Tension quivered through her touch, but his mother's step did not falter.

He bent his head to see her face as she walked, shoulders straight, her dignity restored. His pride in her made his chest feel as if it was being crushed.

"Or marrying me. That might work, too," he heard himself say.

"Oh, Troy." Mom's smile trembled. He knew she hadn't forgotten what she was doing, the distance widening between her and her refuge. But she was happy for him. Taking this walk partly for him.

"Have I mentioned lately how much I love you?" he asked, and she chuckled.

"Not nearly as often as you ought to."

They were nearly to the corner, and despite her fear, Mom was smiling.

MADISON HAD JUST let Troy in the door when her phone rang. "Excuse me," she said, and hurried to the kitchen where she'd set it on the tiled counter.

Aware that Troy followed and was studying his own vase sitting on the windowsill, she picked up the phone.

Her pulse bumped. Oh, Lord. It was her father calling. Instinct screamed, *Ignore it.* Common sense had her wondering if she'd then have to lie to Troy about who the caller was.

With an apprehensive look at his back, she answered. "Hi, Dad."

Troy turned slowly, his gray eyes darkening to flint.

"Madison," Dad said. "Am I getting you at a bad time?"

"I was about to go out to dinner with a friend."

"Friend?"

He didn't, of course, ask if the friend was anyone he knew, because he hadn't met any of her friends or colleagues in Frenchman Lake.

"No, I've begun dating Troy recently."

Troy's eyes narrowed a flicker.

"Is it anything serious?" her father asked.

Oh, boy. Between the rock and a hard place. "He's actually standing here, Dad."

He chuckled. "I see. I'll let you go, then. I didn't have anything special to say. You've been on my mind lately, that's all."

The flash of bitterness surprised her. "Are you sure it isn't Mitchell King who's been on your mind?"

Any denial was too slow coming.

"I thought so," she said flatly. "Dad, I do need to go. I'll talk to you later."

"You're wrong," he said. "You haven't sounded like yourself recently. I think something is wrong."

Yes, she wanted to say. *Yes, it is. Funny thing, I'm a little rattled to find out you have something ugly in your past. And, hey, to discover that Mr. Righteous is fully capable of lying to his daughter. Other than that, no problem.*

Um…except for the cop standing here listening to every word.

"I'll call you tomorrow. Good night, Dad." She touched End without waiting for a response and dropped the phone in her purse, then lifted her chin. "Shall we go?"

"Do you want to tell me what that was about?"

"No, actually, I don't."

He scrutinized her for an unnerving minute, then bent his head. "All right. Shall we?"

Madison swept out of the kitchen ahead of him, keys in her hand. Neither spoke until they were in his SUV.

"You have anything special in mind for dinner tonight?" he asked, starting the engine.

"Something casual. I'm not very hungry."

"How about Brannigan's again?"

"Yes, that's fine." In through the nose, out through the mouth. Why was she so upset? *Because Dad is lying. Because Troy gets a cold, predatory expression in his eyes every time I mention Dad. Because I'm scared.*

Because she wanted to trust and believe in her father— but she did trust and believe in Troy.

"I'm sorry." Her hands clenched her purse. "That was rude."

"No, honey. That was honest. I keep telling you I understand."

His voice came out rough and still so tender she could hardly bear it.

"Maybe we shouldn't be dating until, well, this is over."

His foot caught the brake. "Is that what you want?"

Her panic was the finger-in-the-electrical-socket kind. The hair on her arms stood up. "No!" she cried. "You know it isn't. I love spending time with you. But…what if…?"

"I end up arresting your father?" The tenderness was gone. So was all other emotion.

Madison nodded.

"That's something you have to decide. It won't change how I feel about you." Still flat.

She wanted to beg, *What do you feel for me?* Pride wouldn't allow her.

"I know," she said. "I know you're doing your job. And the right thing to honor your father's memory. It's just…if you're the one to prove my father is capable of something so awful…" Throat thick, she broke off again. "If he did something like that, what does it make me?"

Troy's big hand closed over both of hers, still knotted on her purse. "It doesn't change who you are. Your dad may have made mistakes, but he raised you to believe in certain principles. The sad part will be knowing he didn't always live by them, but this is about him, Madison." His voice had firmed; it compelled her to believe. "Him. Not you."

She did some more deep breathing. "Yes. I know you're right. Most of the time I'm fine. It's only sometimes that I freak."

"Like every time he calls."

"Um…yes."

Without her noticing, Troy had pulled into a parking space in the small lot next to the restaurant. Now he took his hand from hers to set the emergency brake and turn off the engine.

He didn't move for a long minute, though, only gazed straight ahead through the windshield at the sand-blasted brick wall of the old building. "Your first instinct when you read what my father wrote was to fiercely insist he was wrong, your dad would never do anything like that."

Madison sat silent, not moving.

He turned his head, compassion in his eyes. "Why the change, Madison? Where did that fierce belief go?"

She had trouble even drawing a breath. When *had* she begun to wonder whether Dad was capable of murder when his reputation was threatened?

"I don't think I've lost it." She was in the grip of a revelation. "I don't." Oh, God, the relief was enormous. "But…I suppose I do believe he was blackmailed, which means he did *something* crummy. Knowing that shakes my image of him. And that has me thinking, and now

I'm seeing shades of his personality I never let myself acknowledge before. Which," she concluded, "makes me mad, because why couldn't *I* ever make a mistake? Why did he pretend he was perfect?"

"I don't know." Troy was smiling at her, as if he was proud of her. "But I think maybe now you have to find out."

She blinked a couple of times, bemused. "Here's where you say, 'That may not be such a bad thing.'"

"Yeah." He smiled a little and leaned over and kissed her, his lips gentle. When he lifted his head, he looked gravely at her. "I don't want to lose you over this, Madison."

She opened her mouth with every intention of saying, *You won't.* But nothing came out.

They gazed at each other. Finally he nodded acknowledgment and opened his car door, coming around to meet her as if nothing was wrong. As if nothing had changed.

CHAPTER FOURTEEN

OVER THE NEXT couple of weeks, Troy was painfully conscious that something had changed between him and Madison. He was doing his damnedest to pretend it hadn't, and thought she was, too, but he couldn't get that one moment out of his mind. He'd known from the beginning that, if he had to arrest her father, her reaction could get between them, but Troy had begun to hope they were solid enough for their relationship to survive anything.

He'd told his mother he wanted to marry Madison, but apparently that kind of outcome wasn't on her radar. She seemed totally fixated on the outcome of this murder investigation.

He was afraid that if he tried to tell her he was in love with her, it would come across as a demand: *me or him*.

God, he thought, *maybe that's exactly what I would be doing*. He did know he was desperate for reassurance, and had been struggling for weeks to keep himself from begging for it.

Was that pitiful or what?

Madison was under a lot of emotional pressure right now. How would it help if he applied more? Sometimes love meant keeping your mouth shut. Being patient.

Troy had to ask himself whether he'd allowed his innate muleheadedness to drive him into making a huge mistake, one that was hurting Madison. His father was dead. Joe Troyer would never know whether he'd been right or wrong about his friend Guy. If Troy went to Dad's grave to say, "I arrested the killer, Dad," the words wouldn't mean any more than the roar of the mowers that kept the grass down. Dad was deaf to all of it.

And then there was the distinct possibility that he would have preferred Troy to leave well enough alone. To ignite the confession of moral weakness and let it turn to insubstantial ashes.

I was already in love with Madison, even if I hadn't admitted it to myself. And yet, his righteous anger hadn't allowed him to seriously sit back and think, *Who is to be served if I pursue this?*

So now he was stuck with a bigger question. *What's it going to cost me?*

In the dark hours at night, he told himself it wasn't going to cost him anything worth having. If Madison really didn't understand why this mattered to him, she didn't understand *him*. If, in the end, her sense of loyalty to her father was that much more powerful than anything she felt for Troy, it meant she didn't love him. Not the way he wanted and needed.

Not the way his parents had loved each other.

He also knew it was too late to let the investigation go, for a lot of reasons. One was Madison—he knew himself well enough to be aware he couldn't live without finding out where he rated with her. If he quit now, she might say, "I love you. I would have even if you'd arrested my father," but would he ever, gut-deep, believe her? Think how easy the words would be to say once she knew he *wasn't* going to arrest her daddy.

Backing out of the investigation would do some serious damage to his career, too. He was too near to closing in on answers for either the chief or his lieutenant to buy it if he announced one day, "I've asked a lot of questions but I haven't gotten the right answers, so let's just close the book again."

Finally, the truth was that he *was* mule stubborn. He'd started this, and by God he had to finish it. He had to believe that finding answers and achieving justice did matter. Otherwise, why did he bother? What had his life mattered to this point?

And answers just kept coming. Every person he interviewed gave him another name, or several other names. It was like a pyramid scheme. You pass me a name, and that person passes me two, and those two each hand over three…

Most interviews were, by necessity, conducted by phone. He was saving as much of the travel budget—and the time traveling would eat up—for the end when he would have narrowed the suspect list to two or three. With a little luck, he could persuade those two or three to come to him instead, and save the department's bucks.

He finally decided to make an exception to head over to the Seattle area, where he'd been able to book appointments with ten alumni and former employees.

The first two interviewees admitted to having paid blackmail to King. Both were chagrined, a little pissed, but also resigned, which fit the pattern. Neither—if they were to be believed—had committed terrible offenses. One student had been allowed to take an exam early because of a family obligation and had then sold the questions and answers to several fellow students who proceeded to ace the test undeservedly. The other had worked in the café at the Student Union and had swiped some money—including tips that were supposed to be divided with other students.

Another had overheard enough interesting rumors to give Troy the name of a college grounds employee who might have stolen some pretty pricey equipment.

"He was paying King five hundred bucks a month, which had to have hurt. If I had gotten caught, I'd have gone on academic suspension and I would have been real unpopular around campus, but this dude would have lost his job and maybe gone to jail, too. He had serious reason to hate Mitch."

Conveniently enough, that employee had recently retired from the Seattle Parks Department and still lived in Shoreline. He didn't sound real happy to hear from Troy, but agreed to let him come out to the house.

In his mid-sixties, Leonard Hickman was one of those little guys who got smaller with age. It wasn't hard to picture him twenty years down the line, wizened like an Egyptian mummy. His brown hair was mixed with gray in a crew-cut bristle. His eyebrow and nose hairs were damn near long enough to be braided, though, which occasionally distracted Troy from what Hickman had to say.

"It was bullshit!" he exploded. "That little scumbag had somehow manufactured evidence against me. We did have some equipment missing, and one of the other guys must have found a way to blame me. I didn't see what I could do but pay the asshole for a few months until he was outta there. Then I planned to job hunt."

"You didn't consider going to the college administration and laying it all out?"

"Hell, no! Who'd believe me? A prissy ass college like that, the guys they pay to do the dirty work don't get any respect. They wouldn't have cared about truth. They'd have been happy enough to fire me."

He reeked of bitterness, the smell so strong Troy was reminded of sweat socks long past laundry day.

"How many payments had you made before his death?" Troy asked quietly.

"Four. Two thousand dollars. He was killing me."

He seemed unconscious of how telling that last bit was. *He was killing me, so I killed him?*

"I see that you did leave Wakefield College at the end of the academic year even though any threat from Mr. King was gone."

Furious brown eyes met his. "I still had to think about which guy I worked with had set me up."

If his side of the story was true, it would indeed be off-putting to head to work every day knowing one of the other guys was not only a thief, but had also thrown you under the bus to deflect suspicion. Or maybe to get a cut of the payments from Mitch King?

Now there was a thought. Just about everyone Troy had talked to said the same thing—I don't know how he could possibly have found out/seen me/known. What if King's scheme was even more sophisticated than Troy had guessed? What if he had a network of spies and therefore a payroll to record in that ledger?

Well, hell, Troy thought, *what if I need to be identifying those subcontractors, too?* Once they realized King had recorded their names and the less than admirable parts they'd played in his little business, some of them, too, would have had motive to eliminate him and make the damning ledger disappear.

He asked for more information, and elicited the names of two of Leonard Hickman's fellow employees he had suspected—or had disliked most, it was hard to tell. It didn't sound as if he'd gotten along well with *any* of his coworkers.

He blew up when Troy asked for his whereabouts the night of the murder.

"I was goddamn home and in bed with my wife where I belonged. You know, I was trying to help out here. I wouldn't have talked to you at all if I thought you were going to try to finger me for killing the little creep."

He crowded Troy over the threshold and onto the porch.

"May I speak to your wife?"

"We're divorced," Hickman snapped, and slammed the door. A dead bolt slid into place.

Golly gee whiz, Troy thought sardonically, *I wonder why the wife didn't stay with a nice guy like that?*

Troy got back in his Tahoe and made a note to track down the ex. Glancing at the next address on his list, he set out.

This was a woman who had allegedly been at McKenna that night and yet somehow remained unknown to the police.

On the phone, Sally Yee sounded reluctant to talk to him, but after a long silence she'd said grudgingly that she could take a quick coffee break if he dropped by her workplace, which was a law firm. Ms. Yee, he saw with interest as he studied the brass directory just inside, had made partner at some point.

He was stopped by a guard. After a low-voiced phone call, he told Troy, "Ms. Yee will be down shortly."

She appeared so quickly that she must have hustled. Troy's first thought was that she looked way younger than he knew her to be. All the then-students were in the fifty-three to fifty-eight-year age range. Like Mitch King, Joe Troyer and Guy Laclaire, she'd been a senior.

In a stylish poppy-orange suit, she was still a beautiful woman, her skin smooth, her glossy black hair cut in a wedge that followed her jaw. Heels clicking on the marble lobby floor, she came straight to him.

"I wondered when you mentioned your name. You look a good deal like your father."

He inclined his head. "So I'm told."

"There's a Starbucks halfway down the block. Or a Tully's at the next corner."

He wasn't surprised. No block in downtown Seattle was complete without at least two coffee shops. God forbid workers had to stretch their legs to find a caramel macchiato or espresso con panna or whatever.

"Either's fine. I'm not that much of a connoisseur."

Starbucks was closest so that's where they went.

He chose a breve, she went for something sweeter and creamier.

They sat at a small table in the rather dim back of the room. No near neighbors. "What's this about?" she asked, brisk but wary.

He politely repeated some of what he'd said on the phone before he got to the point. "Another student says she saw you at McKenna Center the night of the murder, although it appears investigators didn't have your name."

"You mean I didn't come forward."

Yeah, that's what he meant. He didn't say anything.

He wasn't surprised that a high-powered attorney like Ms. Yee hid what she was thinking and had the self-control to mull over what she wanted to tell him before she opened her mouth again.

"Yes. I went intending to swim some laps."

Well, that was intriguing. She'd intended? "Do you recall what time you went?"

"Yes, I left my dorm room at one forty-five. It wouldn't have taken me more than five minutes to walk to McKenna."

He loved precise.

"It sounds like you didn't stay."

An emotion crossed her face that was surprisingly sharp, even if muted by time. "I'm surprised anyone saw me. I never even got inside the sports center."

"Do you mind telling me why?"

"It didn't have anything to do with Mitch King, which is why I didn't bother speaking to investigators."

"I'd still like to know. I'm attempting to put together the big picture. If I can get every single player on the board, then I'll be able to see which pieces moved where."

She nodded, understanding completely. She likely worked the same way when she planned a presentation to a jury.

Still, she hesitated for a moment. "What I'm going to tell you doesn't reflect well on me."

"If, in the end, it has no relation to what happened to Mr. King, I can promise that anything you tell me will remain confidential."

Her mouth tightened, showing for the first time fine lines that betrayed her age. "Very well. It scarcely matters anyway, after so many years."

He took a swallow of his drink.

She gazed down at hers. "I imagined myself in love with a young professor at Wakefield. I also imagined that he was in love with me. We had…relations."

Troy tried hard not to give away his increased interest.

"That night, I had reached the outside door, which was well lit, when I glanced to one side and saw a couple in a clinch. I must have made a sound, because the man turned his head. It was that professor. He was being quite careless," she added dispassionately, "because he was kissing another student. I'm sure you're well aware that having sexual or romantic relationships with students is taboo for professors."

"Yes."

"He and I had been exceedingly cautious. So cautious the whole thing had begun to feel…sordid. But I was still in love, in that painful way a young woman can be." She sipped her own coffee, then set it down. "I fled. There is no other way to put it. My heart was shattering." She was trying to sound amused, but didn't completely succeed. "It was all very dramatic."

"Did you confront him the next day?"

"Not until the next semester. I'd already had my final exam for his class. When I did manage to be alone with him, he apologized, told me what a lovely young woman I was, but admitted he had fallen for someone else. He should have told me instead of allowing me to discover it that way." She rolled her eyes. "As I said, none of this had anything at all to do with the murder."

"Except," Troy said thoughtfully, "that those two people might have gone into McKenna Center."

"The woman didn't. She fled, too. Which, in retrospect, seems rather sad. He's the one who should have been ashamed."

Yeah, he should have been. Troy wondered how many other female students the guy had seduced. And just think, he'd had another thirty-five years to enjoy the hunting grounds colleges offered to someone like him. Troy kind of hoped that he'd been shocked to discover one year that he was too old to appeal to the students anymore.

"I really need the names of both the student and the professor."

Ms. Yee smiled wryly. "Yes, I imagined you would. Her name was Margaret Berlongieri. He was Stephen Coleman. I minored in Psychology and had a couple of classes with him. Abnormal Psych my senior year."

Troy recognized the name. The elderly English prof, Herbert Wilson, had included Coleman on his list of teaching staff who were particularly athletic and also young enough to conceivably be interested in swimming or playing racquetball in the middle of the night. Coleman, Troy seemed to recall, was a weight lifter.

"I don't think he stayed at Wakefield for long after you graduated."

"No, I heard he took a job at Western. I wondered if he'd been forced to resign. I couldn't imagine why he'd take that jump otherwise."

Troy nodded. Western Washington University was an excellent state school, but it didn't have the reputation Wakefield College did. Joining the faculty there was a step backward, not forward.

"Would he have gotten a job anywhere if he was fired for sleeping with a student?"

"Oh, if they didn't have him cold, they might have encouraged him to resign with the understanding they'd stay quiet. They wouldn't want him to sue, after all. Colleges don't like to remind parents that things like this happen."

Her cynicism didn't surprise him, but her tone of disgust did. He'd have thought an attorney would get past that.

He thanked her, left his card and they parted ways outside her building. He had one more interview scheduled today and two in the morning, but he felt revved. In the past hour and a half, he'd acquired two excellent suspects: Leonard Hickman and now Stephen Coleman, two men who had had one hell of a lot more at stake than any of the students did.

Except possibly for Gordon Haywood, whose dreams of a political career would have depended on a sterling reputation.

Guy Laclaire would have dropped well down Troy's list, if only he hadn't bared a little too much anger to his daughter, and if he weren't acting so damn edgy about where the investigation was going.

Troy had parked in a huge concrete garage half a dozen

blocks away. By the time he located his Tahoe, he'd decided to find out whether Stephen Coleman had by chance stayed at Western Washington. Bellingham was only an hour and a half, maybe a two-hour drive north toward the Canadian border. Hey, Troy thought, he was the on the western side of the state already. He'd make time for the professor who'd had one hell of a secret—one right up Mitch King's alley.

And he'd take the time to call Margaret Berlongieri if she was on the list that contained contact info.

He flipped through that folder first, only to find that Margaret wasn't there. Another name for Madison to research, he thought.

It took him only ten minutes to find out that Coleman hadn't lasted long at Western, either. It was always possible he'd risen again in the academic world—but somehow Troy doubted it.

Tracking him down was going to take time, which he didn't have right now if he was going to make it to the Phinney Ridge neighborhood in—he glanced at his watch—fifteen minutes.

"YES, I'LL SEE what I can find out about this Margaret in the morning," Madison promised. "It sounds like you made some really good progress." She heard her own eagerness and winced.

Lounging at the far end of her sofa, Troy looked at her.

"You know I'm going to have to talk to your dad. I've put it off as long as I can."

Unless he needed her to hunt through college archives for contact information on someone, he no longer told her the names of the people he interviewed. Tonight, his description of his three-day trip to Seattle had been especially bare bones. He hadn't even said why Margaret

Berlongieri was a person of interest to him. In fact, Madison noticed that a couple of vertical lines between his eyebrows seemed deeper than usual, making him look tired. He'd made the long drive back across the state this afternoon and had reason for fatigue. Madison had wanted to believe he was preoccupied with everything he'd learned, too, but now she knew better. Really, he'd been working his way up to telling her something she hadn't wanted to hear. Was that the only reason he'd stopped by?

She wouldn't let herself acknowledge the hurt. Dad was what counted here. Most of the time she was able to forget that Troy was a threat to her father. Right this minute, Troy felt like the enemy. Only by clutching at anger as a defense could she bear this terrible sense of alienation from him.

"You'll just tell him his name has come up?" Her voice had come out sharper than she'd intended.

Troy's expression became guarded. "No. I think the time has come for me to quit keeping secrets."

Her breath stopped for long enough to make her dizzy. "You're going to show your boss what your dad wrote?" she whispered.

"Yes. I'll tell him Mom was reluctant to open it. Once she did, she showed it to me right away."

"But you promised…"

His jaw tightened at her shrillness. "I've gotten far enough that your father isn't the only, or even the most obvious, suspect. Not even given what Dad saw. That's the best I can do, Madison. You have to see that."

"I thought you wanted to protect your dad's reputation, too." She flung it at him like an accusation. "Don't you care about your father?"

"If this investigation has taught me one thing, it's how damaging it is to keep secrets. I'm done with that." Troy paused. "I hoped you'd understand."

She sat frozen. "Will you tell Dad I've been working with you?"

He scowled. "Of course not! What do you think I am?"

The hurt blazed in her now. "Will you think less of me if *I* keep that secret?"

He looked astonished, as if only now did he realize he was dealing with something way more powerful than panic.

"You didn't do anything wrong. It's not the same thing."

"Do you really think my father will see it that way?" She had fire and ice inside her now and didn't know which would win. "That he won't feel betrayed if he finds out?"

"How will he?"

"Because once I know…" Madison stopped, confused. "No, you're right. I *don't* have to say anything." Dad and she could go on the way they always had—her mostly obedient and trying so hard to win her father's approval. Grateful when he gave even a grain of it. Hiding resentment and her longing for something more.

Or she could finally speak out and risk losing him entirely. Risk being left with, for all practical purposes, no family at all. Unless Troy… But Troy wasn't acting as if he wanted to be her family.

Her confusion increased. She *knew* the increased distance between them was her fault, but how could she trust that he would love her when she wasn't even sure her own father did?

Am I that big a mess? she wondered, appalled.

The anger she had needed to protect her was gone, which was no surprise when it always had been a false front.

"You do what you have to." The weariness was obvious in Troy's voice now. He stretched and then rose from the sofa.

"It's only nine. Do you have to go?" Oh lord, now she sounded pathetic. No, it could be worse—she could have begged him not to go.

"I need to hit the sack."

Madison hated that she couldn't read his face. His expression was closed down entirely, but not, she sensed, in cop mode. It was more as if she'd annoyed him. Or disappointed him.

"I said something, didn't I?"

A muscle twitched in his cheek. Finally he shook his head. "I'm getting the feeling you're more interested in the investigation than you are in me. You and I are never alone, Madison. Your father's always here, too."

"Isn't your father?" she shot back.

"No. I'm letting go." Troy's throat worked. "He was a good man, he screwed up and I'm willing to admit it. I love him anyway, and I miss him like hell. He's not alive and present."

She squeezed her arms around herself, trying to hold in the pain and fear. "Shouldn't I feel protective about my dad?"

His gaze was even more remote now. "I'm not in the mood to do this tonight."

"Please don't go." The words came out small and husky, perhaps because of the lump in her throat. She scrambled off the sofa. "Not like this."

"How should I leave?"

She took the leap. "Don't leave at all."

Oh, goddamn it, Troy thought. There'd been nights he'd have cut off his right arm for that invitation. This one wasn't any different—except he didn't trust her motivation for asking him to stay.

"We both know you're conflicted," he said flatly. "You

don't have to prove anything to me." Or offer her body to—what, to make sure he kept talking to her? Had she been stringing him along all this time and only now was desperate enough to go the last mile?

God, he didn't want to think that.

She shook her head frantically. "Dad's not here, Troy. I feel like I'm losing you. I can't. Please. Please tell me you still want me."

Were those tears in her voice? He wouldn't be able to stand it if she cried because she thought he was rejecting her. Not this woman who never cried, who kept all her pain inside.

With a groan he took the couple of strides to her and gripped her shoulders. "Of course I want you. Are you kidding? But it has to be mutual, not..." He couldn't even figure out how to say it without insulting her unbearably.

She gazed mutely up at him, waiting for him to say what he meant. The caramel brown of her eyes was filled with anxiety. There she was, laid bare—the little girl who had never been able to trust in anyone's love.

Troy couldn't do anything but draw her slowly into his arms, bump his forehead gently against hers and whisper, "I want you more than I've ever wanted anyone or anything in my life."

She shivered and turned her face into his neck. "Please," she said, just audibly. Then she kissed his throat, openmouthed. He felt the damp tip of her tongue against his skin, and a shudder racked his body.

"Madison." That was the last thing he said before his mouth found hers. He kissed her with desperation and the aching hunger too long pent up. She rose on tiptoe, wrapped her arms around his neck and answered him with equal urgency. He'd never been part of a kiss that felt like making love without either of them having removed a stitch of clothing. Their tongues stroked and teased and dueled; she sucked on his and he could have come right then. He gave up needing to breathe; it would have taken a force of nature to make him rip his mouth away from hers. Short as his hair was, she had a good grip on it, and the pain of that hard tug was part of the pleasure. He was squeezing her buttock, lifting her, trying to position her to ride his thigh.

She writhed, and as they grappled, he realized there was no way in hell they were making it upstairs. Still kissing her, he lifted her from her feet and laid her back on the sofa, his knee planted beside her. She was tugging at the hem of his T-shirt, and he finally backed off enough to let her wrench it over his head. She cooperated as he peeled her T off, too.

At the sight of her sexy, low-cut black bra, Troy groaned. Madison's breasts swelled above the lacy edge, and he couldn't do anything but nuzzle the lush curves. He slipped a hand beneath her to find the clasp, struggled with it and finally triumphed. He lifted himself enough to look as he stroked her shoulders, sliding the bra straps off, down over her arms, freeing the most beautiful breasts he'd ever seen, round and creamy, the nipples dark and hard.

He tried to tell her how gorgeous she was, but wasn't sure how it came out. Mostly he was making ragged sounds. He had to kiss her breasts, lick and finally suckle. *She* was the one making the sounds then, gasps and whimpers and a few pleading words.

"Troy. Yes. Oh, please. Oooh," she groaned as he tugged hard, his mouth filled with *her*.

Her nipples glistened by the time he roved lower, kissing her smooth, bare belly, feeling muscles shift beneath his touch. He used the heel of his hand to rock between her thighs until her hips rose and fell and she did some more whimpering. He skimmed her thin knit pants down, taking skimpy black panties with them. Then he had to stop for another long look at the woman sprawling wantonly, one knee raised, hair spilling over the sofa cushion. Her mouth was soft and even swollen, her eyes somewhere between shocked and dreamy.

The words *I love you* came closer than ever to spilling out of his mouth, but he stopped himself from saying them. He wanted her desperately, and believed she wanted him, but the doubts were still there, forming a hard ball in his gut that would have made him sick if he let it.

She startled him by sitting up. "You, too," she said in a throaty voice he'd never heard from her before, and reached for his belt buckle. He stared down at her hands as she worked to free him from his trousers. Those hands were so much smaller than his, delicate but strong, the fingernails painted today with a red gloss. She managed to stroke him as she eased the zipper down. For a moment Troy had to close his eyes and drop his head back, fighting for control.

"Wait," he said as she pushed the trousers and boxers down. "Condom."

"Oh." Her eyes widened. "I didn't think."

He wasn't doing one hell of a lot of thinking right now, either. Lucky he'd planned ahead. He pulled a packet out of his wallet and let the wallet fall to the floor. It only took a second to shed pants and socks. Getting the condom on was becoming a desperate matter, the way Madison kept smoothing her hands over his thighs and belly, grazing her knuckles down his erection and watching in apparent fascination as it jerked at her touch.

Somehow he managed to last long enough to slide his fingers into her wet, warm center, working her until her eyes were dilated near black and she was grabbing for him, trying to pull him over her. Troy lifted her legs and sank into her body, a spasm shaking him at the purest pleasure he'd ever known.

One of her feet ended up braced on the sofa back; he hooked her other leg over one arm as he drove into her. *Gotta hold out* was all he could think. *Wait for her, wait for her,* but damn, he didn't know if he could.

And then she arched, convulsed and cried out, and he buried his face against her neck and let himself go. Every muscle in his body locked tight, his teeth were clenched, and somehow still a guttural groan escaped.

When the tide let out, he sprawled heavily on top of her, too weak for a minute to move.

I love you. And his next thought—prayer—was, *Please don't let this have been a payoff.*

CHAPTER FIFTEEN

"I'M SORRY. I DON'T understand why you want to talk to me," Margaret Chaffee nee Berlongieri said, voice stiff. Troy would swear he heard alarm.

Damn, he wished he could see her face. Unfortunately, she lived in Boise, Idaho, so he'd decided to make this first contact via telephone. Once Madison had called him with Margaret's married name, he'd been able to track her down even though she'd had no contact with the college in twenty-plus years.

"I'm trying to talk to everyone who was at McKenna Center that night," he explained yet again.

"I didn't see anyone else."

"You did see Sally Yee."

Silence.

"Ms. Chaffee, I'm making no accusations here. Please talk to me."

"I can't do this," she said, and hung up on him.

Well, now, wasn't that interesting? He'd scared this woman. So far, Troy had gotten a lot of reactions from the people he'd interviewed, ranging from friendly interest to hostility, but he didn't think he'd scared the crap out of anyone yet.

Tomorrow… No, damn it, he'd have to wait and see. But sometime in the next few days, he was either going to drive or fly to Boise and surprise Margaret Berlongieri Chaffee.

An hour later, he was deep in conversation with a more cooperative Wakefield alum.

"Yeah, I'd have to think about who I was living with that semester." Art Hampton made a humming sound. "There were four—no, five rooms in the suite."

Troy hunched over, notebook on his knee, one eye on the receptionist at the psychologist's office, where he was waiting for his mother. He didn't want to be overheard, but he couldn't afford to waste the hour she was in there, either, especially not during the middle of the day.

"I remember three of us hooked up," his informant said. "Buddies of mine, I mean. We were trying to find five so we didn't get stuck living with someone we didn't like. We ended up bringing a couple of guys in we didn't know that well. Juan Hernandez—man, I'd almost forgotten about him. He was okay. The other one was Gordon Haywood. You know, the guy who is a senator now, from—I forget what state."

"Utah."

"Right." Hampton sounded amused. "Conservative as all get-out."

"Was he then?" Troy asked out of curiosity.

"He was a stuffed shirt, all right. Not that bad, though. He'd just retreat into his room if the party got too loud, or we lit up…" He cleared his throat. "Guess I shouldn't say that."

Troy repeated his usual line about not being real interested unless the drug use—or substitute whatever crime the interviewee was getting shy about—pertained to the murder under investigation.

With a few conversational nudges, he moved Art Hampton around to the night in question. Hernandez hadn't been there at all; he'd had a girlfriend in a house off-campus and by late in the semester had been spending most nights with

her. One of the other guys had been at the library studying for an Organic Chemistry final with some classmates.

"But Gordie, Drew and I all had Constitutional Law.
Another guy from the class joined us. Bob Schuler. Hey,
he's an attorney there in Frenchman Lake. All four of us
went to law school. Anyway, we stayed up till…had to be
three or four in the morning."

"None of you left for any length of time?"

He laughed. "No, why would we have? We had a refrigerator and a john. I didn't even hear about the murder until after the final the next day. I don't think any of
us did. Maybe Bob, I don't know, but Gordie, Drew and I
walked over together."

"You've been very helpful," Troy told him. "You've
saved me having to talk to any of those people, since I
know they weren't anywhere near McKenna Center that
night."

"Glad I could help," the other man said. "You really
think you're going to figure it out, after all these years?"

"Yes." Troy heard the steel in his voice. "It's past time."

He ended the call and brooded over his notes for the
remaining ten minutes of his mother's appointment. She
came out smiling, although he thought she looked a little
shaken. This was her first appointment. But they had taken
a couple more short walks—the last time they made it all
the way around the block.

He took her arm on the way out of the restored brick
building that housed several doctors' offices and gave her
a gentle boost into his SUV.

"I suppose having lunch would be pushing it?" He
couldn't help noticing how tightly she was gripping the
seat belt strap.

"I think maybe, if you don't mind." Then she took a
breath. "You know what I'd love?"

Troy cocked his head at her tone, which was mildly defiant. "What?"

"A cheeseburger and French fries. And a root beer float. I haven't had a lovely, greasy, fast-food meal since... Well, in a long time."

He grinned at his mother. "Now you're talking my language."

Of course, she lectured him on his eating habits and cholesterol all the way to Dairy Queen, but the price was worth paying.

He knew when they ordered that she wouldn't come close to finishing her entire meal, but he liked the way she laughed and slapped his hand when he stole some of her fries.

When he pulled up in front of her house, she sighed. "Oh, that tasted so good. I'll probably be queasy half an hour from now, but it was worth it."

He leaned over and kissed her cheek. "When's our next appointment?"

She met his eyes squarely. "You don't have to take me to every one, you know."

"I probably won't be able to," Troy said honestly. "You know how it goes with my job. But for now, I'm mostly talking on the phone and making charts. These first visits have got to be the hardest for you. I'd like to help as long as I can."

"You're a good son."

"I'm not sure I have been." Being honest felt more important these days than it ever had.

"Nonsense." Mom shook her head. "If you think you should have noticed sooner, I can only tell you that I worked very hard to make sure you didn't." She paused, sadness shadowing the gray eyes so like his. "I almost succeeded in fooling myself."

Maybe fooling ourselves is a family talent, Troy thought grimly as he drove away a minute later.

He yanked himself back. He'd made up his mind he wasn't going to think about Madison today, and by God he'd stick to his vow. He'd call her one more time—once he reached her father, so she'd know the plan—but after that, she would have to decide for herself how much Troy mattered to her.

His phone rang as he was pulling into the lot behind the police station. He braked and reached for it, immediately recognizing the number. Speak of the devil.

"Detective Troyer," he said matter-of-factly.

"Guy Laclaire. Returning your call."

Troy found a parking spot and turned off the engine. "Mr. Laclaire, I imagine you've heard that we have reopened the investigation into the murder of Mitchell King."

"My daughter told me," he said tersely.

"I'm going to need to speak to you, face-to-face. A witness places you at McKenna Center that night." He braced himself for the blast.

It never came. "May I ask what witness?" Laclaire sounded tense but civil.

"My father. Joe Troyer."

"What the hell...?" The shock was easy to hear. "I understood he'd passed away."

"Yes, he did. However, he left a written description of the events of that night." Troy had debated how much to say up front, and decided to keep it to the bare minimum. "I can come to Portland this week, if you'll be available."

Madison's father gave a harsh laugh. "Are you going to recommend I include my attorney in this interview?"

"That is entirely up to you, Mr. Laclaire."

The other man swore. There was a long silence. "I'm

sure you're aware my daughter works at Wakefield College."

"Yes." Shit, he thought—what if Madison denied to her father having any close acquaintance at all with Troy? His teeth ground together. *So be it.*

"I think," Laclaire said slowly, "that I'd prefer to come to you, Detective. Let me check my calendar." Another pause ensued. "Would Friday work?"

This was Wednesday. Friday suited Troy just fine. They made an appointment for early afternoon. Neither man said goodbye.

Speaking of shit—it was about to hit the fan. Troy suspected Guy was calling his daughter even now.

He rubbed his belly as he got out of the Tahoe and locked it. Fast food hadn't been a good choice. Then he grunted. Maybe he should be glad he could blame a cheeseburger for the uneasy stirring inside.

"DID YOU KNOW this was coming?" were the first words out of her father's mouth, cold and cutting.

Anger burst in her chest, but Madison couldn't trust it to last. Had she ever stood up to her father when he was in this mood?

"What is *this?*" she asked carefully.

"A goddamn cop has the balls to inform me that I'm a suspect in Mitch King's murder."

Shocked, she repeated, "A suspect? He said that?"

"Not in those words," Dad said impatiently. "He told me his own damn father saw me running away from Mc-Kenna that night. What's the department thinking, letting him investigate when he has that kind of bias?"

"Why would that give him a bias?" she asked. "His father's dead."

Silence. Madison realized her mistake.

"You knew he was investigating."

"Of course I knew," she snapped. "Everyone knows. I told you there was a witness. You blew me off." The anger carried her on, however stunned she was to be speaking like this to him. "No," she corrected herself. "You lied to me, didn't you?"

"Watch yourself." This was close to a snarl.

Madison discovered she was shaking. Cowed, the way he intended—but not so much that she wasn't still mad.

She didn't have to listen when he was like this. She didn't have to talk to him at all.

Feeling numb and more than a little shocked at herself, she took the phone away from her ear, although he was now saying something else, and cut him off. She dropped the phone in her purse and didn't even check to see who was calling when it rang again a moment later.

Opening the file on her desk, she stared at it blankly for a moment, then with an effort of will made herself focus. Making reservations at a restaurant in Memphis, Tennessee, that had been recommended to her because it offered excellent food and a room large enough to accommodate an "On the Road With" evening. Yes, that's what had been next on her to-do list.

For this event, Wakefield Assistant Professor of Geology Jared Andrus would be talking about the confluence of science and man, specifically as it related to controlling the Mississippi River. Madison was considering joining him; she had yet to visit the South in her role as director of alumni relations. If she made the trip, she'd extend it with some meetings with prominent alums in a three- or four-state area.

The phone in her purse rang again. Without looking, she reached in and muted it. *Take that.*

She double-checked details, then made the call to the

restaurant manager, who was delighted to accommodate
her event. She recommended a neighboring hotel should
Madison wish to reserve a small block of rooms. A glance
at her notes confirmed that the particular hotel was already
on her list. She took another look online, then made that
call, too. All she needed was a few more details from Professor Andrus about his talk, and she'd be ready to write
the letter to be sent to alumni within a five-state radius.
She should be able to get a save-the-date message on the
website by tomorrow....

Her purse jumped and vibrated. She pushed it farther
under her desk with one foot.

Troy might be calling... But Madison didn't want to
talk to him, either. Not yet, anyway. She still hadn't come
to terms with last night or what it meant. Making love with
Troy had been the most astonishing experience of her life.
But she couldn't forget the way she'd begged. Or the question he'd tried to ask her.

It has to be mutual, not... Not what? What had he
thought?

God. He hadn't made love to her out of *pity,* had he?
He'd certainly been reluctant.

*I'm getting the feeling you're more interested in the in-
vestigation than you are in me. You and I are never alone,
Madison. Your father's always here, too.*

She'd tried to deny it. That's when she'd begged him
not to go. *Not like this,* she had said.

How should *I leave?* She hadn't entirely been able to
pin down what his tone meant, but now she thought it was
contempt. He'd been impatient, even disgusted. Because
she was so pathetically hung up on her daddy's opinion.

The quiver she felt, a kind of shriveling, made her *feel*
pathetic. The next minute, her chin came up. She didn't
deserve his contempt. *He'd* been obsessed with his father,

too. They'd sympathized. He kept saying, "I understand, Madison." Apparently, like her father, Troy had lied, or his compassion and understanding had limits.

No, she definitely didn't want to talk to him, either. Not yet. Not until she understood better why she was scared and furious and confused, all at the same time. Why a part of her *wanted* to find out Dad had done something really sleazy, as if that would justify all the anger she'd tamped down so well she'd hardly known it was there.

Oh, heavens—Dad and Troy would be sitting down together, and not in a friendly "meet the family" way. She could just hear her father, tone and words intended to freeze the insolent young police officer who dared to question *him*. And Troy—she already knew what Troy thought of her father, and that was partly her fault.

She supposed Troy would be going to Portland. Would the interview be at Dad's office, high in the U.S. Bancorp Tower? Personally, she believed that office was designed to intimidate, although her father would deny it. She'd always thought it funny that the skyscraper itself was built out of rose-colored granite; even the windows were tinted pink. *So* not Dad. It went without saying that the tower was one of the most prestigious addresses in Portland—Dad wouldn't have picked it otherwise—but mostly she believed the appeal had been the view. With tall windows all around him, he could stand astride the city, the Willamette River at his feet, and in every direction see the volcanoes that defined the Northwest—Mt. Hood, St. Helens, Adams, even Rainier.

Dad's offices, of course, were done in severe black and gray with touches of gold. His desk was a huge slab of granite.

Would Troy be intimidated?

No. Her certainty let a little warmth begin to melt the ice that seemed to be encasing her.

She only hoped he remembered that the man he was confronting was her father. And that, she thought, was assuming Troy actually cared about her and hadn't been using her, for information, for connections, for… No, she couldn't accuse him of that. He'd waited patiently for her to be ready for sex. And yes, he'd even been reluctant; she couldn't let herself forget that.

The warmth seemed to spread a little more as she thought, *of course he cares.* Kind, funny, intelligent, stubborn—those qualities were Troy. But the tenderness, that had been for her.

Then why, if she didn't have any doubts about how he felt, was she so uncertain?

"I love him." She jumped at the sound of her voice and was relieved to see her office door was closed. "I'm in love with him," she said more softly, less tentatively than she'd expected.

But, however betrayed she currently felt, she loved her father, too.

Focus, she reminded herself, and managed—mostly— to do her job for the rest of the day.

She swam her usual laps then went home, where she nibbled at a salad for dinner. Not until she was done, the kitchen clean, did she listen to her messages.

To her surprise, the first was from Troy, not Dad. It was brief and to the point.

"I spoke to your father. You may have heard from him by now. He chose to come to Frenchman Lake to talk to me. I'm assuming he'll be staying with you." There was a pause. "Call me, Madison. I'd like to see you tonight."

Next message.

"I can't believe you hung up on me. What is wrong

with you?" Scathing rather than furious, Dad had obviously taken at least a few minutes to rein in his temper before leaving this message. "I'm driving over to Frenchman Lake Friday morning, meeting with this detective in the early afternoon. I assume we can have dinner? If you don't have a guest room, I'm sure I can find a room somewhere." He, too, paused. "I really would like to see you, Madison." His voice had changed, become hesitant. "Give me a call."

Madison's chest felt constricted. She couldn't help noticing how much the two messages echoed each other. *Call me. I want to see you.*

Dad didn't know that there was a rivalry happening, but Troy did. *Your father's always here, too,* he'd said, and now Dad would be, in the flesh.

She hugged herself, trying to keep it together when she seemed to be falling apart.

TROY HAD COMMANDEERED a conference room for the upcoming interview. While he waited, he used the long table to lay out the map he'd constructed of the campus and of McKenna Sports Center in particular, with notations on who was verifiably where at what time. He was good at keeping it all in his head, but he liked to see it in front of him, too.

In the course of the week that had passed since he returned from Seattle, he'd eliminated more people. A part of him was still a little disappointed to have crossed Gordon Haywood off his list, but he knew his dislike had been petty. Hickman, the grounds maintenance guy, wasn't looking like a suspect, either. Troy had reached the ex-wife, who confirmed that he'd been home that entire night. It was thirty-five years ago, he'd reminded her, but Mrs. Hickman insisted the news of a murder on the campus had been so shocking, she'd have recalled anything out of the ordinary the evening before.

She didn't sound real fond of her ex, so Troy didn't think she'd lie for him, although he couldn't be sure. There was the possibility she had known her husband was paying the blackmail and had conspired, if only by her silence, to free them from a money drain they couldn't afford. Or, more innocently, that she was a heavier sleeper than she'd admit and hadn't noticed Leonard sneaking out for an hour. They'd lived less than half a mile from the campus.

His gut said no, though; he thought she was straight-up, and that while Leonard Hickman wasn't a very nice guy, he also wasn't a murderer.

His phone vibrated and he answered.

"Mr. Guy Laclaire is here, Detective, and says he has an appointment with you."

"Thanks, I'll be right out."

Troy didn't often let himself get nervous, but he discovered as he walked to the lobby of the police station that today was an exception. Grimacing, he rotated his shoulders to ease some of the muscle tension. There wouldn't be as much of it if he'd felt more confident in Madison, but, reality was, he was scared to death he'd made a big mistake with her.

She had called him back the night before last, well after dinner, and said, "Yes, Dad left a message saying he'd like to stay with me Friday night. I haven't talked to him yet. I'm actually surprised he's coming to Frenchman Lake. I suppose you were hoping he would, so you wouldn't have to waste your department budget on a trip to Portland."

A half day's drive, maybe one night in a hotel. Sure.

"He surprised me by offering."

"Well, his only child does live here, after all."

"Except that in the year and a half you've been on board

at Wakefield, he hasn't yet visited you." The biting words were no sooner out than Troy wished he'd left them unspoken. They'd sting, and he hadn't meant them that way.

"Are you suggesting we're not close?" Her voice held astringency. "And yet you claim he's always here."

"Damn it, Madison, I'm sorry—"

"I'm afraid I have plans tomorrow night," she said coolly. "Why don't we talk once my father has left?"

Approaching the front of the police station, Troy reflected wryly that he had only himself to blame. He'd made passionate love to the woman, then instead of calling the next day to say, "That was the best night of my life, I hope you feel the same," he'd left her a crisp message about her father. He had let his own insecurities get to him, and in doing so had scraped at the scar tissue—or was it only a scab?—that covered hers.

He was an idiot.

One who was now going to interview her father.

And, by God, he would be completely professional. He wouldn't wonder if Madison had already lied to her father and told him she'd met Detective Troyer only in passing at the time capsule opening.

He'd found pictures of Guy Laclaire online, so he knew him immediately. The golden boy had aged well, becoming a handsome man who obviously worked at maintaining his lean, athletic physique. He stood as Troy approached, his face impassive but his expression watchful. The dark suit he wore probably cost twenty times what Troy had ever paid for anything in his wardrobe. The fit in the shoulders and the drape were way too perfect to be off the rack.

Guy had passed on his coloring to his daughter, the mahogany brown hair and brown eyes, the slight golden tint to the skin that suggested a Mediterranean heritage. Somehow, though, the pictures hadn't revealed the resemblance, but in person it was obvious. Something about the cheekbones, the distinctly high forehead. If anything had come from her mother, it was the lush figure.

"Mr. Laclaire," Troy said, holding out a hand. "I'm Detective Troyer. Thank you for coming." He glanced past him. "Do you have an attorney with you?"

"No. However, I will stop the interview if at any time I think I need one."

"Fair enough. This way."

They walked silently through the squad room, Laclaire's head turning as he took in the busy officers and detectives, the sobbing young teenage girl who had been just been picked up for shoplifting—as if clerks at J.C. Penney weren't going to notice a thirteen-year-old browsing the store when she was supposed to be in school.

"Bigger than I would have expected," Laclaire commented, nodding at their surroundings.

"I've explained to your daughter that even sleepy college towns have domestic violence, robbery, rape and pretty much every other crime you get in a city."

Those sharp eyes turned to him. "Madison?"

Oh, hell, did his surprise mean she had *lied?*

Troy consoled himself with the possibility that she and her father might not yet have really talked.

"Yes," he said evenly, "we met when I was assigned to be the police department liaison to the college for the time capsule opening. There was more concern than usual because a couple of the alumni coming were well known. And, of course, I'd have been there anyway in my father's stead."

"I see." He nodded.

Troy held open the door to the conference room and stood back to let Leclaire go ahead. The papers were still spread out on one end of the long table, so Troy gestured to the other end. He was aware that Laclaire took a look at the spread as he walked by before choosing to sit at the very end of the table, as if assuming that the chairman's position was naturally his. Or else it was a tactical move.

Troy, who didn't care about crap like that, pulled out another chair.

"Do you intend to tape this interview?"

"No, actually I don't," Troy said, "but I can if you'd prefer it."

Laclaire watched him flip open his spiral notebook with mild incredulity. "You take notes."

Troy smiled. "Works for me."

Laclaire drummed his fingers on the table, looked down as if in surprise and stopped. "Is your father the only one who saw me that night?"

"Yes, although I'd have gotten around to interviewing you anyway, as you were seen with Mitchell King in circumstances that suggest he was blackmailing you."

He grunted. "All these years."

"You must have suspected my father saw you."

"No. Yes. Hell, I don't know." Suddenly, he sounded human. "I knew something was wrong. We were friends, you know."

"So I gather."

"I thought he was pissed because I'd stood him up. We were supposed to meet for a game of racquetball."

Troy only waited.

"I was paying the little prick. Not your father." A sharp glance. "You know the worst part? It wasn't the money. It was the pleasure he took in bringing everyone down to his level. He insisted on monthly payments made in person, just so he could rub it in. And then there were the games he'd play. He'd keep you standing there while he laughed and joked and pretended you were buddies. But, Jesus—"

He lifted a hand that had a faint tremor and rubbed it over his face. "Not even he deserved that."

Lightbulb on. "You saw his body."

"Yeah. That's why I was running. I got there early, didn't see Joe—who *always* got there ahead of me anywhere we went—and so I stuck my head in the john, the sauna, you know. And I saw Mitch."

"Were you certain it was Mr. King?"

"Not a hundred percent. His face…" He stopped, shook his head. "I suppose you've seen photos. He wore this bracelet, though. Braided cord. That arm was flopping off the bench…."

To his credit, he looked as if the very memory made him queasy. Troy understood. The crime scene photos had been ugly, even to a man relatively conditioned to such sights.

Thinking hard, Troy studied Laclaire. "Let me ask you something, Mr. Laclaire."

The man raised his eyebrows.

"You're making no effort to deny that you were present that night. I appreciate you being forthcoming." Troy was careful to keep his tone entirely bland. "However, I have to wonder why you chose to admit being there, when thirty-five years ago you were unwilling to do so, even though your testimony would have been an enormous help in pinning down a time frame for the murder."

Laclaire's jaws flexed. "I was twenty-one years old, and terrified that someone would find out I'd cheated for a grade. I'd shocked even myself by my behavior. When I saw Mitch, all I could think was that if anyone found out he'd been blackmailing me, I'd be suspected of killing him. I was there, wasn't I? I did what most kids my age would have done in the same circumstances—I ran like hell and prayed no one had seen me." He grunted. "Where was your father?"

"Sitting on the edge of the fountain waiting for you."

Laclaire gave a bark of a laugh. "Assuming he'd beaten me there, of course." There was a wry kind of affection in his voice.

Troy had to fight any softening.

"How long had Mr. King been blackmailing you?"

"Since the beginning of the semester. I'd made four payments."

"Did you have any reason to suspect you were not his only victim?"

That earned him an incredulous look from those sharp eyes. "I knew there were others. He had a ledger. I assume the killer took it, since the police never made reference to the possibility that he was anything but an innocent college student. If they'd found the ledger, they'd have seen my name."

"Did it cross your mind that, had you shared what you knew, you could have made it possible for the police to catch the killer?"

Guy Laclaire stared back at him. "Yes. Goddamn it, yes. But I couldn't take that risk."

"How great was the risk, Mr. Laclaire?" Troy allowed the knife edge to sound in his voice. "What did you do that forced you to pay up?"

The flick of muscles in his jaw was again the only sign of discomfiture. "I told you. I cheated in a class."

Troy raised his eyebrows.

"It was a senior seminar in my major. I had been flattered to be allowed to take it a year early. I thought I walked on water. I'd gotten so cocky that I thought I could get straight A's with one hand tied behind my back. I'd turn out a dazzling final paper for the class, I was sure. But I kept putting it off. I'd been shaken by a B on a midsemester paper. The professor had written all over the damn thing. Even I could see that he was right. So I kept procrastinating. I finally did write one, but it was shit. I asked for an incomplete in the class, claimed to have had mono."

"And then?" Troy prodded.

"I found a brilliant, incisive paper written by some grad student somewhere that had been published in an obscure magazine focused on literary analysis. I typed it and turned it in a few weeks after the semester had ended. I received an A on the paper and in the class." He grimaced, making him look more human. "And from that moment on, I had this rock in my stomach. I swore I would never cheat again, never permit myself to take shortcuts. I have lived my life by that vow, Detective Troyer. I did not hurt Mitch King. I considered him my penance."

Troy had heard that before. "But you hated him."

"Yes." Madison's father met Troy's eyes unflinchingly. "He was scum, preying off other people's weaknesses. Ultimately, however, I believe it might be more accurate to say that he stood in as a symbol of how I felt about what I'd done."

Troy ran him through what he'd done and seen. He was able to make a good guess as to what time he'd found the body. Running away, he'd been carrying his racquet in his hand.

"I had my own," he said simply. Somehow, Troy wasn't surprised.

He listed names of some fellow students he'd suspected were also being blackmailed. Only one name was new, and it was a woman. Her gender made her an unlikely killer. He hadn't seen anyone on his way into the gym that night, had heard voices in the locker room but no one was visible and he thought he'd escaped the building entirely unseen.

In the end, Troy had no choice at all but to thank him for his cooperation and say that he'd be in touch if he had further questions.

"Are you returning to Portland today?" he asked.

"No, I'm staying with Madison tonight. I don't see her often enough." A hint of pain sounded in his voice, or maybe only regret.

Troy hoped for Madison's sake that her father did feel bad for all the times he'd hurt her. He walked Laclaire out and watched him go, aware of too damn much churning inside him. What rose to the top was something he could only call jealousy.

He resented like hell the fact that her father was the one who'd be having dinner with her tonight, spending the entire evening with her, joining her at the breakfast table. The one who'd get first crack at cementing the bonds of love and loyalty.

Troy hated knowing he was capable of feeling something so petty.

He stalked back to the conference room.

CHAPTER SIXTEEN

"DID YOU ENJOY wandering the campus?" Madison asked her father.

They were eating at a bistro she had recommended after he insisted on taking her out to eat, saying it was the least he could do. That afternoon he had stopped by her office briefly, looked around curiously, then waved off her offer to leave work early and said he'd tour the college and maybe town, too, to see how much had changed. "If anything," he'd said sardonically, which made her roll her eyes.

Madison now regretted suggesting a restaurant where she and Troy had eaten together. Out of the corner of her eye, she could see the table where they'd sat. Had she talked about Dad? She couldn't remember.

"It brought back memories," her father admitted, his expression reflective. "I see they took the wrecking ball to Cheadle."

"Yes, I think the whole community turned out to watch." She certainly had. The great event had happened the week before, and a crew had been stripping the site of bricks and debris ever since. Madison had heard the college was doing a brisk business selling the weather-worn bricks from the demolished building. They were probably destined to pave garden paths and courtyards. "It was sad, in a way."

"Sad some idiot architect's mistake is costing the college a small fortune," he said acidly.

Oh, well—that was Dad. She only smiled at him. "Did I thank you for your donation?"

His face softened. "You know you did. Officially and unofficially."

He'd surprised her by giving fifty thousand dollars. He'd surprised her even more when he told her on the phone, "My years at Wakefield were good ones. I haven't been as faithful in giving back as I should have been."

"Did you run into anyone you know?"

He chuckled. "Old man Wilson. I thought he was tottering toward retirement when I was a student here."

She laughed. "By most people's standards, he probably was. He's been heard to say he intends to die in his office at the college." Madison wrinkled her nose. "Which is, unfortunately, in the dank basement of Welk Hall right now."

"So he told me." Her father talked while they ate their salads; he'd seen a few more of his former professors, although none in the English department. "I think Herbert Wilson may be the last who was here when I was," he said thoughtfully.

"Several of the current professors have been here a long time, though." She grinned at him. "It's just that you graduated an eon ago."

"Brat."

The waiter brought their entrées and took away the salad plates. When they were alone again, Madison asked about the afternoon's interview. She tried to hide how tense she was and hoped she only came across as concerned.

"I gather you know the detective."

"Yes." Oh God, she realized, the moment of truth had arrived. But she'd discovered recently that she wasn't as great a coward as she used to think she was. And denying

Troy felt *wrong*. Even so, her fingers clenched the napkin on her lap. "Did he tell you we've been dating?"

Her father's eyes narrowed. "No. And neither have you. No, you said the man you're dating is named Troy. I thought the detective's name was John."

"Nickname." She challenged him with raised eyebrows. "And I rarely tell you when I'm dating. You never ask."

"Seems like something you should talk about with your mother," he muttered.

"If I ever talked to her."

"You were never willing to give her a chance."

"She left me." Madison heard how flat that sounded, how unforgiving. She saw his mouth open and shook her head. "No, I know that's not fair. But at that age, all I knew was that she had abandoned me. And when she came to get me and I saw that she was already pregnant..." She made a face. "I never felt the same about her."

"The fault is rarely one-sided when a marriage fails," her father said—once again taking her aback. He seemed different tonight, perhaps shaken off his usual pedestal by the reason for his visit.

The thought troubled her, though, and she finally figured out why. No, this *was* the father she knew. When she went long stretches without seeing him in person, she forgot how the twitch of his mouth and the flicker of expression in his eyes changed how his words affected her. He sounded cold on the phone, but he really wasn't. Sitting across the table from him, her daddy, it was easier to remember the father who had struggled to French braid her hair because she had desperately wanted to wear it that way, who had buried their ancient tabby cat Calypso in the back garden after Madison found her dead one morning. He'd been wearing one of his fine suits, she remembered, and had sworn to himself as he went upstairs to shower and change after they held their brief service and he held his sobbing daughter. But he'd done it.

"Why didn't you remarry?" she heard herself ask.

He stared at her. "What in God's name brought that up?" His expression changed to what might be shock. "Detective Troyer. You're serious about him."

She lifted her chin. "Yes." And braced herself for what she knew would come.

He set his fork down. "Are you aware I was friends with his father?"

Madison nodded, eyeing him warily. Wasn't Dad going to ask incredulously what she could possibly be thinking of to date a lowly cop? She cleared her throat. "Yes, Troy told me."

"He looks uncannily like Joe—his father."

"I saw a picture of Mr. Troyer, taken not that many years ago. The resemblance is strong."

"Joe wasn't ambitious the way I was." Dad sounded reflective rather than condemning. "He was smart enough, but too laid-back." His eyes zeroed in on hers. "This Troy can't be very ambitious, either, if all he's interested in is small-town law enforcement."

"I'm not so sure ambition and happiness go hand in hand." *Did I really have the nerve to say that to my father?* she thought, shocked.

He dipped his head stiffly.

Had she hurt his feelings?

"But I think you're wrong about Troy," she continued. "He was with Seattle P.D. for something like eight or ten years, rising to detective. He only came home to Frenchman Lake in the past couple years. It's good that he's been here for his mother, after his dad died."

Her father gave a one-shoulder shrug in acknowledgment.

"I have no idea whether Troy is ambitious—whether or

not he wants to rise to police chief here and then move on to a larger jurisdiction. What I do know is that he's dedicated to his job. He's smart and stubborn and he doesn't give up when he sets his mind to something." She paused. "Like solving the King murder."

Again they stared at one another. It felt disconcertingly like two fencers facing off. Madison sensed that, this time, she'd surprised her father.

And maybe herself.

"It could be a mistake to underestimate him." Again Dad sounded thoughtful.

She stiffened. "What does *that* mean?"

His eyebrows rose. "Exactly what I said. He wasn't quite what I expected."

Madison had to ask. "What did you expect?"

"What I think of as the typical cop mentality. Linear thinking. No subtlety. In his case, young and therefore cocky."

She blinked. "So that means you think he's subtle, capable of complex thinking and the opposite of cocky?"

His mouth curved in a rare smile. "Possibly. He is certainly very thorough."

An involuntary memory of Troy's lovemaking made her think—*yes*. It also made her face warm.

"I won't ask what you were thinking."

"Please don't," she said sincerely.

He grinned, but ruefully. "I don't ask about who you're dating because, I suspect like most men, I prefer not to think of any man relating to my daughter."

Her heart gave a funny squeeze. "It never occurred to me…"

"You thought I didn't care?"

This was the strangest conversation they'd ever had.

"Not that, exactly. I know you love me."

He searched her face, then nodded finally, but not as if he was satisfied. "You asked me why I never remarried," he said abruptly. "I suppose that's why. I'm not good at intimacy. My own parents weren't warm people. Being affectionate with you was a struggle for me. And your mother needed something I couldn't give her. I tried harder for your sake than I did for hers, I'm ashamed to say."

Madison's smile felt crooked. "Because I needed you so much."

"Yes."

She sighed. "Did she have an affair while she was still married to you?"

Her father's face remained impassive. "I'd rather not answer that question. Talk to her. She does love you."

Madison crumbled her bread. "Maybe I will."

He picked up his fork and began to eat again. She followed suit, although her appetite was MIA.

"You didn't answer my question about your meeting with Troy," she reminded her father.

He set down his fork again and looked at her. "Because the answer is...I don't know. I told him what I did and saw. I have no idea whether he believed me. And if he didn't, what he can do about it. I can't prove I didn't kill Mitch King, and your detective can't prove I did, because of course I didn't."

Madison nodded, relieved to discover that—of course—she believed him.

"You know he was blackmailing fellow students."

"Troy told me," she agreed warily.

"I was one of them."

"I...suspected. I could hear your bitterness when you talked about him."

"I suppose you wonder what I did that justified blackmail."

Not a question, but she nodded, anyway. Despite the extraordinary nature of this talk, her anger was alive and well. "I've spent a lifetime listening to your lectures on personal standards, on the conduct you expected of me, of how nothing short of perfection was acceptable."

He frowned, and she sensed that she had disconcerted him. "I never said that."

"That was my take."

"Then I'm sorry." When she didn't respond, the muscles of his face seemed to sag. It was as if he aged before her eyes. "I cheated in an advanced English seminar," he said bluntly. "I'd gotten so full of myself, I didn't think I had to work to get the grades. I procrastinated until I had no time left to write a paper with the quality I needed to get an A. So I stole a paper published in an obscure journal." Despite the careful lack of inflection, his tone was dark. "I made a hasty decision to do it, and lived to regret it."

"Because somehow Mitch King found out."

He started to nod, then shook his head. "Because I was disappointed in myself. Shocked, even. Horrified to be caught, yes. Mostly, I discovered I wasn't the man I had believed myself to be, the man I wanted to be. I've tried very hard since to be that man." His mouth twisted. "Too hard, perhaps. The lesson was a harsh one."

"And you wanted to be sure I didn't have to learn it myself."

He watched her closely, as though gauging her reactions. "Yes. I didn't want you to find out what it's like to despise yourself."

"It would have worked better if you'd told me you screwed up. *Why* it mattered so much that you never make that kind of mistake again." She had to say this, if only once. "Instead I was left trying to measure up to a father who presented himself as godlike."

The years settled even more heavily on him. "That was never my intention."

The best she could do was nod. She believed him. Forgiveness was another issue.

But he was also the father who had taken vacation so they could go to Disneyland when it was probably the last thing he wanted to do. He'd at least pretended to have fun so she could.

And poor Dad dealt with her shock and embarrassment when she started getting noticeable breasts well before most of her classmates. A boy had teased her and she'd come home in hysterics. Dad had bravely taken her shopping for her first bra that evening. She was with him when her first period came, too. Mom had prepared her, at least, and made sure she had supplies, but she'd been freaked enough to need to talk to *someone,* and Dad was there. She still remembered him gravely listening, and talking to her about what being a woman meant. He had even told her stories of how his own body had changed, so she knew the boys' points of vulnerability and had some defense against them.

The silence had stretched. Dad's eyes were veiled by his lashes as he slowly turned his wineglass around and around. Madison's heart hurt.

"I love you," she blurted out. "Sometimes I'm mad at you, too, but…I do love you."

His smile held all the complexity of the emotions she struggled with herself, but it was a good smile. Warm. Without giving herself time for second thoughts, Madison stood up and went around the table to hug the difficult man who was her daddy.

He swiveled in his chair and his arms closed around her hard. Despite the awkwardness of her position and the fact that they were in the middle of a restaurant, they stayed like that for a long time.

TROY DIDN'T EXPECT to hear from Madison Friday night, although he would have given a lot for a brief phone call. All she had to say was, *I know it's weird with Dad here, and you probably can't tell me what he said, but...I wanted to hear your voice.* He would have felt better.

But okay, he understood why she didn't call. The situation *was* awkward, given the reason for her father's visit and Troy's adversarial relationship with him. But she didn't call Saturday, either. And that's when he realized he knew exactly what his problem was.

Before, when he'd claimed her father was always there with them, he'd been speaking metaphorically. That had made him uneasy enough. Now, Dad was literally here. In Madison's house. His actual, physical presence had Troy's doubts biting deep. A part of him was thinking, *Crunch time.* Madison had to make a decision.

And the longer the silence continued, the more he feared she had made it already.

Troy finally gritted his teeth late in the morning on Sunday and phoned *her.*

"Oh, hi." Madison sounded less than enthusiastic to hear from him. Imagination? He didn't know. Her voice was low, almost a murmur. "Um...Dad's still here. This isn't a good time."

Troy's eyes narrowed. She hadn't said his name. *So Dad doesn't know who she is talking to?*

"He stayed the whole weekend?"

"Yes. Yesterday we toured wineries and we're just heading out the door to have brunch at Cordray."

Cordray was the fanciest—and priciest—restaurant in

town. Troy hated to think how much even brunch there would run.

"I won't keep you then," he said.

"Dad's been really opening up to me." Nearly whispering, she sounded awed.

He wondered what he was supposed to say to that. *How nice?* When what Troy was thinking was that the timing of Dad making nice was suspicious, given his curiosity about the investigation. Troy wanted to say, yeah, that's great, but why didn't Dad open up to you twenty years ago, when you really needed him? Or even ten years ago?

Angry and frustrated and yes, damn it, jealous, he still managed to clamp his mouth shut. After a minute, he said, "I'm going to be out of town the next day or two."

"Oh?" But she didn't sound very interested. In fact, he heard a murmur, as if she'd momentarily covered the phone. "Listen, I really have to go now," she said into the phone.

Troy had to work to get any words past the ball in his throat. "See you" seemed enough. He ended the call without waiting for a response. Small of him, but, goddamn it, his hands were shaking.

His worst fears had just come true. With Daddy here, "opening up" to her, Troy might as well not exist. He hadn't heard even a hint that she'd missed him, had been thinking about him. Nothing.

He'd been afraid all along that he couldn't compete with the asshole of a father who filled her world.

So now I know.

Despite everything, Troy was stunned. Sick. Hurting.

After talking to Madison, he went out to his garage-studio with the intention of sitting down at the wheel for the first time in weeks. But instead he looked blindly around and knew he wouldn't throw any pieces worth firing.

For the first time, he got a genuine glimmer of what his mother had been going through, why Dad's death had completely wrecked her. Grief was one thing; this was something else. If a buddy, devastated by a breakup, had said to him, "I can't live without her," he would have considered it romantic drivel.

He felt as if he'd been in a car accident, was in shock but had somehow stumbled out of the car. The pain would hit any minute. Right now, the worst was the disbelief.

Even with all his recent doubts, he had believed Madison loved him, too. Underneath the fear had been a completely unjustified faith that they were meant for each other.

Troy walked back into the house and straight to the refrigerator. A beer or two or six sounded real good right now.

Mom, he thought, *I am so sorry. Now I get it.*

He tossed his phone on the kitchen counter and carried the first two bottles out to the patio.

HE FELT LIKE shit the next morning when he boarded a twenty-seat commuter plane that took him to Walla Walla, where he caught a flight on a slightly larger plane to Boise.

There was a good reason why he rarely drank alcohol, aside from the example his parents had set and the fact that he hated feeling out of control. He also didn't metabolize it well and got hangovers.

Wouldn't you know, the airplane bounced and bucked over scattered cumulus clouds like a ride at the county fair, making his stomach lurch. Even at his best, Troy wasn't a fan of flying. His fingers dug into the armrests and he braced his feet on the floor, as if that would do any good if they went down. He closed his eyes, then slitted them to verify that there actually was a puke bag in the slot on the back of the seat in front of him. Then he shut his eyes again and endured.

The airplane bounced a couple of times on the runway, too, an appropriate ending to a flight he'd rather not have taken. Head throbbing, stomach rolling, he exited the plane and headed straight for the car rental place.

Troy made himself stop for lunch before bearding Margaret Berlongieri Chaffee in her place of business. A sandwich settled his stomach enough for him to tolerate a couple of ibuprofen for the headache. At this point, he wasn't letting himself think about Madison.

Who had finally left a timid message last night.

"I'm sorry I couldn't talk this morning. It was sort of a strange weekend, but good. Um, I don't think you said where you were going." Her voice had become more and more hesitant. "Well, I guess I'll wait until you call."

When hell freezes over, he'd thought, his mood savage. *She guesses she'll wait?* He guessed she'd eventually get the point when he *didn't* call.

And yeah, Troy knew his behavior wasn't very mature, and probably he'd get over it, convince himself he'd misinterpreted her end of that last conversation and call. Because he was pathetically in love.

But right now, he had a job to do.

He parked and walked into the hospital where Ms. Chaffee worked in the business office. He showed his badge and asked to speak to her. Wide-eyed, the receptionist scuttled away and a moment later a rather plump woman with improbably red hair emerged from one of the small offices. Radiating shock and dismay, she hurried forward.

"You!" She turned her head sharply when the receptionist returned. Her eyes were so dilated, he'd have suspected a head injury if he hadn't known better.

"I'm Detective Troyer," he agreed. "It's not very private in here." The offices were little better than cubicles. "I saw a coffee place across the street."

After a moment she nodded jerkily. She collected her purse and excused herself to the now avidly curious receptionist.

The coffee shop was empty enough; they had it almost to themselves. It wasn't a Starbucks, but otherwise the ambiance wasn't that different from the coffee shop in Seattle where he'd sat down with Sally Yee.

This time he ordered an iced chai tea, Margaret one of those frothy sweet drinks that were really desserts laced with caffeine.

They sat at the back and looked at each other. Troy saw a woman who looked her age and maybe a little more. He wondered if she really was a redhead. She was buxom, which would have appealed to a womanizer like Stephen Coleman.

"I thought I made it clear I didn't want to talk to you." Margaret's voice shook with the force of her emotions.

"You'd be better off if you'd said, 'yes, I saw Sally Yee and was so embarrassed I ran away, so I don't know what else I can tell you,'" he said mildly. "I'm afraid you made me curious, Ms. Chaffee."

"I don't understand why." Her stare was defiant, but the fear was there in her hazel eyes. "I never went into the gym. I *did* run away."

"Did you know Mr. Coleman's previous lover had been another student?"

After a moment she shook her head dumbly.

"But when you saw Ms. Yee, you understood."

She bent her head and looked down at her cup. "Yes."

Where the hell was this going? His instincts told him she was telling the truth—she hadn't gone into McKenna. So what could she possibly have seen or done that, thirty-five years later, she still didn't want to say out loud?

"What did Mr. Coleman do once you pulled away?" Troy asked.

"He called after me, but I didn't stop."

"Did he follow you?" Hell, maybe this wasn't about Mitch King at all. Had the bastard raped this woman?

She shook her head, still not looking at him.

"Did he go on into the gym?"

Her answer was almost inaudible. "Yes."

"You're sure?"

A nod.

He filed that away. Why had no one seen Stephen Coleman once he entered the building?

Chance. Killers got lucky, like anyone else.

Refocusing on Margaret, he thought, *Okay. Now what?*

"When did you hear about the murder?"

"The next morning at breakfast." She didn't mind telling him that. "Everybody in line at the cafeteria was talking about it."

"Did you know Mitchell King?"

"I sort of knew who he was."

She'd been a sophomore, he recalled from his notes. No reason she would have gotten to know a senior. Unless, of course, she'd been a blackmail victim. Troy didn't believe she was, though; if anything, she'd relaxed subtly when he asked about her relationship with King. She felt safe there. So whatever had her wound so tight wasn't personal between her and this mostly unknown senior.

"Did you have a final that morning?"

She visibly tightened up again as she shook her head.

She really, *really* didn't want to meet his eyes, which intrigued Troy.

"What did you do after breakfast?"

For a long time, she didn't move. Maybe a minute passed, second by second. And then she did lift her head, and he saw torment in her eyes. He was careful not to move a muscle.

"I went to see Stephen. I knew where he lived. I'd... been there." Shame stained her cheeks, but her voice was growing stronger. "I thought...maybe I had misunderstood Sally's reaction."

"Where did he live, Ms. Chaffee?"

She named a street and he nodded. "It was only a couple of blocks from my dorm."

"Was he home when you got there?"

"I didn't think so at first." All the misery her youthful self had felt was there on her face and in her voice, but something else now, too. Resolution, and maybe relief. "Then I smelled smoke."

He must have twitched. Or maybe something happened to his expression because she flinched, retreating until her back must have been pressing painfully against the hard chair.

"From his chimney?" Troy asked, as if merely curious.

Margaret eyed him warily for a moment, then shook her head. "It seemed to be coming...over the house. So I went around and saw him in the backyard. He had a rake in his hand, but he wasn't burning that much. It was weird because, you know, it was almost Christmas. I mean, the leaves would have long since fallen. And the smoke smelled funny. I remember gagging."

"Did you look closely at the fire?"

"I think he was burning clothes," she said flatly.

"When he saw you, how did he react?"

"He seemed crazy. His hair was standing on end and his eyes were wild. It was like he'd slept in his clothes. He said, 'What are you doing here?' in a rude voice."

She was staring into the past. Troy had seen people like this before, reliving an experience they had suppressed for too long. He was careful to speak softly, not to make any big movements.

"Did you ask him about the night before?"

"First I said, 'What was that with Sally Yee?' And he said nothing, as if he didn't know what had gotten into me. I asked what he was burning and he said it was trash and none of my business." Her eyes focused suddenly, intense and burning, on Troy. "I said, 'Did you hear about Mitchell King? You didn't have anything to do with it, did you? Like see what happened, or…'" She swallowed. "He started yelling at me—was I nuts, how could I even say something like that? And I clapped a hand over my mouth because the smoke had drifted my way and I gagged. Then I noticed his shoes. They were white athletic shoes, I think pretty new, and they were splashed with something I at first thought was paint, but it was a rust color."

"Did he lay a hand on you?"

She shook her head. "I got scared and turned and ran." Tears sparkled in her eyes. "I was in love with him," she said so quietly he had to lean forward to hear her. "I told myself what I saw couldn't be what I thought it was. I think I almost believed it."

"Did you continue your relationship with him?"

Shame-faced, she shook her head. "I withdrew from his class the next semester. I avoided him and never talked to him again. I talked to my parents about changing colleges, but I couldn't tell them why and they patted me and said look what good grades you're getting, of course you don't want to leave. When I got back that fall for my junior year, I heard he was gone. I was so relieved."

Troy smiled at her. "You have been an enormous help, Ms. Chaffee. Thank you for having the courage to tell me this."

"He did it, didn't he? He killed Mitchell King."

"I think it's possible he did," Troy said carefully. "I will need corroborating evidence that may be impossible to find, however. But yes. I also think you were very smart to run that morning."

Her breath hitched. "I should have told."

He didn't have to say, *Yes, you should have.* It wasn't necessary. She knew.

"Why did he do it? He was a *professor.* And Mitchell King was only a student."

Troy told her about the blackmail scheme, and her expression became even more stricken. "The whole thing happened because of *me?*"

"No. It happened because of him." Troy let his voice grow hard. "Coleman preyed on female students. You weren't the first, or probably even the second or third. You were a kid. Nineteen years old."

"Eighteen." Her smile twisted. "I graduated high school a year early."

"Do you have children? A daughter?"

"Two, in their twenties."

"What if you'd found out one of them was sleeping with a professor?"

Her mouth tightened. "I'd cut off his balls."

Troy grinned at her. "I repeat—not your fault. It was his, and to some extent it was Mitch King's, because he was a predator, too."

He watched as she processed his words and accepted them. Finally, she nodded. When he asked whether she would testify if it became necessary, Margaret Bergonieri Chaffee, now older and wiser, said, "Yes."

TROY CALLED CHIEF Helmer from the airport and told him what he'd learned.

"Well, damn." There was a pause. "Proving it…" the chief said thoughtfully, "that's another story."

"There might be traces in the soil where he burned the clothes and the ledger."

They both knew how unlikely that was.

"You'll go talk to him?"

"Oh, yeah," Troy said grimly. "Tomorrow."

"This was a very cold case. I didn't really think you could do it," Helmer told him. "You've done a hell of a job, Troyer."

Troy hardly noticed the turbulence on the flight to Portland.

CHAPTER SEVENTEEN

"TROY?" MADISON'S VOICE was dignified but somehow… diminished. "Will you tell me what's wrong?" That was all she said. Her message was the only one in Troy's voice mail, which he checked as he walked from the gate to the board that listed Portland hotels.

He knew he should call her, but he was weary to the bone. It was lucky he'd brought a duffel bag with a change of clothes in case he had to overnight in Boise. As it was, he'd stay at an airport hotel in Portland, then catch the first morning flight to Medford. He hoped like hell Coleman hadn't suddenly jumped ship, but he was still listed among the faculty of the two-year Rogue Community College.

After checking into the closest hotel, Troy ate a late dinner at a chain restaurant, then returned to his room to shower and lay in bed with the intention of plotting his strategy for breaking Coleman once they were face-to-face. Usually, at this point in a case, he would be consumed by a fierce sense of satisfaction that the pieces were all coming together.

Instead, all he could think about was Madison.

He knew he'd overreacted to being sidelined by her, but he couldn't seem to get past the hurt. At the same time, he was ashamed to know he was responsible for whatever she'd been feeling earlier when she left that message. The longer he thought about it, the more ashamed he was. What was he, one of those possessive jerks who was jealous of his woman's friends and family because she was supposed to be entirely focused on *him?*

God, he hoped not. He didn't think he'd ever felt jealous in his life before. And yes, he thought, he would like to believe that he could heal some of her insecurities. Love her enough she'd *know* she was lovable. But he'd been a fool.

He loved his mother. There were times she'd have to come first, and he knew Madison would understand. So why hadn't *he* understood that this was one of those times she had needed to treasure the rare experience of a weekend with her father?

He groaned, punched the pillow and wadded it up under his head.

Because, where she was concerned, *he* was insecure. He really didn't know whether she felt as much for him as he did for her. The answer was that simple. If they'd both said "I love you" and he believed her, Troy wouldn't have had any problem with a single distracted phone call or a few days of silence when she had family visiting. There wouldn't have been any trouble understanding why, under the circumstances, she wanted to avoid the awkwardness of talking to him while her father was there.

As he lay looking at the streetlights leaking in around the drapes, a lot of things came together in his head. He'd been telling himself jealousy was a foreign emotion to him, but he remembered the time Madison had suggested he *was* jealous because his mother was so utterly focused on her loss, she seemed to have forgotten her son. He'd known then she was right, and had let her prod him into moving past that unacknowledged resentment to be the son his mother needed.

What he hadn't done was understand that, maybe, he'd always felt a little excluded by his parents' intense love for each other.

Troy groaned again and laid a forearm over his face. Was that why he and Dad so often saw each other during the day, separate from Mom? Had he suggested lunch so often, not because it was simply convenient, but because he was hungry to have his father all to himself?

His chest filled with a whole lot of complicated and not very comfortable feelings. How could something so obvious have passed under his radar? *Because I didn't want to know?* Yeah, had to be. Because now he was smacked in the face by the truth. While he'd felt loved and supported by his parents, he'd also known he wasn't essential to either of them, not in the way they were to each other.

Yes, he wanted a marriage as committed as theirs, as passionate, as happy—but he was going to be damn sure his kids never felt left out.

There was a real irony in discovering that he was as screwed up about his parents as Madison was about hers, and her excuse was a hell of a lot better.

Man, he wished he was home. That he could drop by her office tomorrow morning to persuade her to take a break and go for a walk with him or out for a coffee. He wanted in the worst way to say, "I'm sorry." To ask what her father had told her, whether she'd resolved any of her issues with him.

He grunted aloud. He wanted to give her what she needed from him, which right now might simply be understanding. So why had he been thinking only about himself and what *he* needed from her? Why hadn't he'd learned his lesson when he had discovered his mother did need him and that he'd been letting her down?

I'm better than that, he thought, and hoped it was true.

In person, Stephen Coleman didn't look anything like the photo Troy had seen of him in a Wakefield College alumni magazine published back when he'd taught there. A weight lifter then, he'd let his muscles go to fat. He had to be carrying an extra hundred pounds or more on a large frame. Drooping bags under his eyes changed the contours of his face. The beard was familiar but graying, and Troy suspected it now was grown to hide the jowls.

After calling, "Come in," Coleman half stood from his chair behind the desk in his faculty office, but when he realized Troy was a stranger he froze halfway. "I was expecting a student." The chair creaked as it accepted his weight when he sank back down. "What can I do for you?"

Remaining on his feet, Troy took his badge from his belt and held it out. He watched as a flush crept up Coleman's neck to his cheeks.

"Frenchman Lake P.D." Coleman sounded hoarse. "Why would you want to talk to me?"

"We've reopened the investigation into the murder of Mitchell King." Troy paused. "You do remember Mr. King?"

Coleman seemed unaware of the beads of sweat that had popped out on his forehead. "No one who was there then could forget." His eyes met Troy's with clear reluctance. "That doesn't explain why you're here. I never even had him in a class, as I'm sure you can verify."

Troy had decided to apply pressure early and hard. Seeing the physical manifestations of fear confirmed his instinct.

"I have reason to believe King was blackmailing you, Mr. Coleman. And you had reason to pay him—until you could think of another way to get him off your back."

"What in the hell are you talking about?" Coleman shoved his chair back and lumbered to his feet. "Why would I pay him a penny?"

"Because you believed his threat. If you hadn't paid

him, you would have lost your job and you knew it. What's more, it would have been hard to get hired anywhere else, wouldn't it, Mr. Coleman?"

"I don't know what you're accusing me of...."

"Colleges take it quite seriously when professors abuse a position of power to have sexual relations with their students." Troy kept his voice hard and didn't try to hide his contempt. "I have spoken with two of those students, Sally Yee and Margaret Berlongieri. Both were frank about their relationships with you."

Sweat trickled down Coleman's face. It must have burned his eyes, because he swiped his forearm across his forehead. "You're crazy."

"No. And I'll tell you why I'm here, Mr. Coleman. I came all this way so that you could tell me what you were burning in your backyard the morning after Mitch King was bludgeoned to death. So brutally his killer must have been splashed with blood. And let's not forget about the ledger he carried everywhere. That was probably soaked in blood, but the writing still would have been legible. I think police would have been able to read the names of his victims, don't you?"

"Jesus, Jesus." Coleman stumbled backward, striking a shoulder against a bookcase, staggering so that he had to reach out to steady himself.

Troy took a couple of steps around the desk, just enough to be intimidating. "I suspect the killer's shoes were splattered with blood, too." He gave that a minute to sink in. "I believe Ms. Berlongieri described them as 'rusty splotches.'"

The big man had begun to shake. He backed toward the window. "She didn't see anything. She was a stupid little bitch who imagined she was in love with me. I was burning trash, that's all. Trash!" he howled.

The door opened behind Troy. "Mr. Coleman?"

Troy half turned, not taking his eyes off Coleman, who was big enough to be dangerous if he went on the offensive.

"This is a private meeting," he said coolly.

"Oh," the timid voice said. "I'm sorry, I, well, I thought…" The door clicked shut. Footsteps rapidly receded.

"Trash," Troy said softly to the bastard who'd murdered Mitchell King to hide his own unforgivable transgressions. "Trash that smelled really bad when it was burning. Bad enough to make that young woman gag. Acrid, maybe, the way bloody clothing would smell when it was on fire."

"Her word doesn't mean anything." The defiance in his voice was a spark, nothing more. Easily stamped out.

Or drowned. Troy had never seen anyone sweat that much. Coleman's beefy face was shining with it. He'd need a towel to mop it up.

"Oh, it's plenty adequate to justify a warrant. She recalls exactly where that fire burned in your backyard, Mr. Coleman. We'll have our own little archaeological dig. Any scraps of the clothing—assuming it was cotton—will probably have decomposed, but leather endures surprisingly well. The soles of those athletic shoes will definitely have survived." He shook his head. "The metal rings holding the pages of the ledger together. I think it's real likely we'll find all kinds of bits and pieces once we start digging. You really should have burned that bloody clothing somewhere else, Mr. Coleman."

He turned and punched the wall, once, twice, three times. Going right through the wallboard, slamming knuckles against a stud, seemingly unaware of the pain. And then he swung around, fixing eyes that burned with soul-deep despair and fury on Troy.

The next second, Coleman charged, those raw knuckles flying. He was howling again, this time wordlessly.

Even though Troy dodged, a fist struck his shoulder and he lurched into the wall. Coleman had crashed into the door, turning with shocking speed to come at Troy again.

Troy leaped behind the desk. "Goddamn it, *think!* I'm a police officer!"

The desk shuddered and the huge man came around it. *I'm going to get the shit beaten out of me,* Troy thought incredulously. The quarters were too close for him to risk pulling his gun.

Troy spun away, knocking the chair to one side, then went on the offensive. Using his shoulder to slam into his oncoming opponent came naturally, even though he hadn't played football in years.

The force of his hit made Coleman expel all his air in a long "oof." He was still on his feet, though, coming at Troy again. This time Troy deliberately let one of those fists connect so he could get his own forearm up and into the other man's throat. Hard. He slammed Coleman backward into the wall. Books fell from shelves and a picture frame shattered on the floor. Troy stared into the beet-red face now wet with tears and snot as well as the copiously running sweat.

"You are under arrest for assaulting a police officer, Mr. Coleman. Not smart. Not smart at all."

Stephen Coleman folded in on himself. That was the only way to describe it. One minute he was staring, vibrating with fury and fear, the next bewilderment overtook him. His legs gave way. Troy had to step back and let him fall. He landed heavily on his knees.

"You don't understand," he whispered.

Troy used his forearm to wipe blood off his face. "What don't I understand?"

"He wanted more money. He laughed at me and said, 'You'll give me whatever I want, won't you, *Stephen?*'" Even now, the mimicry of the way Mitch King had said his name was stunningly nasty. It said, *I've got you, a high-and-mighty professor, right in my hand, and I can squeeze if I want.*

Mitch King had finally miscalculated how much pressure he could apply. In his pleasure at humiliating a professor, he had underestimated the man and how much he had at stake.

None of which justified what Coleman had done to him.

"Were you carrying a weapon when you went to talk to him in the sauna that night?"

Swaying, Coleman shook his head. "I brought my payment. He wouldn't take it. That's when he said he was doubling his charge. He was still laughing when I turned and walked out. I knew where the rack of equipment was. The student who should have been behind the counter wasn't there. I grabbed a bat and went back. He looked so surprised when I opened the door and started swinging."

The last thing Troy wanted to do was interrupt this, but he felt compelled to say, "You do know you have the right to remain silent. You have the right to an attorney. We can stop this conversation until you have one."

"What difference does it make?" he said dully. Still on his knees, he swayed as if barely able to hold himself upright. "Look what he did to my life. I was brilliant, you know. I could have been at Harvard by now, instead of this. Every single night, I dream about him. He haunts me. Forget Mitchell King?" Coleman began to laugh, and it was a long time before he began choking and quit. "I haven't been able to forget him for a single minute. I would have kept paying him, you know." Coleman had been brought down, shattered. His expression pleaded for understanding. "If only he hadn't asked for more."

Troy shook his head and dialed 911.

NOT UNTIL TROY ended the Sunday morning call so abruptly did Madison realize he was upset with her. She immediately had the awful, sinking realization that he hadn't known her father had decided to stay for the whole weekend. He must have assumed she'd ignored him since Friday because she was mad about how he'd treated Dad. And then what did she do but seem completely uninterested in him when he phoned her!

I am an idiot, she thought, wanting only to call him back immediately. But her dad was waiting impatiently, they had reservations at the restaurant, and she needed privacy when she talked to Troy anyway.

But after Dad left midafternoon and she finally had a chance to call Troy, he didn't answer. Unlike most people, he never went anywhere without his phone. He once told her that it was the most important tool he carried for his job.

He might be in the middle of an interview, she tried to convince herself.

Uh-huh. On Sunday afternoon?

Okay, maybe he was with his mother.

The alternative was that he'd glanced at the screen, seen she was the caller and muted the ring. As in, he didn't want to talk to her.

No! She didn't believe it.

Maybe she should have left a message, but he must check to see what calls he's missed, right? Madison hated the anxiety that gripped her as she debated calling again, leaving a message, or... *Or what?*

Finally she couldn't stand it any longer and did call

again. Still no answer, but this time she waited for his prompt and started talking.

"I'm sorry I couldn't talk this morning. It was sort of a strange weekend, but good. Um, I don't think you said where you were going." Oh, God, what did she say now? "Well, I guess I'll wait until you call." She winced, thinking how lame that had sounded, and hastily ended the call.

Her phone didn't ring all evening. Or the next day. There were calls at the office, but none on her mobile phone. She checked it half a dozen times to make sure it still had battery life.

By evening, she was mad. Troy hadn't said the words *I love you* but he'd made her think he did. And then what? Did he think she shouldn't have let her father stay with her? She had absolutely no idea. She kept thinking back to when he said her father was always in the room with them. He couldn't possibly resent her for spending time with Dad, could he? If so, well, then he was a jerk and she didn't care if she ever heard from him again.

By morning, mad segued into worried and even scared. Where had he gone? He must have found more people to talk to. About Dad? Oh, dear God, what if he'd *arrested* her father? No, Dad would have let her know, surely.

What if something had happened to Troy? He was a police officer, at high risk of getting hurt or even being killed. Would anyone let *her* know?

But there was no way she was embarrassing him or herself by calling the police station to check up on him. His mother? She shuddered at the thought. He hadn't even introduced the two of them.

I could leave another message.

Pathetic.

When he finally did call, wouldn't you know she had been in the shower and didn't hear the phone ring. Once she was dressed, she compulsively checked the screen and learned there was one new message.

"Hey," he said. His voice sounded a little strange. Thicker than usual. "I just got back in town. I was hoping to see you. Uh…I'm at home. Call me."

Not a little strange, Madison decided. A lot strange. Her eardrums seemed to shiver with the beat of her heart. *It's Dad.* Troy must have found evidence that he thought proved her father's guilt. No wonder he hadn't wanted to talk to her, to tell her. Considering their relationship, those words would be hard for him to say.

I'm sorry. I have to arrest your father for murder.

She stood stock still in her kitchen, absorbing his message, then snatched up her purse and raced out of the house. She had to see him. Otherwise she had a very bad feeling Troy would distance himself to save her from… Him? Or did he assume she'd hate him?

Oh, God. She'd given him enough reason to think she would. Be honest—she hadn't known herself how she'd feel if it came down to it.

Now she did.

Maybe they *shouldn't* have gotten involved. Maybe her first instinct had been right, but it was too late now. She didn't know if she could bear it if Troy was working his way up to ending things with her for *any* reason.

She found his block but wasn't positive she'd have known which town house was his if his SUV hadn't been parked in front. Madison pulled in behind it and barely remembered to turn off the engine before she hurried up the walk. Not until she was on his doorstep did she feel a thump of fear. What if she saw dismay on his face when he opened the door and saw her?

No. Stupid. Why would he? He'd called, hadn't he?

She rang the bell and heard it on the other side of the

door. It wasn't more than thirty seconds before the door opened. Troy appeared with bare feet, wearing nothing but faded, clay-stained jeans that hung low on his hips. His hair was disheveled. And—oh God—he *had* been injured. His right cheek was red, scraped and swollen, and his mouth on that side was swollen, too, making him look askew.

"Madison?"

"Oh, my God!" she whispered. "What happened to you?"

He lifted a hand self-consciously to his face. "I got punched. It's not a big deal. I barely felt it then. I'll look better by morning."

Aghast, she stared at him. "Who punched you?"

"Ah...long story. That's one of the things I wanted to talk to you about."

Aware she was still standing on his doorstep and he hadn't invited her in, she said awkwardly, "I got your message."

His expression changed, became warier. Or maybe she was misreading it, given the way the swelling changed his features.

"I...take it you have something to say."

"Yes, I do."

He shook his head and stepped back. "Sorry. Come in."

She walked past him. "Were you working on your wheel?"

"What?" He glanced down at himself. "Oh. No. Just showered and threw on the most comfortable jeans I could find. Let me go grab a shirt."

Madison wanted to say, *Not on my account,* but didn't. She loved looking at his chest, but it might be easier to talk if she didn't want so desperately to touch him.

He left her in the living room and loped up the stairs,

returning a minute later wearing a T-shirt as faded as the jeans. "Coffee? Tea?"

She shook her head, wishing he'd take her in his arms. After a moment, she set down her purse on a side table and faced him.

"You were mad at me on Sunday."

"Yeah." A muscle on his jaw twitched. "It was dumb. I got my feelings hurt. But it doesn't matter now. I'm sorry."

He said that so simply, her heart cramped.

"I didn't mean to hurt your feelings. I let myself get excited because Dad really seemed to want to spend time with me, to talk to me and to listen. I said things I should have told him years ago." She tried for a smile. "The fact that I could is thanks to you, you know. You…made me realize I deserve better than the way he treats me sometimes. He told me what he was being blackmailed for, and it made me sick."

Troy took a step toward her. "It wasn't that bad."

"He convinced me he was perfect." That was what she couldn't get past. "But I'm not, so I never felt I could measure up." She shook her head. "But you've heard all that, and you know what? I'm glad Dad and I talked, and that I understand him a little better, but I'm done obsessing about it. You were right. I was letting how I felt about him be a lot more important than it is anymore. I mean, I love him, but my life isn't about him. I'm good at my job, and I like myself, and, well, I didn't come to talk about my father."

Troy gave a low, rough laugh. "That isn't quite what I expected."

"What did you expect?" she had the courage to ask.

He only shook his head. "Come here."

She moved, he moved, and the next instant they were holding each other. The horrible tension Madison had been living with disappeared in the huge relief of being able to lean against Troy, feel the strength of his embrace, the heat of his body, his breath ruffling her hair.

"We should sit down," he said finally, and when she nodded he guided her to the leather sofa. He didn't let her go, keeping her tucked under his arm. After a minute he tilted his head so he could see her face. "There's something I need to tell you."

"Can I finish first? In case…" She didn't want to speak those words out loud: *in case you're going to say, "I have to arrest your father."*

Troy nodded.

"Dad told me what happened that night, how Mitchell King was already dead and Dad saw his body." She didn't wait for Troy's face to change, to become cop-guarded. Instead she hurried on. "I believe him, but I know maybe you don't."

"Madison…"

She laid her fingers across his lips. Gently, not wanting to hurt him. "Not yet. Please?"

A smile seemed to twitch at his mouth, swollen as it was. He nodded again.

She took a deep breath and talked really fast. "What I came to say is, whatever happens with Dad won't change how I feel about you."

Troy quit moving at all. He couldn't possibly even be breathing. All he did was stare at her, his eyes made more shockingly turbulent in contrast to his complete stillness.

"How do you feel about me?" he asked, voice hoarse.

Her fingernails bit into her palms. "I'm in love with you. You have to know that."

For a moment his lashes veiled those intense eyes. "I… wasn't sure."

When he didn't say anything else, she stiffened. "You must be tired if you just got home. I won't stay. I only came because I didn't want you to feel…I don't know, worse if you still suspect my father."

She didn't make it to her feet. Troy's grip on her arm stopped her.

"You think I'm letting you get away after that?" The vibrancy in his voice and the smile that lifted one side of his mouth—the uninjured side—healed her hurt instantly. "I love you, Madison. God, I've been so afraid you didn't feel the same." The smile was gone. He sounded shaken. "I thought, if it came down to it, you'd choose your father."

Suddenly tongue-tied, she shook her head.

"Will you marry me? Whatever happens?"

She felt as if something were breaking inside. It was as if a giant dam had cracked and then split up, and the huge flood of emotions were free to tumble out. It should have been painful, but instead the experience was glorious.

"Yes. Oh, yes!"

Troy groaned and bent to rest his forehead against hers. Smile shaking, she lifted a hand and slid it around his neck to his nape. She squeezed, and finally bumped her nose against his, nuzzling. He did the same.

"I want to kiss you, but, uh, I'm not in such good shape for that."

Her giggle felt like a champagne bubble popping. "I noticed. But, you know, I bet we could make love without kissing." A thought occurred to her. "Unless…" She pulled back. "Are you hurt anywhere else?"

"A few bruises." There was that tilted smile again. "There's nothing stopping *you* from kissing them. I'll bet you could make me feel a lot better."

"I will." Her rational brain had started functioning

again at the thought of his big body being battered. "But first, I'd like to know what happened."

"Ah." Troy's eyes gleamed with what she swore was triumph. He started to grin, winced and cupped his cheek. "I arrested the man who murdered Mitch King. He didn't go quietly."

Madison sat back, gaping. "What?"

"You heard me." It was obvious how much he wanted to smile. "It's over, Madison. And no, I didn't arrest your father."

The air whooshed out of her. "Who?"

"Stephen Coleman."

Weirdly, she didn't recall the name. She would have sworn she'd recognize the name of every single student who'd been at Wakefield then.

"He was a professor." Troy kept talking, telling her every step that had led to his conclusion. Professor Wilson mentioning his name. Sally Yee. Margaret Berlongieri Chaffee. And finally, that morning's violent confrontation with Coleman himself.

"He said 'Mitch King ruined my life,' and it's true, in a way." He shook his head. "It's never easy seeing someone completely break down. He told me he grabbed the first available job, thinking if he left Wakefield right away he could put what he'd done behind him, but it's not that easy. I talked to many people who learned a lesson after King caught them in whatever petty offense they'd committed. They didn't like him, but after all this time they were able to shrug because they had consciously set out to be better people after that."

Madison frowned. "Dad said something like that."

"If Coleman could have walked away…" Troy shook his head. "But I doubt he could, for a lot of reasons. He hadn't been caught doing one dumb thing. He'd likely been preying on female students since he was a grad student. I can't believe Sally Yee was the first, or Margaret was the last. I suspect he did the same after he left Wakefield."

"He couldn't stop."

"No, and didn't want to. He didn't have enough conscience to believe he was doing anything wrong. When Mitch King dug his hooks into Coleman, he had way more at stake than anyone else I talked to. He wouldn't have just lost his job, his career would have been dead in the water. But probably he would have kept paying until King graduated and moved on to bigger and better things. It was King who made the mistake, deciding he could turn the screws a little more, not for the money but because he enjoyed doing it. So then Stephen Coleman finally did do something that was completely impulsive. While he was filled with rage, he grabbed a baseball bat and beat Mitchell King to death." Troy took her hand, holding it as if he needed the connection. "And then he had to live with what he'd done."

"Dad horrified himself because he'd cheated in a class. Once. Having to remember yourself slamming the bat into someone's head…" Shuddering, Madison didn't like to think about it.

"Over and over and over. And then he had to have the presence of mind to scoop up the ledger, wrap it in a towel that was probably bloody and get himself carrying that bat out of the building without anyone seeing him. He was bloody, too. He went home, showered and gathered everything that had blood on it, wrapped it up and waited until morning to burn it. He was afraid the fire would draw more attention in the dark. He saw it as his bad luck that Margaret came by. He'd have still been okay, but somehow he hadn't realized his athletic shoes had gotten spattered, too. He said his head was filled with this roar that wouldn't let him think. It wasn't until Margaret stared at his shoes that he saw the blood on them, too. After she ran away, he ripped them off and threw them on the fire. He convinced himself that he was safe once everything incriminating was nothing but ashes. His real luck was that she still imagined herself in love with him, enough that it was a long time before she really let herself confront the knowledge that he was probably the murderer. And then she thought it was too late. Would anyone even believe her?"

Madison held his hand tightly. "You did."

"But she didn't come to me out of the blue with her story. I tracked her down because I had good reason to suspect him of being the killer."

"I wish you'd called me."

"I couldn't have told you anyway, not until I arrested him."

"Did you bring him back with you?"

"No, it's not that easy to transfer someone under arrest from one state to another. He's in jail in Medford. It may take weeks to get him up here."

"Does everyone know now?" she thought to ask.

"It'll hit the papers tomorrow. Chief Helmer called your college president late this afternoon. You'd probably already left the office."

"You're a hero." She smiled, but she had a lump in her throat. "Think how relieved your father would have been to know."

"Yeah." He cleared his throat. "That occurred to me." He hesitated. "There's no reason you can't call your dad if you want and tell him."

"I will." For no good reason, Madison had tears in her eyes. "Later. Right now, I think I'd like to kiss you everywhere you hurt."

Half a smile could still be plenty wicked. "And maybe a few places that don't?"

She tucked herself back into his arms and whispered, "Oh, definitely a few that don't."

* * * * *

If you liked this WAKEFIELD COLLEGE *novel,*
look for the next book set here by Janice Kay Johnson!
From this Day On will be available August 2013
from Harlequin Superromance.

COMING NEXT MONTH FROM

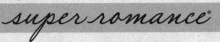

HARLEQUIN®

superromance®

Available June 4, 2013

#1854 HIS UPTOWN GIRL by Liz Talley

For the first time since Hurricane Katrina, Dez Batiste is in New Orleans. But he's not here to play jazz—his music left him when the levees broke. Then he encounters Eleanor Theriot—a woman too rich for him—and suddenly his muse starts whispering in his ear again.

#1855 A TIME FOR US • *The Texas Firefighters*
by Amy Knupp

Grief is the cruelest form of guilt. Especially for Dr. Rachel Culver and her complicated feelings for her dead twin's fiancé. The attraction to Cale Jackson is wrong—she knows that—but he's also helping her cope. And the more they're together... Well, maybe they can heal each other.

#1856 THE FATHER OF HER SON
by Kathleen Pickering

Evan McKenna has never had to work this hard to get a woman to go out with him! The only guy Kelly Sullivan pays attention to is her young son. Lucky for Evan he's buddies with him and that friendship just might be the way to this single mom's heart.

#1857 ONCE A CHAMPION • *The Montana Way*
by Jeannie Watt

Matt Montoya longs to be a champion again. Not only has the tie-down roper suffered a crippling knee injury, he can't reclaim his former glory without his best rope horse. But Liv Bailey, who tutored Matt in high school, is Beckett's new owner—and she won't give him back!

#1858 A WALK DOWN THE AISLE
A Valley Ridge Wedding • by Holly Jacobs

Sophie Johnston and Colton McCray are about to say "I do" when chaos erupts. Take two people who are perfect for each other, add one shocking guest with a wild objection, mix with a pack of well-meaning friends and there's no way they can't find their way back to love!

#1859 JUST FOR TODAY... by Emmie Dark

Jess Alexander won't see him again, so what's the harm in spending one night with Sean Patterson? After all, she deserves some fun after the hurt caused by her ex. But when Sean shows up at her door offering a temporary dating deal, she can't resist his one-day-at-a-time offer....

YOU CAN FIND MORE INFORMATION ON UPCOMING HARLEQUIN® TITLES, FREE EXCERPTS AND MORE AT WWW.HARLEQUIN.COM.

HSRCNM0513

SPECIAL EXCERPT FROM

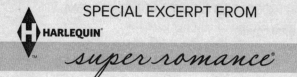

HARLEQUIN

superromance

His Uptown Girl

By Liz Talley

It's time for Eleanor Theriot to get back into the
dating scene. And now a friend has dared her
to chat up the gorgeous guy who's standing
across the street! How can she resist that dare?
Read on for an exciting excerpt
of the upcoming book

She could do this. Taking a deep breath, Eleanor Theriot
stepped out of her shop onto Magazine Street. She shut the
door behind her, gave it a little tug, then slapped a hand to her
forehead and patted her pockets.

Damn, she was a good actress. Anyone watching would
definitely think she'd locked herself out.

Hopefully that included Mr. Hunky Painter Dude, whom
she intended to ask out. Like on a date.

She started toward him. The closer she got, the hotter—and
younger—the guy looked.

This was stupid. He was out of her league.

Too hot for her.

Too young for her.

She needed to abandon this whole ruse. It was dumb to

pretend to be locked out simply to talk to the man. Then he lifted his head and caught her gaze.

Oh, dear Lord. Eyes the color of smoke swept over her. That look wasn't casual or dismissive. Oddly enough, his gaze felt…profound.

Or maybe she needed to drink less coffee. She had to be imagining a connection between them.

Now that she was standing in front of him, though, she had to see this ridiculous plan through. She licked her lips, wishing she'd put on the lip gloss. Not only did she feel stupid, but her lips were bare. Eleanor the Daring was appalled by Eleanor the Unprepared who had shown up in her stead.

"Hey, I'm Dez. Can I help you?" he asked.

You can if you toss me over your shoulder, and…

She didn't say that, of course.

"I'm looking for a screw." Eleanor cringed at what she did say. *So* much worse! "I mean, a *screwdriver.*" *Please let this nightmare end.* "I'm locked out."

Turns out Dez is *not* just a random guy and there's more than attraction pulling these two together! Find out what those connections are in HIS UPTOWN GIRL by Liz Taley, available June 2013 from Harlequin® Superromance®.

REQUEST YOUR FREE BOOKS!
2 FREE NOVELS PLUS 2 FREE GIFTS!

HARLEQUIN

super romance

More Story...More Romance

Wild hearts are hard to tame....

Matt Montoya longs to be a champion again. Not only has the tie-down roper suffered a crippling knee injury, he can't reclaim his former glory without his best rope horse. But Liv Bailey, who tutored Matt in high school, is Beckett's new owner—and when their tempers clash over who stakes claim, sparks fly in more ways than one!

Enjoy the latest story in The Montana Way series!

Once a Champion
by Jeannie Watt

AVAILABLE IN JUNE